CREW II

RESISTANCE

MARTEL SMALLS

Crew II: Resistance

By

Martel Smalls

Published by **Martel Smalls**

Copyright © 2023 by Martel Smalls

CHAPTER 1

Calynda stepped out of the SUV dressed in a pair of 95 Air Max, skin tight black cargo pants and a long sleeved black compression shirt. A Glock. 23 rested on he hip holster with 4 extra clips in a mag holster as well as a stiletto strapped to her outer thigh. Her hair blew wildly in the evening breeze as she watched from behind her designer frames as her men stormed the hospital with one order; kill Friday and anyone standing in their way. Her two top henchmen, Solas and Chepae, were at her side after giving the final kill order. Calynda caught a hint of movement in the distance and noticed an unmarked police car with an officer yelling in his radio looking in her direction just as the first sounds of gunfire erupted inside of the hospital.

"Can my day get any more fucked up?!", Calynda sighed as she pat Chepae on the shoulder and nodded at the squad car.

Solas chambered a round inside of his .223, ready to get active with the law when he witnessed a fleet of SUV's pulling up recklessly at the far entrance of the hospital.

"La jefa!", Solas spat, directing Calynda's attention to the unwanted company.

As the SUV's doors opened, men with dreadlocks carrying AK47's rushed into the hospital. Calynda's face twisted in confusion and frustration as she watched

1

the scene unfold. Lastly, a tall man with skin as black as tar emerged from a SUV with another dread at his side as the rest of his men carried out their mission.

"What in thee fuck is going on?", Calynda wondered out loud.…

Iggy's driver drove the Infinity truck like a four wheeler as they navigated through the streets and pulling up at the hospital. His men were given one directive; kill 3-T and anyone who stood on the way. Before Boogey, Iggy's right hand man, could get out of the truck to give the ok to storm the hospital, gunshots could already be heard coming from the inside.

"Sounds like we not da only ones er'.", Boogey said as he walked up and stood next to Iggy.

Hearing Iggy stuck his teeth, Boogey followed his boss's gaze and saw what appeared to be three hispanics, one female and two males standing at the far entrance of the hospital looking back at them. The two Hispanic males were holding what seemed to be assault rifles and it wasn't hard to figure out where the shots were coming from.

"Dey muss be er' to protect the pussy boi from us.", Boogey spat.

"But why da shoots before we come", Iggy asked. "No one in der but regular people." "Wha ya wan do?"

"We do wha we come to do.".……

C2

Hearing the beeping of the monitors seemed worse than hearing the tick of a bomb counting down to explosion. Nicole never imagined that she would be on the shitty end of the stick but her she was, watching her man's life hang in the balance. The results of Friday's gunshot wounds landed him in a coma in I.C.U. with no signs of his condition getting any better. Nechelle sat in a chair asleep and would sit awake when Nicole got tired. Someone had to stay alert because they were being hunted. 3-T was also suffering from gunshot wounds but he was fully conscious on the second floor, one floor before Friday. As Nicole's head began to nod from dosing off, she heard what sounded like firecrackers began to sound off. Wanting to stay awake incase Friday came to, she decided to open a window to get some fresh air. As soon as the window opened, Nicole instantly became aware that what she was hearing were not no damn firecrackers.

Somebody was fucking shooting! She knew her crew was strapped and the only reason they would be shooting was if they were engaged.

"Bitch you need to wake the fuck up!", Nicole panicked, shaking Nechelle out of her sleep.

"Girl, what the hell is your problem?", Nechelle said with much attitude as she looked towards Friday.

"Somebody shooting!" "Shooting?"

"Yes! Get up!"

"What you mean shooting?", Nechelle asked, still shaking off the sandman. "Shooting! Like POW! POW!

3

BOOM! BANG! Bitch get up!"

Now, more gunshots could be heard coming from the window as they both recognized the sounds of footsteps running outside of their door.

"Where Dullah at?", Nechelle asked now fully awake and alert. "How the fuck would I know? I'm in here with you!"

"Stay here with him. I'll go see what's the deal ok?"

"Nu-uh! You ain't leaving me here! This nigga in a coma. It'll take us both to protect him."

"Protect him!?", Nechelle hissed. "Bitch you better protect yourself first! Anything that comes through that door that ain't crew, you dropped their ass off!"

"Please hurry back Nechelle."

"Girl, you making my pussy itch with all this soft ass scary shit you got going on." "Suck my dick bitch!"

"That's my bitch!", Nechelle laughed as she smacked Nicole on the ass, then peeked both ways out of the door before creeping off.

"I should fuck you in yo sleep.", Nicole said looking at Friday. If she was gonna die, she wanted to go out with a nutt.....

"Secure the perimeter! Cover all of the exits! No one leaves out without being cuffed! I don't give a fuck if they come out hopping missing a fucking leg, cuff em!"

Lt. Pines showed up on the scene barking orders to the SWAT team. The hospital was in complete chaos as injured civilians continued to pour out of every exit. Dead bodies and a bloody mess could be seen laying in the lobby as they geared up to move in.

"What the hell is going on here Lee?", Lt. Pines asked as the defective walked up.

"Your guess is a good as mine sir. Griggs and I came to serve a warrant on a suspect and saw a group of Mexicans storm one entrance and a group of what looks like Jamaicans stormed another, then all hell broke loose." Lee explained.

"Jesus fucking christ!"

"What do you wanna do sir? It's your call.", Griggs asked.

"What the fuck do you think we're gonna do? It's about time that you got your cherry popped anyway cupcake.", said Pines before joining the pack leading into the hospital….

"Can you believe this shit ma nigga? Seems like yesterday we were teens in the hood park, now we got mufuckaz gunning for us.", Dullah stressed to 3-T who laid in the bed hooked up to monitors and an I.V.

"I know right. This shit done got outta hand bruh. The big homie in a coma, I'm stitched the fuck up, and ain't no telling where the next bullet gonna come from.", 3-T admitted.

"Didn't you say it was some dread heads that pushed up on you?" "Hell yea. I bet it's Chedda Head peoples."

"It gotta be ma nigga. Plus Nicole said Friday was saying it was some Mexicans that got at him." "Mexicans?"

"Yea, Mexicans.", Dullah confirmed. "Penny said some Hispanics were at the club the other night looking for some coc and Friday served them. We're thinking that they tried to jack the homie."

5

"Maaaannnnn, this shit is just too much to….."

"Shit! Shit! Shit! Shit! We gotta move!", Penny panted as she burst through the door cutting 3-T off.

Dullah had a weird look on his face. "The fuck you mean we gotta…." "Now! Motherfucker!", Penny screamed.

"Penny, babe. What's going on?", 3-T asked now on full alert.

"I was heading to the first floor to check on the rest of the crew and as soon as I stepped off of the elevator, there were dead bodies everywhere! Those Hispanics that I mentioned at the club were all over the place tearing shit up. I got stuck for a second because the elevator doors closed behind me and that's when I saw men with dreads shooting everything moving as well. And just when I thought that shit just couldn't get any worse, SWAT stormed the place and now every fucking body starts shooting at every fucking body!"

"This shit ain't hard to figure out. L", Dullah spoke up. "The Hispanics are here to finish Friday off, the dreads are here for you 3-T. And SWAT is here obviously to kill whomever ain't SWAT."

"We gotta get outta here.", 3-T said.

"The whole place is likely surrounded.", Penny advised. "The whole crew needs to be in the same…."

"I don't know what the fuck is going on but I am too cute for this shit!", Nechelle panicked as she barreled through the door.

"Who is with Friday?",Dullah asked Nechelle. "I left Nicole in the room."

"Nicole!?", they all screamed in disbelief.

"Yea! I heard gunshots and wanted to see what was going on."

"Penny, group tx the crew and have them meet us at Friday's room on the third floor.", Dullah directed. "3-T, can you move around on your own?"

"Yeah, I'm good ma nigga. I gotta take a shit though."

"Lol. You always gotta shit when it's time to get active. Nechelle, take him up to the room with Friday and Nicole and stay on point. Penny, me and you gonna see if we can help the crew get up to the third floor."

"Got it." Penny then turned to 3-T. "Baby I love you. Are you gonna be ok?" "We got this. Just stay focused and make it back upstairs, you hear me?"

"Yes daddy." Penny then gave Holm a sloppy kiss and headed out the door with Dullah.

"Now that you're done putting yo lip lock on that cracker bitch, can you please remove that I.V. abs the rest of them damn wires so we can go?", Nechelle sassed.

"I think you jealous.", 3-T teased.

"And I think you need to hurry the fuck up."

"Tyler, you, Tonia, and Karen make your way to the parking lot and stay put. Me and bro gonna make sure that the rest of the crew is straight.", J.J. directed once they all were in a janitors closet on the first floor.

One minute they were eating in the hospitals café, and the next minute, it was Call of Duty in that bitch! Police were shooting Hispanics who were shooting jamaicans who were shooting civilians. It was a total war zone and they had no idea why.

"O.K., but why y'all can't come with us?", Tyler whined.

"Because me and bro get paid to protect, not run. Everyone in here is strapped and knows how to use it but we all ain't built for war. Me and bruh been doing this shit. I need you to do what I told you to do and get up outta here before it's too late."

"I'll tell you what", Karen said as she moved towards the door. "I'll let y'all two corny assess figure that shit out but I'm but I'm outta here."

Karen opened the door and a nurses headed exploded as she ran pass the janitors closet. The headless corpse shook violently before curling up and bleeding out at Karen's feet. Everyone stood frozen in shock looking down at the dead body when a dread head appeared and began to raise his AK47 in an attempt to cut down everyone in the closet. Karen went straight into survival mode and grabbed the barrel of the assault rifle with both hands and put all her weight on it so that it would point to the floor as Tyler ran up, put her ruger under the dreads chin and popped his top off. Tonia quickly dragged the body by its feet inside of the closet as Tyler shot the door and a Karen took his rifle.

"Who the fuck this nigga playing with? Talking bout we all ain't built for war!", Tonia asked rhetorically. "I know right!", Karen agreed. "They ass still on stuck. Looking like a couple of pussies!"

"Y'all was closer.", Pepp mumbled.

"Yea, yea, yea. Anyways,", Tyler dismissed him. "Do what you gotta do babe, I'll be waiting for you." "That's all I need. Now y'all stay close to each other and get outta here.", J.J. ordered.

Tonia, Tyler, and Karen left the closet to make their way to a safe place. J.J. and Pepp checked their weapons and vests and prepared to make it to the crew alive.

"Aye bruh, Penny just sent a tx saying meet up at Friday's room.", Pepp said.

"They must be on point too. Come on, let's get this shit over with."

J.J. was armed with a folding AR15 which he unfolded and chambered a round and Pepp was strapped with a MAC 11. They both were huge as fuck so as soon as they stepped out of the closet, they were spotted. The twins had been in the field more than a few times so verbal communication was not needed. The duo moved as one as they made their way to the elevators. Pepper moved in a crouch as J.J. stood tall over his back as they moved together, giving every target double the fire. They made sure that their weapons were on semiautomatic to conserve ammo but were gone fucking the triggers as if that were working a fully auto. When they got to the elevators, the number pad was shot to shit so they had to use the stairs. And to their luck, the stairs were on the other side of the floor. Noticing that the AK47 on the dead bodies had shoulder straps with 100 round mags, Pepp picked up one and draped out over his shoulder and J.J. did the same. Picking up a few mags and stuffing them on their waist, they continued stepping on everything breathing on the way to the stairs.

"Why the fuck are these grease balls shooting at us?!", Calynda yelled on frustration. She and Chepae were crouched behind a nurse's station on the first floor trying to get to the elevators. She had a nurse give her the 411 on Friday's room before knocking her melon loose.

"I do not know la jefa but please do not move hastily. We must keep a….."

"Fuck this shit!", Calynda spat, cutting Chepae off as she dove over the counter of the nurse's station.

With her glock. 23 glued to her palms, she scanned the area quickly and counted at least 6 men with dreads who were shooting at cops as well as her men. Wasting no time to get active, Calynda ran full speed then slid across the tiled floor and tangled her feet between the closest dreads legs in a scissors motion, causing him to drop to his knees and kiss his nose goodbye as Calynda knocked it off with a hollow point. Another dread heard the all too close blast and turned just in time to see his comrade head to the upper room.

Bringing his AK to aim at Calynda, dread number two cut loose with the rifle only to have Calynda use his boy's body as a shield and pumped two in his chest. Before he could even drop dead, Calynfa had already used a chair to leap into the air and wrapped her legs around dread number three's neck, swimming her body in a downward 180° motion, causing the dread to crack his skull in the front on the marble floor as she stood over him and pulled the trigger twice, blowing the back of his head open.

Seeing that she had single handedly cut the enemies numbers in half, Calynda made her way towards Friday's room……

"Lt. are you ok?", asked Lee.

"I'm fine, I'm fine! It didn't go through the vest!"

"We gotta get this shit under control and bring it to an end!", Griggs shouted over gunfire.

"You're fucking right!", Lt. Pines agreed. He then got on his radio barking orders.

"Everyone make a wall with your shields! Move in pairs of fours! Three men crouched with connected shields and one man behind them shooting these cock suckers! Split up and move down every hallway until we clear this fucking place out!"

"Roger!" "Copy that!"

"Loud and clear sir!"

Affirmations came through the radio as SWAT team assembled a rolling wall through the hospital with orders to eliminate all threats. Let. Pines took a team of his own as well as Griggs and Lee.

"O.K. boys!", Lee spoke up. "We got our orders. Light em up!"

And with that, SWAT team took no prisoners. If you were armed and not an officer, you were a target.

The twins ran into Dullah and Penny in the stairwell and met up with Nicole, Nechelle,

Friday, and 3-T on Friday's room. With Friday being in a coma, he would need to be carried out of the hospital. That was a job for one of the twins. 3-T was mobile, but still seriously injured so someone would need to be by his side at all times. The goal was to make it out of the hospital alive, they would have to fight another day. J.J. stepped up to the plate and said that he would carry Friday and Penny would lead the way as

Nechelle covered the rear. They would head down the east stairwell. Pepper would shuffle 3-T out and Dullah would lead the way as Nicole covered their rear. They would head down the west stairwell. Gullah thought it'd be best to split up because if anything went wrong not everyone would be in jeopardy.

"Wait a minute!", Dullah halted before they left the room. "Where's Aisha?" "Oh shit! Aisha!", Nechelle panicked.

"I sent her a text with everyone else's. We gotta find her!", Penny said.

"Fuck it! We gotta move forward.", Dullah announced. "Just keep your eyes open for her while we try to get the fuck out of here. Ain't much that we can do for her at this point, but don't count her out, she's trained remember? So let's do what we do."

And with that the crew crept out of the room and went their separate ways.

Iggy gave no fucks whatsoever as he marched through the hospital's halls airing shit out. If you moved, you got hit, simple shit. Boogey had a slightly different agenda. He wasn't shooting civilians, but if you were Hispanic or the jakes, her got with you. They already had the low on where 3-T's room was so they made their way up and over.

"Aye Iggy!", Boogey yelled out as he stood sty the elevators. "We gotta take the stairs." "Wha da pwoblem wit de elevator?"

"It broken mon!"

"Rasklat!", Iggy yelled in frustration.

Boogey ordered three of his men to follow them to

the stairs. The lead goon got to the foot and swung it open, catching a bullet to the throat. Dullah pumped three more slugs in the goons chest, yanking him in the stairwell and shutting the door. Iggy and his crew cut loose on the door on the stairs, damn near tearing it off of the hinges. Nicole back pedaled up the stairs and opened the second floor door to clear an exit route because there was no way they were walking through that door with Iggy on the other side. They would have to use the other exits. Nicole made sure it was cool to walk the second floor and the crew left the same way they came.

CHAPTER 2

Calynda found herself between a rock and another rock as she and her two henchmen exchanged gunfire with Penny and Nechelle. Cheapae and Solas stood behind two wide pillars as Nechelle shot relentlessly at them while crouching behind an overturned soda machine. J.J. laid over a comatose Friday to shield him as Penny shot rationally while moving from one cover spot to another, as she was trained. She wanted to get as close to Calynda as possible for an easy kill. As if God wanted everything to come to a halt, the room was suddenly filled with sounds of guns clicking. Nobody moved or made a sound as each party waited for the gunfire to come back to life.

"I have 20 more men on the way chica!", Calynda yelled from the doorway of an empty patent room. "I came for Mr. Friday and that's all. Hand him over and I'll let you live!"

"Fuck you motherfucker!", Penny screamed. "Suck my dick bitch!", Nechelle joined.

"I guess we'll do this the hard way.", Calynda said as she stepped out of the room, empty gun in hand.

"And what eay is that?", Penny asked standing erect with an empty gun also. "Penny!", Nechelle hissed.

"What?"

14

"What the fuck are you doing? Wet her ass up!"

"How?", Penny asked. "You want me to play with my pussy and squirt on the bitch?" "This shit is not happening right now…", J.J. mumbled.

Chepae and Solas stepped out into the open ammoless and was ready to throw down alongside their boss. Nechelle peeped the move and was not about to let Penny go out alone and stood out beside her girl. Penny didn't know that Calynda was a walking nightmare when it came to hand to hand combat, and Calynda had no idea that Penny was a trainwreck looking for a place to happen either.

"Nechelle.", J.J. called out. Nechelle looked in his direction. "He needs you.", he said motioning to Friday laying on the floor. Nechelle slowly walked over to Friday while grilling the ops and dat down Indian style while laying Friday's head in her lap.

"You're a pretty big fella.", Solas snickered sizing J.J. up. "I'm glad that I got help." "Check it.", J.J. said pointing at Chepae, "Ima take your head and shove it up his ass!"

Silas and Chepae were good fighters but J.J. was a whole nother kind of action. And all three men engaged in combat like their lives depended on it.. Because it did….

"Now that the boys are getting along well, maybe we should have some girl time." Calynda toyed.

"You're going through all of this to steal some cocaine?", Penny asked.

"Steal? Bitch he stole my cocaine, robbed my stash house and killed my workers!"

15

Penny was stunned. All along the crew was under the impression that they had robbed Pusha, when he was actually a nobody. Nechelle heard Calynda's accusation and immediately recalled one of the workers at the money spot saying that they were fucking with the Puerto Rican princess.

"We had no idea that we were robbing you!", Penny admitted. "We thought they were some locals. You could've came to us and we would've made everything right!"

"There are rules in this game when you take someone else's shit!" Calynda spat. "And rule number one is 'eye for an eye'!"

"Well, I only got two eyes and I'm trying to keep em so now what?", Penny said sarcastically.

Without another word, Calynda sprinted towards Penny and threw a right hook that was blocked and a high kick that was easily ducked. Rising from a crouch, Penny hooked Calynda's kicker leg before it could touch the ground and lifted her into the air. Taking the quick steps forward, Penny hopped into the air and brought Calynda down hard in her upper back, knocking the wind from her lungs. Calynda had underestimated her opponent and laid in shock as Penny straddled her and began raining blows to her face.

Calynda timed it perfectly and caught one of Penny's punches in an elbow lock, and wrapped her legs around Penny's shoulder blade in an attempt to break her arm. Feeling the pressure build up to the point of breaking her bones, Penny lurched forward and rolled with the pressure, landing on her knees as well as bending her elbow in a curl. Landing on her back,

16

Calynda curled at the abs and kicked Penny in the face then hopped up to her feet. Penny shook off the blow and stood up as well.

With her earbuds in, music turned up to the maximum, Aisha sat like a princess taking the best shit that life had to offer. Something about the meatball marinara sub that she ate gave her booty the runs. Aisha had no clue that world war three was unfolding right outside of the bathroom door until a 7.62 slug came flying through one side of the stall and out of the other. She dam near fell into the toilet bowl when she jumped back from the lemon sized hole in the stall. With a wet booty, she cleaned herself up as best as she could and stored stepped out of the stall without flushing. Looking towards the exit door of the restroom, bullet holes were visible across the door and wall.

"What the fuck?", she whispered.

Aisha was so stunned that she still had her earbuds in and when she removed them, she heard hella gunshots which caused her to recoil. She knew that the cops were coming, so no need to call her own. But when she pulled out her phone, she saw a text from Penny.

"How the hell am I gonna get up the?", she asked herself.

Thinking that things couldn't get any more difficult, her belly rumbled and watery shit came knocking at heavens back door.

"Fuck that! Y'all just gonna have to wait.", she decided and shuffled back in the stall holding her ass.

C2

Chepae and Solas were giving it their all but couldn't seem to wear down the monster in J.J.. The two Puerto Ricans were wearing an ass cutting like it was the new fashion.

Everytime J.J. would connect, it felt like something would break. J J. Was taking a beating as well and felt fatigue begin to kick in. But he would door fuckin shit up before he threw in the towel. He knew he had to give it his all because Penny was looking like a fuckin avenger the way her and Calynda went at it and he had to admit, he was proud to fight along side of her. Solas made a grave mistake of attempting to play it close with J.J. and found himself being choke slammed on a counter of a nurse's station, knocking him unconscious. Turning to deal with Chepae, J.J. found himself staring down the barrel of a rifle that Chepae saw in the hands of a dead man. He knew him and Solas couldn't defeat J.J. at the rate that the fight was going and thought to improvise.

Lost for words, J.J. held an impassive stare at the Puerto Rican, sitting his fate.

Nechelle could not believe what she was seeing and prayed for a way out for J.J., but knew her prayers would not be answered when she heard the blast, saw the flash, and witnessed J.J. staggered backwards but didn't fall. Calynda and Penny recoiled and backed away from each other as they turned just in time to see Chepae hot J.J. three more times in the torso. J.J. fell to his knees and looked towards Penny with warning on his eyes but it was too late. Calynda took three distraction as an opportunity and took the stiletto off of her thigh and buried it once in Penney's lower back and twice in her lower ribs while holding her in a choke hold from behind. Seeing the blood spill from Penny's mouth sent Nechelle over the edge. Knowing that she was next, Nechelle stood up and welcomed death with a can of whipass. She was not going willingly. She took a fighter's stance without saying a word, her body language spoke for her.

"This one here looks like she got a lil tiger in her eh la jefa?", Chepae joked.

"Only thing her and a tiger got in common is that their both pussy!", Calynda spat. "You pull a knife when her back was turned and you", she pointed at Chepae,

"scrambled for a gun when J.J. was busy pulling his foot out of the other ones ass, and I'm pussy?", Nechelle asked sarcastically. "Put the gun down and I'll fuck you up first!"

Cheaper threw the rifle down and held his arms out as if to say- take your best shot. Huge mistake. Nechelle threw a left jab, right cross hook, and a left upper cut on his ass so fast that Calynda backed up and cringed with a fist up to her mouth. As if on cue, about ten of Calynda's men rushed the area ready to tear shit up. Nechelle finally dropped her guard and sat on the floor next to her man, ready to take her final breath.

Chepae hopped up off of his ass full of embarrassment and started kicking and punching Nechelle in the face and chest. Tired of the kitty games, Chepae took a rifle from one of his goons and pointed it at Nechelle's head.

19

"Cabron!", Calynda barked halting Chepae from knocking Nechelle's noggin loose. "Hahahaha haaah!", Nechelle laughed hysterically.

"The fuck is so funny puto?", Chrpae asked. "Lol! You hit like bitch!"

"Enough of this bullshit!", Calynda interrupted. "Where is the gold?". "At the end of the rainbow bitch!", Nechelle spat through a swollen lip.

Calynda squinted with death on her eyes and pulled the stiletto from her thigh and crouched down face to face with Nachelle. Grabbing Nechelle by her ponytail, and coming eye to eye, Calynda slowly drove the blade between her ribs as Nechelle's shook violently and her series became wide as the steel slowly took her life. Blood crept down the corner of her mouth as Calynda applied as much pressure as she could on the blade, cutting into Nechelle's lungs. Snatching the weapon out of her victim, Calynda gave the final orders.

"Chepae, have the men bring Friday with us. We have to find Amelio's gold and he's gonna tell us where it is. Somebody grab Solas and get the choppers to meet its on the roof."

And with that, Calynda and her crew made their way to the roof for the great escape.

Once alone, Nechelle dragged Penny over to J.J. who laid in a pool of blood with eyes wide with death.

"Hold on Penny. Someone will be her soon to help us. Just stay woke." "I kicked that bitch's ass didn't I?", Penny said weakly and raspy.

"Lol. You did girl. That's why you gotta stay with me so that we can finish the job.", Nechelle pleaded.

"Dam right! I saw you pop that guy in the mouth too! You should've seen the look on his face when you sat him on his…..", was Penny's last words before she faded to black.

"Penny….", Nechelle whispered through tears. "Penny pleeeaaasse…..AAAAAHHHHHHH!!!"

Nechelle let out a blood boiling scream. Her man was just abducted, no telling she the other half of her crew was while this half lay here dieing. But she was not ready to go.

Nechelle took all the life that she has left in her and made her way around the floor finding everything she need to patch her wound up. She barricaded herself in a room with an I.V. in one arm and an assault rifle in the other and waited for help or hell to arrive.

"We can't let dem pussy boys get away mon!", Boggey shouted to Iggy.

"Split up! ", Iggy commanded. "Dey have ta come down once of dem stairs so cova dem all!"

"You lead the way and I'll cova da back.", Boogey said.

"Let's get this shit ova wit.", Iggy replied then headed to the north stairwell.

No sooner than he turned the first corner, he saw SWAT with shields moving towards them in a crouch. The length of the connecting shields reached from wall to wall so nothing could pass. An officer in body armor stood protected above the shields ready to fire at the first sign of a threat.

"Turn around mon", Iggy whispered. "We have ta go up da north side. Too many devils headed me way."

The duo jogged to the other stairwell and quickly ascended the steps. Slowly opening the door, Iggy peeked around and saw that the coast was clear. But not for long. Boogey spotted the Hispanic woman from the parking lot with a small army and what looked like a dead body thrown over one of the men's shoulder. His beef was not with her shit, he didn't even know why she was here but her men had started shooting at them first.

Seeing that he was outnumbered, Iggy decided to let them pass but Boogey had a different objective. He had witnessed a number of his goons get cut down by the hands of the Hispanics and wanted revenge. Iggy was none the wiser until he heard the familiar sound of an AK47 rattle off from beside him. Seeing that he's was without option, Iggy was committed and let that stick talk as well. Calynda heard the shots, saw the bullets ricochet all around her and hit the deck instantly. Four of her men took fatal blows from the surprise attack, including the one who carried Friday.

"Get Friday and get him to the roof!", Calynda screamed to Solas over the gunfire from both crews.

"Chepae! Cover me!"

"But la jefa!.   ", was all her could say as Calynda went kamikaze once again.

Calynda spotted five more dreads coming up the far side of the hospital and gave warning signs to her men. Seeing that Iggy one her position but the new comers didn't, Calynda decided to use the element of surprise to get advantage and pull a sneak attach on the fresh meat. The first two goons came around the corner and came across what looked like a dead body. Thinking nothing of it, they stepped over and around it. Grave mistake.

Calynda slowly rose to her feet and threw the stiletto in the back of the neck of the first gon. Soon as goon #2 spun around he caught a punch to the throat, kick to the belly and a flying knee to the chin. Once the goon was on his back holding his throat and broken nose, Calynda snatched the blade out of the dead goon and knelt beside his homie.

"Why are you here?", Calynda hissed at the busted dread with the steal to his neck. "Fuck you! Me die fore me speak to da devil!"

"Oh really?", Calynda smiled with raised eyebrows.

Calynda quickly reached in the goons pants and grabbed a fist full of his balls. She squeezed, twisted, then pulled abs the goon thought that he would faint. He could not cry out because Calynda had covered his mouth to muffle any altering screams. Even though he could not speak, his eyes told Calynda that he was more than ready to cooperate. Only loosening her grip just a smudge, she uncovered his mouth and gave his nutts a jerk, prompting him to speak up.

"De robbed us! De kill his brudda!", the goon cried out.

"Who robbed and killed who?", Calynda hissed with another jerk of his nutts. "Da nigga Tony! He kill Chedda and took the weed mon!"

"Well why the fuck are you shooting at us?"

"We thot ya was er protectin Tony.", the goon panted.

"I know this is not the time to dwellon this, lol. But you got a fat fucking dick that you'll never get to use again."

And with the speed of light, Calynda drove her stiletto into the goons skull while releasing his mutts. Even though her beef wasn't with the dreads, they were now at war, so it is what it is. But now was not the time to engage. She had what she came for and decided to fight another day.

Dullah found himself and the crew trading shots with the Hispanics not long after they escaped the dreads. Looking for an exit rout, he noticed the same dreads busting at the Hispanics. Seeing that Nicole was holding her own, Dullah made his way over to 3-T and Pepp.

"Man, some freaky ass shit is going on ma nigga. ", Dullah said to 3-T. "Fuck you mean?"

"The dreads and Hispanics shooting at each other too bruh!" "Huh?", Pepp asked unbelievably.

"I said the same shit!", Dullah admitted.

"Well somebody better chooses fuckin side and fast because that looks like the jakes!", 3-T said, pointing all the way up the hall. "Shit!", Dullah spat. "Nicole!"

Nicole saw the crew clicked up and made her way over. "We gotta get outta here!", 3-T told her.

"I agree because I seriously need to change my tampon." "We did not have to know that.", Pepp frowned.

Dullah shook his head smirking, leading the way, with Nicole covering the rear. As they headed towards the stairs, Dullah spotted a dread dragging another towards the same stairs. It seemed like one was shot, who continued to shoot as his goon dragged him to safety. A bullet ricochet passed his head and Dullah noticed the Hispanics advancing from the rear. Nicole was doing her best but she was only one gun. Looking ahead, he noticed more Hispanics closing in on the two dreads. He quickly decided to deal with the lesser of the two evils and made his way over to the dreads and shot at the Hispanics as one goon dragged his homie into the stairwell. Boogey didn't know who this man was but as he dragged Iggy into the stairwell, he was thankful for him. Iggy's AK had just clicked empty as the man joined their side of the battle and saved their lives. Once on the stairs, Iggy and Boogey witnessed three more people run in behind him, one of them looked to be injured. A female was the last to enter who came in shooting until the door closed.

"Tyler just text me and said they're in a parking garage for the staff under the hospital.", 3-T said.

"We gotta get down there then.", Dullah said.

"What the fuck was that?!", Pepp screamed to Dullah. "You helping these niggas out when they're gunning for us?!"

"Now is not the time bruh.", Dullah said.

"Well we need the understanding that you got because the last time I checked, these muthafuckaz flipped my truck and shot me the fuck up!", 3-T defended Pepp.

"You wanna run from two crews or one?!", Dullah asked. "They're running from the same muthafuckaz we're running from so we got a common enemy plus the Jakes are everywhere. So yea, I made am executive decision to help them get to safety because they came here with an army and we didn't. We can't afford to keep running into muthafuckaz with dreads and they can call them off. So if any one of you geeked up muthafuckaz got a better idea then let me know. Otherwise, let's help them to the garage so we can get the fuck outta here!"

Nobody had much to oppose to what was said so Nicole helped 3-T, Pepp carried Iggy, and Dullah and Boogey led the way to the garage. Once down there, 3-T called Tyler, who was with Tonia and Karen in an ambulance.

"Where's everyone else?", Tyler asked, but really looking for J.J.

"Don't know but we gotta move.", Dullah said. "Y'all got the keys to this shit?" "No but all I need is a few seconds.", Tonia advised.

"Why the fuck are they with us?", Tyler whispered to Dullah. "Not right now Tyler. Not right now."

Tyler shook her head and walked off glaring at Iggy and Boogey. Once the truck started up, everyone hopped in the back except for Tyler. She put in a spare cap that was on the inside and headed to the garages exit. Turning on the lights after several attempts, she pulled up to the exit and was let through without hassle.

"Open this door or we're coming in ugly!", an officer yelled from the other side of the barricaded door. Nechelle was in and out of consciousness but when she headed the jakes threatening to tear shit up, she got all the way on point. Knowing that the rifle she was holding has crazy bodies on it, she chucked it out of the window after wiping it down.

"I'm removing the barricade! Don't shoot! I'm unarmed and injured!", Nechelle yelled through the door. It wouldn't have mattered if she was missing her kneecaps because when she opened that door, that cracked dam near snatched her soul away as he grabbed her by the collar and pinned her to the ground. With his knee on her back, the nasty SWAT officer cuffed Nechelle at the wrist, nearly cutting off her circulation.

"I need a doctor!", Nechelle screamed.

"And I need a fucking Ferrari! Shut your fucking mouth before you need braces bitch!", the officer threatened.

"All clear!", another confirmed.

"On your feet!", the nasty officer commanded Nechelle. "What are you doing here?"

"It's a fucn hospital! The fuck you think I'm in here for you ignorant pencil dick son of a bitch?!"

"One more word and I'll fuck you up!", he threatened, yanking Nechelle's head back by her ponytail.

"Stand down officer!", Detective Griggs ordered. "can't you see that this woman is dam near bleeding to death!"

"Orders were to apprehend everyone no matter the condition." "Apprehend! Not batter and abuse! I'll take it from here."

The SWAT officer spat at Griggs feet, mugged Nechelle and walked off. Griggs uncuffed Nechelle after a quick pat down and ushered her out of the run room.

"I really appreciate what you did.", Nechelle thanked Griggs once she was seated outside of the room.

"No problem ma'am, just doing my job. Medic!",

Griggs called out. Once the medic began to deal with Nechelle, Griggs went through the formalities. Asking her name, age, and what did she witnessed. Nechelle only gave him what she knew that the camera would show and nothing more. Before he stepped off, Griggs gave her his contact card, advising her to reach out to him if she remembered anything else. Once Griggs was put of sight, Nevhelle looked to where she left J.J. and Penny. J.J.'s body lay under a white sheet but Penny's was nowhere to be found.

"Now would be the perfect time for somebody to explain to me what the fuck just happened back there!", Tyler fussed.

The remainder of the crew, which were Dullah, 3-T, Nicole, Pepp, Tyler, Tonia and Karen, had taken Iggy and Boogey to the club to figure out the next move. Still no word from J.J., Nechelle, or Penny. And only God knew what the deal was with Friday.

"Me bruddah needs a doctor mon." Boogey advised no one in particular. "Fuck you and your BRUUDA!", Tyler barked.

"Lemme kill em Dullah.", asked Pepp.

"Everybody just calm the fuck down! Please!", Dullah ordered. "Nicole, patch this nigga up the best you can. If he goes to the hospital, his ass is leaving the in cuffs!"

"So why the fuck should we care?", Tonia spoke up.

"Since when we started locking muthafuckaz up?", Dullah asked sarcastically. "But these niggas tried to kill me!", 3-T screamed.

"And you kill me lil bruddah!", Iggy yelled through

tears. "You killed all me had left and took me weed! Wha ya expect?"

As Nicole went to work on Iggy, who now clutched a bottle of rum for comfort, Boogey stood up and addressed the crew.

"Dat mon on de floor right dea is da rest of me bloodline. Not from me momma, but from me heart. Chedda was out little man. And ya kill him." He then walked up on Dullah. "Me tank you for saving our lives mon. But dat don't make us even."

"Well what the fuck you want from us?", Dullah asked.

"We wan da devil bitch dead!", Iggy said from behind. "We saw those devils slay me posse in front me eyes and me no rest until we give her a slow death."

"And what the fuck does that have to do with us?", 3-T asked. "We liked you people, then we saved your lives. I'd say we even if you asked me."

"Give me a minute.", Dullah told Boogey. He then pulled 3-T and Pepp to the side. "Listen ma niggas. We ain't got much of a team and it don't take a rocket scientist to figure out that whoever that bitch is, she coming back! These dread muthafuckas got an army and hella guns and we are in desperate need of both. So unless y'all got a better idea, we

need to roll with these cats."

"How do you know that we can trust them?", Pepp asked.

"Never said that we could. But right now, we need them." "Only on one condition.",3-T said.

"What's that?", Dullah asked.

"I set time on his we deal with these cats." "Then set the tone ma nigga."

The trio made their way back over just as Nicole was done with Iggy. "So what exactly is it that you want us to do?", 3-T asked Iggy.

"Ya know da states betta than we. We give you control of a crew of me men, only ta hunt down tis devil. When she dead, we vanish."

"How we know that you won't cross us once we hit this bitch?", Dullah asked. "If me wan ya dead, me kill ya right now.", Iggy said.

"Nigga please!",Tonia spat. "Ain't shit but the two of y'all and y'all ain't got no guns nigga."

Iggy held up his cell phone. "Me tx me hit squad on da way ova. 30 rastahs sit out ya club waiting on me orders."

Boogey just smiled.

"Here's the deal.", 3-T said. "We'll take your men, and we'll smoke this bitch too. But know that we call the shots and we ruin the show. We don't need y'all interfering or doing all the extra shit that nobody asked y'all to do. If you can agree to that then we good."

"Agree.", Iggy said simply. He then walked up to Dullah. "Me can see in ya eyes ya a good mon. You save me life. Ya save me from police. Me may not like you, but me always respect you."

And with that, he held his hand out for a shake. Dullah shaked his hand without breaking eye contact. As Iggy and Boogey got to the exit, 3-T called out to them.

"So what's y'alls names?" "Me Iggy. Dis er' is Boogey."

"A lot of people counting on me Iggy."

"Wha dat got ta do wit me?"

3-T looked around at the crew who in turn wss staring back, wondering what was on his mind.

"Sheeeeed…Got dam…a nigga need a plug. Sup with the weed ma nigga?" "Nigggaaahh!"

"Girl no he just did not!" "Bruh, you for real right now?"

"Man, we still gotta eat.", 3-T said rubbing the back of his neck.

Iggy just shook his head smirking and walked out of the door with Boogey behind him.

C2

"Any sign of him?", Lee asked Griggs. They were looking for Friday but came up short everywhere they looked.

"None at all. I got someone confiscating the security footage. Should be one hell of a show.", Griggs said as her looked at all of the dead bodies laying around.

"Why would anyone shoot up a hospital? Looks like jamaicans and Hispanics judging by the bodies with weapons beside them."

"So you think that someone shot a rival gang member and came to finish the job while the other gang protected the injured?"

"That's a pretty good analysis Griggs."

"Well, if you thought Lt. Pines was on your ass before, imagine the heat that's coming now."

"Don't remind me, please. Who was the dame that you were talking to earlier?" "Some victim that barricaded herself in a room."

"Any good info?", Lee asked, hoping for something valuable from a living witness. "Not really. Just some shit that we can see on video footage."

"We have to find Smalls Griggs."

"I know Lee. Just be easy until we get the footage. In the meantime, we have to deal with the public's response. We can't let this shit get out of hand."

"Tell me about it. Well, I'm outta here. See you at the office on the morning." "Drive safe bro."

Griggs took one last look around at the carnage before making his way out of the hospital.

CHAPTER 3

Hearing the beeping of the monitors let him know that he was still alive. But where was he? The hospital, yea, it had to be. That's the only place where you would hear the beeps right? But where was the pain? He didn't feel any pain at all. Finally, he cracked his eyes open and the bright sunlight dam near blinded him. Trying to hold his hands up to his eyes, he finally felt the pain in his shoulder. The beeps from the monitor quickened its pace because his heart rate was picking up speed, a reaction to the pain. Suddenly, a young nut pretty woman appeared in the room dressed in scrubs holding a clipboard.

The hospital!, he thought. This nurse must be an intern because she is so young. Looking around the room, he realized that this was no hospital room. Sheer curtains, 60 inch flat screen, king sized bed, and her was butt ass naked. No. No fucn way he was on a hospital. But where at? As he tried to speak, he found his throat to be as dry as dirt.

Shaking his head from side to side, trying to get the nurse's attention, his heart rate sped up more causing the beep to quicken.

"Wa…" his voice was barely a whisper. "Wa…water. Please."

"No problem, sir.", the nurse responded then made a glass of water with a straw in it and held it to his mouth.

As he drank, he felt the cold liquid spread throughout his chest and belly. The nurse raised an eyebrow and smirked as her downed the whole glass in no time.

"More! Please, more!", her requests a little more aggressively than he intended.

Ok, ok, lol. Calm down, I got you.", she said refilling his glass and holding it to his lips. "Thank you.", here said once he was finished.

"No problem, sir."

"Excuse me, but um, what care center is this?"

The nurse did not respond or even look up. She just continued to record his vitals. "Hey! Lady! Where am I?!", he repeated, getting pissed off.

The nurse gave him a quick glance as she walked out of the room. Taking another look around the room, he caught a view of what looked like a body of water as he stared out of the window. The air had a salty ocean smell so he was sure that he was on a coast.

Looking himself over, he noticed bandages over his torso and had no clue as to why he was patched up. Staring off into space, he realized that he couldn't remember shit before waking up today. What the fuck?, her thought. A different lady walked into the room and stood at the foot of his bed and just stared at him. She was one of the most beautiful woman he has ever seen. Long hair, perfect body, and beautiful eyes. Ass for days wonderful breast, and a face of exotic features. But the scowl she wore made him think that she was ready to rip his arms off and beat him to death with it. The beautiful beast slowly walked around the bed and stood right beside him stared a few more seconds, then sat next to him on his bed. The smell of her perfume was intoxicating and her eyes were hypnotic. As his eyes traveled her body, his gaze rested on the red and purple bruises on her knuckles. Looking back up at her eyes, he noticed she had covered a few bruises with makeup.

"Where am I?", he asked the beautiful beast. "You're here with me.", she answered coolly. "Who are you?"

"The question is, sir, who are you?"

He opened his mouth to respond and couldn't find the words to answer her question. Looking around at everything and at nothing in particular, he realized that he didn't even know his own fucking name. What the hell?

"What happened to me? Why am I here?", he asked with a boy of panick in his voice. "I was hoping that you could tell me the answers to those questions."

"Listen bitch,I don't remember ever seeing shit like what's outside of that window. So somebody better tell me where the fuck I'm at, how the fuck did I get here and why the fuck I'm even here in the first place!"

"Let's start with your name and what happened to you, then we can go from there." "I don't fuckin know!"

"Maybe you should get some rest and when you wake up, we'll revisit this conversation.", she said then stood up to leave.

"I don't need any fuckin rest! I need to go home!"

"Where the fuck is home cabron?!", she screamed

back at him. He just stared back at her because he had no response. "Exactly! You don't even know who the hell you are or where you're from so how the fuck do you expect me to help you? You want me to just wheel you out of here and drop you off in the gutter? Huh?" He continued to stare. "Didn't think so. When you remember your story, I'll remember to help you."

With that, she walked out of the room. Looking at the doorway that she just walked through, her noticed an older gentleman smiling a cigar glaring at him with a look of hatred in his eyes. Once the older guy walked away, he laid in bed replaying the conversation with the beautiful beast. Her couldn't remember shit at all. Her stated down at his hands in his lap and his gaze fell on a tattoo on his inner forearm. It said Friday, but he had no clue why….

C2

"Can somebody please tell me again why the fuck we're here and not in the streets looking for my man?", Nicole asked no one in particular.

The crew was silent in the club trying to piece everything together as well as come up with a plan to progress on anything somehow.

"Your man?", Tyler questioned Nicole with sass. "Half of the fuckin crew is missing and all you can think about it one man?"

"I didn't mean it like that."

"Well how do you mean it? Because if I heard

correctly, which I know that I did, you failed to mention anyone else."

"You know what? You're not gonna make it seem as if I'm not for the whole crew. I know it sounded selfish but I just want my man. I want everyone to be ok of course, but it just came out wrong.", Nicole explained.

"Yea, whatever bitch.", Tyler dismissed her with a waive of her hand. "I'm not gonna be too many bitches."

"Bitch! Bitch! Bee-yatch! The fuck you gonna do Nicole?"

"No, no, no. We not gonna do this shit!", Dullah interrupted. "Tyler you missing J.J., 3-T missing Penny, Nicole is missing Friday AND Nechelle, and I'm missing Aisha. We're not getting any closer to finding them by….."

"Nechelle!!", Nicole screamed cutting Dullah off.

Nechelle walked in with the same clothes from the hospital with stitches and bandages underneath.

After a drink, she told the whole story from front to back. When she told them that J.J. got smoked, Tyler lost it. 3-T had a million questions about Penny's whereabouts but Nechelle didn't have a clue. But when they heard that Friday was snatched up and could be alive, the energy in the room shifted. Dullah got a phone call and stepped off as Nechelle continued to try and satisfy everyone's curiosity. 3-T filled Nechelle in on the encounter with the jamaicans along with becoming allies with them.

"Aisha is almost here.", Dullah informed them. "She had a lot to say but I'll let her tell y'all in her own words once she gets here."

"Pepp, baby, are you ok?", Karen asked.

No one noticed Pepp hugging a bottle of Henny or even acknowledged that he had just lost a twin. "When we catch up to these characters….. this Chepae mufucka is mine."

"Respect.", 3-T agreed.

"Say no more ma nigga.", Dullah agreed as well.

Karen walked over to Pepp and wrapped her arms around him the best she could to comfort him.

Karen walked over to Pepp and wrapped her arms around him the best she could to comfort him. Tonia was doing her best to console Tyler but it was futile, she just could not pull herself together at the time.

"We need to find Penny.", 3-T advised. "If she wasn't next to J.J. under a white sheet, she is likely alive. With her connections, we'll have a better chance at finding out who this

bitch is that got Friday and where she's at."

"I heard the bitch telling Penny she came for a Friday for rubbing her coc, gold, and money. And when me and 3-T hot that stash house, one of the ill lil niggas mentioned that we were fuckin with the Puerto Rican princess.", Nechelle informed them.

So Pusha was working for this bitch and we smoked dude but took her shit.", Dullah began piecing things together. "She came looking for her product and found it in the club and figured out that Friday had her shit. So she sent a hit to his crib, that's when Nicole got active then drove them to the hospital. She got word that the hit was failed and came to the hospital to finish the job."

"Same scenario with the jamaicans.", 3-T

confirmed. "They came to the hospital to kick my bucket but the shit didn't work out like that."

The door chimed and in walked Aisha in full uniform. The look on her face let it be known that she didn't have much good news. After tonguing her man down and addressing the crew, she went straight into briefing.

"Before I say anything, I want y'all to know that I was not hiding or avoiding the fight. I had no idea what was going on until I was briefed by my superior. I was taking a shit...."

"You were what lol?", Tonia asked clearly amused.

"Man something about that meatball sub that had my shit all fucked up!", Aisha confessed. "Anyway, I was too dam comfortable with my earbuds in listening to music when a dam bullet came straight through the fuckin stall! I got ready to go out and engage, but my belly started rumbling again and I couldn't seem to get out of that bathroom."

"So what is being said by the police?", Dullah asked, ready to get serious.

"Well right now, to satisfy the public's concern, they're spinning the story to make it seem like it was a random mass shooting. But word is that a Hispanic gang and

jamaicans are at war. But none of that will matter once the footage is downloaded showing the real story. And that's where we need to be concerned. Because anybody who was involved and survived will be hunted until they are judged or buried."

"So what do you suggest that we do?", 3-T asked.

"Shit, ain't too much we can do. All they will have on the footage is faces. If you're prints aren't found on anything then you're cool unless some good samaritan identifies you in the footage." Aisha looked around and saw people missing. "Where's Friday, J.J., and Penny?"

Nechelle gave here the rundown since she had front row seats and Aisha was floored.

3-T informed her on how they came about joining seth the jamaicans and she couldn't grasp how things had woven themselves together.

"We need you to find out where Penny is.", 3-T said.

"I'll do what I can." Aisha assured. "In the meantime, y'all need to keep a low profile.

The club is in Nechelle's name so it's cool to open up. Not so sure about your barbershop Dullah but it's your call. I will advise you to let your employees run it and stay involved from afar. Once we find Penny, we can look for Friday."

"Y'all cannot keep me here! Give me my motherfucking release papers so that I can get the hell out of here!", Penny screamed.

When she blacked out from blood loss, she was transported to another hospital and rushed into surgery. Law enforcement was informed because she was a federal employee and the hospital was directed to hold her until the proper authorities arrived.

"Ma'am, we were instructed to keep you here until the detectives arrived." A nurse informed her.

"Listen to me you little troll faced bitch! I swear to God I will kick your chubby fucking ass if you don't get someone in here to uncuff me now!"

The nurse swallowed hard at the wild eyed fuzzy haired white woman and left to find a police officer. Twenty minutes later, Detectives Lee and Griggs walked in and wasted no time getting straight to the point.

"What were you doing at the hospital?", Lee asked.

"Looking for a fucking unicorn! Why the fuck would anybody be at a hospital?!", Penny sassed.

"Answer the question smart ass!", Griggs snapped.

"And I just did!"

"You were found, dam near stabbed to death, laying next to a known criminal who was shot to shit.", Lee said.

"I could've been laying next to a puddle of poodle piss in the park. What the fuck does that have to do with me being cuffed to a fucking bed!"

"Is there anything that you wanna tell us? We can help you, you know." "Am I under arrest?", Penny asked, ready to end this illegal interrogation. "Don't do anything that you'll regret.", Griggs warned.

"Am! I! Under! Ah-fucking! Rest!" "Not yet.", Lee taunted.

"Well take these fucking cuffs off so that I can get the fuck out of here." "You surely use the word fuck a lot.", Lee said uncuffing Penny.

"Because I like to get fucked! Now please fetch my release papers so that I can go get fucked!"

"Tutoring him will do nothing but piss him off and confuse him more pappa.", Calynda tried to reason with her father Amelio.

Amelio Diaz was an United states fugitive and a

Puerto Rican king pin. He raised in Cuba under the protection of the Cuban government in exchange for money. He was also allowed to run a major cocaine operation transporting to the states under the radar. Because of his issues with the federal government, Amelio elected his only daughter,

Calynda, to head the operations in the states. Now that Calynda had not only failed to secure the product, but lose his gold as well, Amelio felt that his presence was much needed. And having the man responsible for the monkey wrench in his plans was a true test to his self control because he wanted to peel the skin and meat from Friday's bones for disrespecting his prestige.

"Well what do you suggest because the longer we don't have the gold the harder it will be to find it.", Amelio spat back at a frustrated Calynda.

"We just have to be patient pappa. You don't think that I don't wanna get our shit back as well?"

"I don't see you doing anything about it!"

Calynda squinted her eyes in anger and stepped up face to face with her father. "How dare you!? It's me out the, everyday on the front lines, tossing my ass for the familia! It was me in that hospital, knee deep in shit looking for this puto. It was me as well who brought him back, while you sit on your old wrinkled balls and collect the….."

SMACK!!

Amelio bitch slapped DNA out of Calynda's mouth in midsentence. In return, she gave her father a look of death but dared not to respond with aggression. Daughter or not

Amelio had no issues with giving the orders to have her come up missing.

"Seems to me that you've been away so long that you've forgotten who the fuck I am.", Amelio grumbled through clenched teeth. "I run this shit! It was me so gave you the power that you have and it will be me that will take it away if you show any signs of inadequacy."

"So what do you suggest poppa?"

Calynda's eyes held tears that she refused to let fall. She wasn't hurt emotionally from the physical transgression, she was just so pissed to the point of tears because she was powerless to respond in the way that she desired. But this wasn't the first time that Amelio has slapped her lipstick crooked and it surely won't be the last.

"You say that her has no member eh?", Amelio asked, stroking his beard, lost in thought.

"As of now, he doesn't remember anything. How he got his wounds, how he got here, where he's from, not even his first name."

"Then we shall create one for him."

"What are you saying poppa?", Calynda asked, not really grasping his concept.

"We give him a name, age, hometown, and everything else. Shit, we can even give him his favorite color!"

"Poppa, he's not Puerto Rican and even though he's fucked up, I'd imagine that he'd figure out right away that he's not familia."

"Not if you're his wife.", Amelio suggested.

It took a split second for the realization of what Amelio was implying and Calynda's eyes grew wide in disbelief.

"Poppa! No fucking way! You want me to marry that vato?"

"No Calynda. Well, not actually, but engage his memory with the notion that you are."

"So what do you expect me to do when this man's hormones begin to rage, huh poppa?" "Suck his dick and take it up the ass on Tuesday nights! What the fuck do you think

Calynda! Do what you have to do to get the job done!"

"And what exactly is the job Amelio!?""Find my fucking gold!"

And with that, Amelio spun on his heels and made his exit. Calynda could not believe they mission that laid ahead of her. She had not been with a man in years and didn't know the first thing about a relationship, let alone a marriage. She was a drug dealer and a ruthless killer. The fuck she looked like cuddling, eating popcorn and watching reruns? Not to mention that she was expected to fuck a stranger. But she had fucked up and her choices were to either take the necessary steps to find the gold or be a fugitive from Amelio for the rest of her days. She took a few moments to get her thoughts together and left to approach Friday.

When she entered his room, Friday was sound asleep. The medication had kicked in and he was man down. Calynda just stood at the foot of the bed and stared at her mission. This was the man that she had to give herself to and play a role in his life that she felt that she could not conquer. The more she took the idea in, she began you agree that it may not be as bad as it seemed. On the surface, Friday was a very handsome man. His facial hair could use a little TLC but other than that, the man was fine. The more she entertained the thought, the more curious she became.

Looking around to ensure that she was alone, Calynda stepped to the side of the bed and brought the blanket that covered Friday down from his neck to his navel. This man had a body that looked like it was sculpted! Chest so wide and full, stomach rocked up with tattoos, and athletic arms with veins running from shoulder to fingertip. Lost in her lust, Calynda smoothed her palms over his belly muscles and felt a tingle between her thighs that she thought was still on vacation. Letting her curiosity get the best of her,

Calynda pulled the blanket down to his thighs and her vision locked in on that thick curved dick that was attached to this hell of a specimen. Letting a small giggle escape get lips from the thought of what she knew she was about you do, Calynda rubbed up and down the length of his piece with just her fingertips. She could've sworn that she saw it twitch just slightly but noticed that he was still out cold. Taking full advantage of his state of unawareness , Calynda began to stroke Friday's dick until it became a hard piece of man meat. And she had to admit, she was impressed. Looking at her progress, Calynda stroked herself so deep in a trance that when she realized that she wax literally palm fucking him, she looked up and Friday was fully awake looking in her eyes without facial expression.

"Shit!", Calynda hissed and recoiled away. "You were just gonna sit there and say nothing looking all weird and creepy?"

"Wait a minute. You're the one in her dry jacking my dick while im sleep, and YOU'RE calling ME creepy?"

"You act like it's a crime for a woman to play with her husband's dick while her takes a nap."

"Husband?"

"Oh, so you don't love me anymore since I had fun while you were asleep?"

Calynda was thinking fast as the conversation moved forward. There was no turning back now.

"Um…it's just…", Friday's eyes held this far away look. "I'm sorry, I just don't remember."

"It's ok my love. I will do everything that I can to help you get your memory back. But first you must get better."

"But why I'd my ankle cuffed to the bed?"

Calynda was not prepared to answer that. She realized that she had to be very careful and remember everything that she was telling him, exactly how she told him, incase he ever asked again.

"You were in and out of a coma, fighting the help and acting like a maniac. So we had to keep you sedated and restrained until we could get you under control."

"Really? I didn't hurt anyone did I?"

Calyndav remembered him noticing her bruises and decided to use it to soften his heart towards her.

"Well, I was alone with you once and you attacked

me, but it's no real problem my love. My wounds will heal."

A look of shame and regret came over Friday's face and his heart sank.

"Yooo…look, I'm sorry…um.. what's your name?"
"Calynda."

"Calynda. Right. Ok, um…Who am I?"

Another question she was not ready for but had to be quick in responding because this was something that a wife should obviously know.

"Eric. Eric Snipes."

"Eric…", Friday said, letting it roll off of his tongue and set into his memory. "So you must be Calynda Snipes."

"The one and only lol.", she said with a phony smile.

Friday took another moment to let it all register. Then he came with the question if the day. "What happened to me Calynda?"

Yet, ANOTHER fucking question that she wasn't ready for. "You were shot baby."

"Shot? How, why? Why would somebody shoot me?"

Calynda thought to mix a little truth with the dreams she was selling. Because eventually, he would become familiar with the family's operation anyway.

"We are business owners, but you were shot because we are drug dealers." "Geeet the fuck outta here! Drug dealers?", Friday asked in disbelief.

"We run shit cabron.", Calyndav said with all seriousness and Friday caught on quickly. "My popa runs a major cocaine operation and we transport to the states for distribution."

"The states?"

"Yes. We are in Cuba." "So you're Cuban?"

"No my love, I'm Puerto Rican, but it's easier to get everything to where it needs to be from here."

She figured it was best to leave out the part about Amelio being a fugitive, that was not something that he needed to know.

"But you still haven't told me why I was shot. Like what was the motive?"

"You were betrayed and sold out by individuals that you thought were your friends." "I think I deserve more intimate details than that Calynda.", Friday pressed.

Calynda was never in a position to where she had to lie to anyone because she acted with no regards or regrets. So making up a story on the whim was a serious task.

"Me and you are a team all on it's own. But I selected people that I trust to be a part of what we have and so did you. The people that you chose tried to cross you and take over all that you have worked for."

"Fit what though? Wouldn't I choose people that I could trust? Just like you did?", Friday continued to dig for a deeper understanding.

"For what else? Greed! And you chose people that you 'thought' that you could trust. But when the smoke cleared, you were left to die."

"Why an I know in a hospital though?"

"You were my love. But word got out that you

survived the hit and or enemies came to finish the job. That aligned themselves with a hit squad from Jamaica and attempted to assassinate you while you were in a coma."

You're fuckin serious right now?", he asked in disbelief. "What happened at thet hospital?"

It was a nasty bloody battle but I would die before I failed to keep my love safe.", Calyndav said cupping his face in her palms for effect.

Friday was stuck in a state of confusion because everything that was being told to him, he could not grasp. Not being able to remember anything was making it that much more difficult to digest. But all he knew was whatever she told him sup he had no choice but to commit to the one that he was with.

"So what now?", he asked. He was going to have to follow her lead.

"Now, you get better my love. Seeing that you know nothing, I must teach you everything. Once you can move around on your own, you meet the familia. Then we train."

"Train? Train for what?"

"To protect ourselves. Your wife is one hell of a fighter. I will bring someone in to help me out but we will get you back to where you once were if not better."

"Well, I guess that's not so bad. Bit what's after that?"

"One step at a time my love.", Calynda said as she stood. "Right now, you rest and heal. If there is anything that you need, ask the nurse. She is her for all of your needs."

"Um, so, me being your husband, you're gonna let another woman bathe me and handle me naked while I use the toilet?"

Calynda thought about that for a moment and knew that she had to act as the wife that she wasn't.

"When I say needs, I mean domestic. It's my job to scratch any other itch that you may have. Just say the word."

"Honestly, I wanna apologize ahead of time if I seem disconnected. It's just that this is all new to me buy I'll do whatever to get back on track, just be patient with me."

Calynda walked back over to Friday and did get best job kissing him passionately.

Three seconds into the kiss, Friday's hands found their way to Calynda'a soft plump ass and pulled her on top, straddling him as his back rested against the headboard. Even though she knew that this all was a job, she couldn't help but to enjoy herself. She allowed her hands to roam across his chest and abs as her pulled them add cheeks apart, grinding his erection against her lower belly. A moan unintentionally escaped Calynda's lips and she realized that if she didn't cut this shit short, she was gonna fuck this nigga back into a coma. Breaking the kiss with a hint of regret, Calynda gave Friday a weak smile as she stood to straighten out her clothes. Lust glazed their eyes over and the disappointment was evident in the hardness of his dick.

" Rest up my love. We will have our time when the time is right. When you part these lips, I want you to be familiar with the space that you're invading."

Friday shook his head in agreement as he continued to hold eye contact. Calynda pulled the cover back up over his lower half and kissed him once more lightly on the lips. "One more question Calynda."

"What's that my love?" "Who is Friday?"

Calynda thought it'd be best to be honest incase it came back to haunt her. "You are." "I know this is a crazy question, but, why would I call myself

Friday?" "Because for you, everyday is payday lol."

CHAPTER 4

After 3-T left the crew addy the club, he was drained and exhausted. He had yet to hear from Penny and her phone was going straight to voicemail. He had called around to all of the local hospitals and no one had a Penny Austin that was admitted. He thought that maybe they withheld that information for her protection or something but he still worried and had a hard time thinking the worst. When he pulled up to his place, a wild haired crackhead was pacing in front of his door. This wax far from the hood so he didn't understand why a dope fiend was in these parts anyway. Mentally preparing to get rid of this woman, when he got closer, his heart sank. Penny was waiting for him like death had just dropped her off. She hobbled over to him as her sobs louder and louder. Once they embraced, she fell limo into his arms in a full blown wail. A mixture of joy she had for being reunited with her man and them almost losing their lives had her emotions in steroids. She couldn't calm down if she wanted to. 3-T carried her inside and bathed his woman then dressed her wounds.

Penny took her time and told him her version of what Nechelle had told him already. Hearing that Friday was abducted dam near cranked her back up into that crazy white bitch that everyone knew she could be, but

3-T convinced her that there was a time for everything. She still was in much pain and so was he but nowhere was safe so they has to take care if each other. 3-T bathed next and in turn Penny took care of her man.

Having him back in her care has her ready to get nasty. Even though they were both injured, Penny was being honest with the detectives, she wanted to get fucked! 3-T was sitting on the edge of the bed handling business on his phone to never notice Penny walk up in him in a wife beater over her bandages and nothing else on. Just pussy and ass all out everywhere. 3-T looked up as she positioned herself between his legs and was eyes to lips with the smoothest, puffiest kitty he'd ever seen and all thirty two shined bright when he smiled. Picking up a bottle of Jose from the floor, 3-T leaned back on his elbows as Penny slowly went down on her knees. Removing his underwear, Penny wasted no time double fisting his dick then spitting all over it for a slicker stroke. Seeing his hips rise and fall, she new that he was anxious to receive whatever was in store for him. Taking his huge balls in one hand, she spit all over them and began sucking it off still stroking his piece to its full ten inch potential.

"How do you want it daddy?", Penny asked, emerald green eyes low with lust and thick pink lips coated with saliva.

"Show me magic babygirl…"

With a smirk on her face, Penny looked down at her challenge for the night. She knew what he was asking for and was ready to give any magician a run for their money.

Already slick and slippery, Penny wrapped her soul

snatchers around his dick and voila! It disappeared round one and she heard this niggas toe knuckle crack! Clutching two fist full of her hair, 3-T guided her head down as he stroked upwards feeling he throat tighten around him with every dive. Penny squeezed the base of his dick causing it to thicken and swell, making it harder to go down her throat. She knew this would make him force her head down on him, feeling her neck muscles break as he slid deep and it drove him nuts. She moaned and hummed and slurped all around his piece, having him ready to blow her head off of her shoulders and she felt it.

"Not right now daddy.", she panted after interrupting the skull fucking that she was receiving.

Penny stood up and turned her back to him. Reaching between her legs, she grabbed his dick and eased down on it. Placing her hands on his knees, Penny rose and fell slowly on that pipe making crazy pussy smacking noises. The arch in her back gave 3-T a view of her bleached asshole and wide soft ass. The more she bounced on him, the wetter she got. So hypnotized by the view of a lifetime, he never noticed the bandages on her back began to spread with blood. A stitch must have came loose and it almost blew his buzz.

"Slow down baby, chill.", he told her.

"Huh?", she asked out of breath. "What? Why?"

"You're bleeding from the cut on your back."

"Fuck that fucking shit!", she said starting to bounce on that dick again but he held her still.

"What Tony? You're fucking up my nut!"

"Lemme do the work Penny. I don't want your shit

getting worst." "You sound like a pussy!"

Penny stood up, turned around, and straddled 3-T and began fucking him harder. "Penny! You're gonna start bleeding heavy."

"I bleed heavy every fucking month! Now stop fucking talking and fuck me motherfucker!"

Say no more, 3-T thought. Flipping Penny on her back, 3-T gripped the back of her kneecaps, pressed her thighs to the mattress and dived in that pussy balls deep. See, that dick a whole new type of dick when you're laying on your back and all Penny wanted was another chance to change her bandages. She felt that dick touch the top of her cervix area and just gave up on life. For some odd reason this nigga's dick was harder than hard and thicker than a snicker, but she remained grounded and held on for the ride. Seeing the sexy fuck face that Penny made mixed with witnessing her take all that dick, 3-T was falling in love with Penny. After that simple thought, he slowed his stroke down, laid on top of Penny and wrapped her up on a love hug while grinding in that pussy. Penny didn't know the reason for the change of pace but was all too grateful.

"I love you Penny.", her panted in her ears slow grinding in her belly.

Penny's eyes flew open to full capacity. She loved him as well but never thought that he would feel the same about her, let alone let her know so soon. 3-T kept show stroking but lifted up just enough to look in her eyes.

"Tony...are you sure that it's love that you feel and not lust?"

"I want you for life Penny.", he confessed as he palm brushed her scalp. "You're everything that I want in a woman and I trust you with my heart and life."

"I love you too Tony. And trust that I'm not going anywhere but when the time is right we need to have a talk."

"Anything you want Penny." "Anything?", she asked really sultry. "Name it."

"Cum with me."

"Huh?", he asked a little confused.

"Let's cum together to deal the deal. We'll never betray one another or leave each other."

3-T's agreement came in a kiss full of passion and a stroke full of purpose. Penny kissed him back with equal emotion while thrusting upwards to meet him half way.

"Fuck me Tony!", she demanded. "Like fuck me hard!" "But the banda..."

"Fuck me or I'll clip your balls on your sleep!"

Without a moment wasted, 3-T hot that pussy like he over paid for it. Penny gripped his ass cheeks and pulled him in as he choked her. The harder she pulled him, the closer he came to shooting up in her club.

"Look at me.", he whispered.

Penny opened her eyes and they locked gazed as their climaxes build. "Hum cumming!", Penny squealed through the grip in her throat.

"Me too!", he admitted.

3-T started hitting that pussy so hard that it started squirting everywhere like crazy! "I'm cumming Tony! Shit it's cumming!"

"I'm cumming too babygirl, keep looking at me."

Penny felt his dick swoop l swell up as he felt hare pussy tighten up around him and all hell broke loose.

"UUUHHHHH!"

"OOOOOHHHH SSSHHHHHIITTT!"

"Mmmm dam you motherfucker!!"

Penny's face was dam near blue from 3-T's death grip on her neck and he still was in the moment from cumming. She clawed at his wrist and he recoiled like she was poisonous to touch.

"I'm sorry.", her panted. "Sorry babygirl. Was caught up in the moment." "It's ok.", she huffed. "Pussy good ain't it?"

He chuckled and collapsed on top of her. She embraced him and wrapped her legs around his waist and just enjoyed the ride that the wave gave her.

"Wha ya tink bout mon?", Iggy asked Boogey.

The hit squad was now back in Jamaica on a different mission than what they left for.

They left on a death mission and came back to regroup for an even more dangerous death mission.

"Me don no if we cud truss da enemy."Boogey responded lungs filled with tree smoke. "No one say we have ta truss dem. But we need em' to find da gal."

"Den he had da nerve ta all us ta sell em' weed!", Boogey snapped. "Pantie boy got big balls mon!" "We give it to em'."

"Ya fareal mon? Ya gone do bidniss wit da one dat murdah Pontune?"

"If we do bidniss, dey get comfortable enuff ta let

dey guard down. Dey work fa is two ways mon. Dey sell da weed and dey look fa da gal. When we kill da gal, we kill dem too."

Boogey rubbed his bearded cheeks while thinking over the plan that was set. Why not make some money while killing two birds with one stone.

"Me guess it da best way.", Boogey agreed. "Aye, wha ya tink about da gal wit all da tattoos?"

"No Boogey! Dis not time fa playn hide da poonpoon pootah!" "Me no care. Me will have me fun wit her and me gun."

Over the next few weeks, there was still no luck on finding Friday, but life must go on. Dullah helped handle the club's operations and 3-T helped Adrian and Nechelle run the gym. Since Friday owned the gym, the detectives still popped up every now and then because he had an active warrant and they didn't know his status. They tried viewing the footage from the hospital but the main video conductor was so shot to shit, it had to be repaired before thru could recover any evidence off of it. Nechelle was busy helping a member when Detectives Griggs stepped into the gym. Standing 6'3, 235lbs, big brown eyes, wavy ceasar fade and full beard, the man was the sexiest fuck nigga that the hood has seen in a while.

Seeing Nechelle for the first time in workout attire threw him off balance. She looked nothing like the mess he found her looking like the day they met at the hospital.

Nechelle wore a pair of baby blue and white 95'Air Max, baby blue spandex shorts that hugged her camel toe way too tight and her ass crack separated because of how jacked up she wore the spandex in her crotch. A white sports bra was struggling with every thread of its existence to hold then tig ole bitties inside. Her hair was a messy ponytail and her body shined with sweat. She was truly one of the sexiest women he had ever laid eyes on in a while. Nechelle noticed him as he stood ringside in admiration of her skills and physique and thought it was best that she got rid of him as soon as possible.

"How can I help you, fuck nigga?", Nechelle asked with an impassive stare. "It's detective."

"Detective Fuck Nigga."

"What's a fuck nigga?", Griggs asked in irritation. "A straight up lame ass muthafucka."

"And what exactly is a lame muthafucka?" "A fuck nigga!"

Griggs blew out an air of frustration. He was just doing his job. "Where is Mr. Smalls?" "Ain't seen him in a while."

"When did you last seen him?"

"You know what, let's cut the bullshit." Nechelle stated. She stepped out of the ring and walked up to his face. His cologne was intoxicating. "My man was in a fuckin coma. How he got out of that hospital, I couldn't tell ya. I was too busy surviving. You keep coming in my gym on this goofy shit and it's pissing me the fuck off. That hospital was transformed into a slaughter house and you're in a fuckin gym trying to serve a warrant. And there's only one type of person that would do some clown ass shit like that."

"And what type of person would that be?"

A FUCK NIGGA!! Now step yo ass outta my gym. Coming in here smelling like ajax and muscle rub.", she lied because this nigga was smelling like he deserved to get his dick sucked.

Nechelle's face was twisted into a scowl as she looked him up and down then walked away. Griggs was oddly turned on by this sexy ass disrespectful lil bitch. But he knew that he had to lighten up because to continuously show up without a warrant was harassment. He turned to leave and was face to face with Samantha, Adrian's girlfriend. She heard the hold thing and even knew why he came.

"You look like you got something that you wanna tell me.", Griggs fished.

Samantha did her best to control her emotions because she wanted to be understood.

"A black man was abducted after being left in the care of a white man. Another white man sends another black man to fetch his own kind to be exterminated instead of resuming the care he deserved before his abduction."

"And why are you telling me this?"

"Incase you didn't know what a lame ass fuck nigga was."

C2

Friday woke up feeling a lot better than he'd felt in a while. His body was a little sore and he needed a good stretch because he was in bed so much. Deciding not to call the nurse, he got up on his own and headed to the bathroom. Even though it took longer than it normally would, he cleaned himself up and decided to take a tour of the home. He hadn't left the room that he stayed in since he first woke and it felt like a prison. The hallways had plush burgundy carpet that was thicker than lawn grass, walls the color of banana pudding. Pictures of Puerto Ricans decorated the wall as far as he could see. He was in the last room so he just walked ahead, taking in the sight.

As he looked at the pictures, he noticed that none of them were black people. Not even a mixture. He wondered if it was because this may not be his home, but a relative maybe. The first room he came across looked like an office of some sort. He wandered inside and knew that whoever room this beloved to was more likely the head nigga in charge. The 5x5 photo above the Italian leather master chair was a dead giveaway. It was of an older gentleman that looked like he'd seen happier times. His facial expression held one of a killer and his eyes held death on a short leash. He walked over to the desk and a gold cigar box that looked like it cost a life sat on top, which he opened and saw almost two dozen expensive looking cigars. He shut the case and made his way to the office window. If he had to guess, he would say that it was the rear of the home because all he saw was water. As if the home sat on some type of plateau. It was a beautiful tranquilizing sight to see and he wondered what his life was like before he lost his memory.

"Hey Mr.!", a small voice shouted.

Two energetic seven year olds came dashing into the room and started running circles around Friday. One was a handsome little boy and the other was a starry eyed little girl.

Friday thought that it was best not to get caught in the office by anyone who knew better so he made his way out.

"What were you doing in poppa's room?", the young boy asked. "Oh, I was just…"

"What's your name mister?", the girl asked, cutting him off. "I'm um…I'm Eric.", he remembered. "Yea, my name is Eric."

"Nuh-uh lol!", the boy giggled. "Somebody already has that name." "Who has that name already?", Friday asked.

"Our dog's name is Eric too!", the girl responded.

Friday frowned at that. The kids led him into a huge kitchen with all modern appliances. Every countertop was marble and so was the floors. A made was arty the stove preparing something that smelled so good it made him feel like he had to take a shit.

"Nanna! Nanna! Look what we found!", the boy hollered running into the kitchen "Oh child! It's not what, but who you found."

The older lady looked up at Friday with a split second of disgust on her eyes then smiled into her role.

"Good morning senor Snipes. Would you like something to eat?" "Um, yes ma'am. I guess."

"Call me Nanna. Please. Ma'am makes me remember my age lol."

"Got you. Nanna it is.", he agreed. "Have you seen Calynda this morning?" "Senor Snipes, Calynda is here when she isn't, and she isn't when she is." "Wow. Ok. Whatever that means."

"She does it all the time.", a deep voice came from behind. "This woman always speaks in riddles, makes you pay attention whenever she speaks!"

Amelio Diaz stood a short 5'5 and weighed almost 250lbs. But one could tell, even with a few extra pounds, the man was no sloth. Just by the way he walked told you that he could more than likely step foot in ya ass with ease. He came up beside the old woman and gave her a loving kiss on there cheek.

"What's that you're cooking Nanna?", Amelio asked as he stood on the opposite side of the kitchen's island from Friday.

"Does it matter? You cat everything that you see anyway!", Calynda said as she walked into the kitchen.

Her hair has that fresh out of the shower wet look and she wore no make up. This bitch was badder than J-Lo and Cardi-B combined. She walked up to Friday and kissed him really nasty which shocked him, making him keep his eyes open and look at everybody else, who on turn was looking right back at him.

"EEEEWWWW!!!", the kids squealed.

"Come on children.", Nanna announced. "You two have eaten already. It's time to get ready for school."

She knew it was time for Amelio and Calynda to put in work and there in the company of adults was no place for children.

Four months has pass and there was still no signs of Friday or Calynda. Aisha informed the crew that the surveillance conductor from the hospital was almost fully repaired so when she heard anything, they would be the first to know. Dullah was taking Friday's absence the hardest. That was his nigga from day one and it was killing him not to be able to do anything about it. Pepp had always been the quiet type but ever since J.J.'s death, he'd been really distant and secluded. He still did his job, but one could tell that he was not the same. He was really waiting on the time so he could serve revenge to the ones responsible for killing his twin. Tyler was just as broken up as Pepp over J.J.'s demise, if not more. Tonia came around often to help Tyler out and the two had started spending more time together. Not as much as old times, but making progress. Iggy and Boogey kept true to their word and sent a wrecking crew to the states to find Calynda but they had been on standby ever since. Iggy also hit 3-T off with 1500 pounds of some crazy stand of weed that had the city on fire. But the cocaine side of the business was at a stand still. Dullah had taken over Friday's place heading the crew and most operations. He was at the club in Friday's office when 3-T came through the door with a look of in interest.

"Whaddup fool?", Dullah greeted, dapping the homie up.

"Ain't shit. But check this out. You remember that lil bass bitch Treece from the west?" "Talking bout the one with the super phat ass and walk all pigeon toed?"

"Yes lawd! That one!", 3-T tripped. "What about her?"

"Well, you know she sniff a lil white every now and then but she always but at least three pounds a week. So I go to serve the bitch at her crib and she got a big bag of blue getting right. But there thing that's funny, while we're making small talk, she mentioned that she ain't had blow like that since we fell off."

"Alll righhttt. What you trying you say?", Dullah asked a little confused.

"Nigga! If she ain't had blow like that since she got it from us, then somebody selling coc like the coc we had! And it's more than likely from the same people we jacked!"

"Shit! You think them same Hispanics we jacked found somebody to open up shop?"

"One monkey don't stop no show.", 3-T said. "We knocked off Pusha and his crew, all the Hispanics did was wait until the heat died down and found another route."

Dullah sat in thought and evaluated everything that his boy had just laid on him. If this was the same coc that they used to push, then all they had to do was follow the bread crumbs and it would lead them to the connect. And possibly Friday.

"So who did she say that she got the white from?", Dullah asked.

"Some cracker out in the country. Said the muthafucka breeds reptiles or some shit." "You get the addy?"

"You know I did! But the bitch charged me though.", 3-T said. "How much?"

"Ten."

"Ten racks?!", Dullah asked in disbelief. "Naw. Ten inches lol!"

"Geettt the fuck outta here! Lol! She should've let

me paid her. I'd give her a lil more." "Nigga whatever. You ain't rockin like that."

"Ask ya momma.", Dullah joked. "Aye fuck you boy!"

"Lol! Cool out ma nigga. Let's just ride out there and see what this cracked can tell us." "Lego!"

Dullah and 3-T took the trip out to the country side of town to see if they could find out who was the new supplier in the city. They knew that whomever they were meeting was not the actual connect, but just a buyer. But it was one step closer to the connect. The address took them to an old wooden cabin in the middle of west bubble fuck. No neighbors for at least a quarter mile in either direction and it sat on a dirt road. They were greeted before they parked the car because the were heard looking before they were seen. The walked up to the front porch and came face to face with a man who looked as if he hadn't seen a country road a day in his life. Gucci flip flops, Gucci socks, Gucci frame, and wife beater did not fit the description that they were expecting. The white guy was on the chubby side but not in a way that made him out of shape. A glock 33 was on a hip holster and he was smoking on one of the fattest blunts that they had ever seen. The weed smelled very familiar and it didn't take a genius to figure out where it came from.

"I've never been the smartest man in the room but to me, it don't look like you two are from around here.", the cabin owner said. He looked neither friendly nor hostile but he was strapped, so it would be best to play it cool.

"We're looking for Manny.", Dullah informed him. "Oh, I know that part.", the man said.

"And how'd you figure that out?", 3-T asked.

"Who the fuck else would you be looking for out here?", the man snapped.

"Look, we didn't come here on no bullshit, we just need some information and we'll be on our way.", Dullah said.

"I don't have to find you shit and you'll still be on your way!", the man pulled the glock. "Who sent you?!", he demanded, chambering a round.

"Nobody sent us. We just want.."

"Well how the fuck did you find me?!", the man questioned, cutting Dullah off. "All that shit is irrelevant."

"Well you better say something before you become irrelevant."

"Someone robbed us out of our cocaine and it's close to the shit you're selling. We didn't come here to fuck up what you got going on, we're just at a dead end and we need some help."

The man took a long look at the trespassers and reholstered his gun. "Never did like a crook. Come on in, see what we can do."

The man led them into the cabin and it looked like a reptilian zoo! Small gators, lizards, snakes, and all kinds of other shit was either caged or hanging somewhere. The furniture and appliances were modern, but everything else looked like it was used for reproduction.

"I'm Manny. Feel free to have a seat."

3-T and Dullah looked terrified to sit. Never knew what could jump out and attack them at any moment.

Buy they needed Manny's help and didn't want to offend him so they sat cautiously. Manny returned with a sofa only for himself and sat across from the homies.

"So what exactly is it that you want me to tell you?", Manny asked, getting right to business.

"Who sold you three coc?", Dullah asked. "Got it from a woman. Lives out near Bear's Creek."

"Woman? What's her name?", 3-T asked.

"Trina, if I'm not mistaken. Short, brown skinned, thick. But I could tell that she was some sort of runner, not the main plug."

"How'd you figure she may be the runner?"

"Because there plug wouldn't risk dropping off ten bricks." "Yea, you right about that.", 3-T agreed.

"Would you mind helping us contact this Trina?", Dullah asked.

"Naw. I think I've done enough for the both of you. Now act like you was never here and…."

"AAAHHHH SHIT! MUTHAFUCKA!", 3-T hollered jumping to his feet. "What? What the fuck happened?", Dullah asked jumping up as well. "Man, something bit me ma nigga!", 3-T cried, holding his crotch area.

Dullah pointed to 3-T's feet as a big ass green spider fell out of his shorts and scurried under the couch.

"Oh that ain't good.", Manny admitted.

"What you mean that ain't good?", Dullah screamed. "My fuckin spider is loose!"

"Your spider? Fuck your spider! What about this spider bite nigga? What's gonna be the reaction?"

"Ooohh my dick! Madick madick madick madick!", 3-T whined holding his

dick and shuffling in circles.

"Yo Manny! Do you have something for this shit?", Dullah asked. "Naw. Not that I know of."

3-T had now dropped his pants and underwear. His dick had a lump the size of a ping pong ball on the side of it at mid length.

"Man you gotta help me out ma nigga.", 3-T pleaded desperately. "Come on, we gotta get to the hospital.", Dullah said.

"No man, we ain't got time for that shit. I need your help now!"

"I don't know shit about no spider bit! What the fuck you expect me to do?" "You gotta suck the poison out!"

"Suck the say what now?", Dullah studdered not really believing what he'd just heard. "Man ma nigga pleassseee. Just suck on the bump 'till it goes down."

"Bruh…. You seriously can't be asking me to do no shit like that!"

"Man this shit is growing!" 3-T then looked to Manny. "Please Manny please. This shit hurts and all you gotta do is…"

"I am not….sucking your dick bro.", Manny said with his hands raised in surrender.

"I think I'm gonna pass out! Dullah I don't wanna die Dullah please!" 3-T had now begun to shed tears.

"Manny! Get a fuckun knife!", Dullah snapped. "The fuck you need a knife for?", 3-T asked. "We gotta cut this shit off!"

69

"AIN'T NO FUCKIN WAY!"

"Well what else you gonna do?", Dullah asked.

"I'll squeeze the bump and all you gotta do is suck em till it goes all the way down." "If you tell me to suck your dick one more time ma nigga…"

"Bro, you gotta get him to a hospital.", Manny advised. "Pull your fuckin pants up and let's go!"

3-T got it together the best he could and made it to the car. Dullah group text the crew what happened. Some of them found it hilarious and a few serious they'll meet them at the hospital. Once 3-T was admitted, Dullah chilled out in the waiting area. Penny showed up first, then Nicole and Karen. He told them the story again and they died laughing when they heard about 3-T asking him to suck the poison out. He also put them on point about the coc coming from some female names Trina.

"I know the bitch.", Karen admitted. "What's her story?", Dullah asked.

"She was buying from us! I used to drop off to her nigga."

"You think it's the same coc that we took from Pusha?", Nicole asked.

"Don't know for sure, but one way to find out.", Dullah said. Then he looked to Karen. "Can you still get in contact with her?"

"Yup. Got the bitch number still saved in my phone."

"Well y'all two do what it takes for her to tell where she's getting the white from. That should put us one step closer to finding the homie."

CHAPTER 5

"On your feet!", Cheewaus commanded Friday.

Standing 6'2, 210lbs of solid Puerto Rican muscle, Cheewaus was known for fucking shit up. Trained in four different types of material arts, two tours in Afghanistan, one in Iraq, he was an ass whipping looking to be handed out. Cheewaus and Calynda had been training Friday since he could wiped his own ass again. Slow in progression, but progression none the less.

"Bruh", Friday panted as he stood back up. "Your moving like a fuckin ninja and I don't know this shit like that, but you expect me to...."

BAM!

Cheewaus walked up on Friday midsentence and served him a spinning elbow to the jaw. Staggered and stunned, but Friday did not fall.

"Protect yourself cabron!", Calynda snappe.

She joined in and gave Friday a swift kick to the back of the knee caps as Chrewaus followed up with a drop kick to the chest. They were fucking him up!

"This shit ain't fair yo.", Friday complained standing up once again.

He was pissed off and a feeling of rage came over

him. Calynda stepped up and swung a right hook.

Friday ducked the blow and Cheewaus came with a two piece combo which Friday bobbed and weaved. Side stepping towards his largest opponent's weakest side, Friday waited for Cheewaus to deliver the expected left jab, leaned on the backside of the punch and came with a jaw crunching right uppercut. Calynda had swung when Cheewaus did and missed her mark by inches, shifting her balance. Friday peeped her mistake, shuffled his stance, and gave her a left uppercut to the gut, and dropped her with a hip thrown right to the temple. Cheewaus laid knocked out cold with one kneecap stuck in the air and Calynda had a worried look on her face. Whatever happened was not a part of any training that they had taught him. She knew that he was a boxer. Those were moves of a boxer. He was slowly gaining his memory.

"Baby, are you alright?", he asked her. "I'm fine Eric."

"I'm sorry, ok. I mean, I guess I got carried away, you know."

"It's ok. I promise. This is all a part of the training my love. You did great.", she assured. "Well, what about him?", he asked nodding to Cheewaus.

"He'll be fine. You just surprised him, that's all. Now go get cleaned up, I want to show you something afterwards.

After showering and hydrating, Friday met Calynda in one of the many studies in the mansion. She sat at a nice sized wooden round table with paperwork and pictures spaced out across the top of it. She noticed his presence and gave him a light smile.

"Come my love. Have a seat with me." Once he was seated beside her, Calynda placed several photos of men and women in front of him. "Do you recognize any of these people Eric?"

"Naw. Well, should I?"

"These are the people that you selected to help with your operation.", Calynda informed him.

"So I take it that you're about to tell me that these are the people that shot me."

"Not exactly my love. These are the individuals that has you shot. And they are currently under the impression that you are unaware of them being behind your failed assassination attempt."

Friday studied the pictures for a long while but nothing came to mind. They had might as well been random photos of strangers.

"Well, so I guess you have a plan to settle the score then right?"

"Yes. And it's death! But first, we have to recover something highly valuable that they stole from us after they tried to have you murdered."

"What? Drugs?", he asked. "No, gold my love. " "Gold?!"

"Yes, gold. We has 25 pure solid gold bars worth $865,000 each. Our sources, which are very reliable, says that the gold has not been attempted to be fenced. So they obviously have it stashed somewhere." "And we're gonna find out where it is huh?"

"Not we. You!", Calynda said. "Me?"

"Yes, my love."

"But that tried to kill me. They'll try again!"

"They may, but not themselves. They will hire someone. And that's where our hit squad plays a role. We will watch your every move and surroundings. Anything that holds suspicion will be swiftly executed."

"Can't we just go wherever they are, kill them and take it?"

"We do not know the exact location of the gold. So it's your duty to go back like you're none the wiser of their treason and inform me of the gold's whereabouts."

"Naw, we ain't doing it like that.", Friday said after giving it some thought. "What's the problem? Why not?"

"Because that's the dumbest shit I've ever heard!"

"Eric! This is the only way to find the gold!", Calynda snapped.

"Gold?! Fuck that gold! These muthafuckas tried to kill me. So instead of using my absence as an advantage to reappear on some low key goofy shit, I'll use my absence in a way to stay invisible. I'll follow each and every one of them until I know their routines. One by one, I'm knockin em' off until I have my revenge! The gold will have no choice but to show up once we take back everything that was once ours."

Friday stood to leave Calynda with her thoughts and his plan. "Now get me the info that I need on each of them so that I can get this shit over with. In the meantime, I need to know more about my role that was played in this cocaine operation. I want all my shit back the way that it was Calynda."

And with that said, Friday walked out. This was not how Calynda planned for things to work out and now she would have to get him more involved with Amelio's operation in order to keep the lie alive that she's painted as him being a man of status in her family. She knew that Amelio may not be happy with her decision, but it was one that could not be undone.

C2

"Dam Tonia! Girl you're putting on a little weight huh?", Tyler joked from the kitchen.

The two has set their differences to the side and decided to give their relationship another try. Ever since J.J.'s death, Tonia made it her business to stay sniffing up Tyler's ass and it paid off.

"Shit, ever since Friday's been gone, ain't been much to do but lay around. Guess the time off wasn't such a good thing.", Tonia replied.

"Well, the food is almost ready. This won't help either lol."

Tonia had been a bit on the lazy side ever since the war at the hospital. The crew thought it'd be a good idea to lay low for a while, so there was nothing really to do but lounge around. When the food was ready, Tyler fixed two plates and that sat to eat.

"This shit looks really good babe.", Tonia complimented. "I know. I'm about to fuck this shit up!"

"Me too!"

Tonia took her first bite of BBQ ribs and her stomach lurched. She stopped chewing to take a few easy breaths. Tyler saw the awkward look on Tonia's face and got suspicious.

"Nuh-uh! Don't play with me. My food is not nasty!", Tyler sassed.

Tonia looked off into the distance, tilted her head to the side, chewed once more and bolted towards the bathroom. By the time Tyler caught up with her, Tonia was faced down in the toilet bowl.

"Dam! Was it that bad?", Tyler asked.

"I don't know what's wrong babe. I feel sick as a dog."

Tonia gagged up more fluid until all she could do was dry heaved because there was nothing left to come up. She sat flat on her ass and leaned up against the tub. Tyler looked down at her lover with a look of disbelief on her face. Tonia noticed it and twisted up her mug.

"The fuck you looking at me like that for?!" "Bitch you pregnant!"

Nicole and Karen pulled up to a condo complex on the upper class side of town.

Expensive vehicles were parked in designated parking spots so all visitors had to park in a vacant lot next to the complex. The two women exited the car and made their way to the condo. Karen knocked on the door and it was answered moments later. Trina was a hood booger, turned hood rat, turned drug mule. All the bitch cared about was another dollar and glitter. Basic recipe for a double cross. Trina invited them in and the girls were slightly impressed. The condo was quite nice and beautifully furnished. Trina offered them drinks, which they declined, and Karen took the lead since she was the one familiar with Trina.

"Listen, I'm not here to take up much of your time so I'll get straight to it.", Karen said. "You still working with the white?"

"Girl you know I am.", Trina said all friendly. "Without the white, can't pay the lights lol." Nicole rolled her eyes.

"I know that's right. So what you getting them for?", Karen asked.

"Well, you know my man does all the negotiation buy I overheard him saying he gets then for 20k each."

"Dam! That's 5k cheaper than what we had them for." "And the shit just as good too!", Trina bragged.

"Well we trying to get plugged in so what's up with the connect?"

"I don't really know about that Karen. I mean, I fuck with you but things have changed you know. We on some low key shit and ain't really trying to do nothing new."

"Come on girl, we better than that.", Karen said trying to butter her up. "We made a lot of money together in the past, let's get this bag and stop bullshitin."

"Lemme talk to my nigga and…."

"Look bitch!", Nicole snapped. She'd been quiet too long and could tell that Trina was spinning Karen. We need that connect info like Pronto! You drive a Mercedes Maybach with front and rear cameras that records everytime the car is in park until the engine dies.

So we're gonna need that footage for the last two months too!"

"Bitch?!", Trina said to Nicole standing up. She then turned her attention to Karen. "I don't know who your silly ass friend think I am but I'll...."

WOP!!

Nicole hopped up and popped Trina square in the nose. "You'll what bitch?!", Nicole taunted.

WOP!! WOP!!

Nicole did her signature move, slinging Trina on the floor by her hair, dove on top of her and split her lip with a two piece.

"Where is your phone?", Karen snapped. "Get this bitch off of me!!", Trina screamed.

WOP!!

"Bitch, where there phone at?!", Nicole hissed through clenched teeth after popping her in the eye.

"On the kitchen counter!"

Karen got the phone but it was locked. "What's the password?"

Trina looked up at Nicole who in turn raises an eyebrow and drew her first back. "Pussy Power.", Trina mumbled in defeat.

After opening the phone and saw the Mercedes app already logged into, Karen threw it in her purse. "Come on girl, we got what we need. Let's slide."

Nicole got up off of Trina and fixed her clothes. Trina wrote a scowl on her face as she watched the two make their exit.

"Fix your face bitch! Fore you make me beat that

ass.", Nicole threatened. "Just leave please.", Trina mumbled as she looked away.

When the girls pulled away from the complex, Nicole called Dullah on speaker. "Whaddup?", Dullah answered.

"We got the bitch's phone.", Nicole said with attitude.

Dullah sighed. "Please explain to me why you have this women's phone." "The bitch bucked. Plain and simple."

"Oh my gawd. Is she still alive Nicole?" "Yea, she alive lol."

Karen snatched the phone. "But she fucked up though!" "Just get y'all ghetto asses back to the club alright!"

"YES DADDY!!", they laughed in unison then hung up.

Dullah rubbed his temples in frustration. He didn't know how Friday was able to deal with all of this shit but he saluted the homie. After taking on the load Friday left behind, Dullah was constantly on edge and easily annoyed. He knew he needed to do better or he would never stay focused enough to get a lead on Friday.

"Hey baby!", Aisha beamed walking into the club's office. She wore a tight black thigh high dress with black wedges. That tiny waist, juicy breast and phat ass had Dullah forgetting all of his problems.

"Ain't shit. Just waiting on some new leads. What's good with you?" "Well, it's my day off so I thought I'd hang out with you for a while."

"Yea , I'm just here busy as usual.", he sighed.

"Anything I can do to help?", she asked with a hint of freaky in her voice. "Mmm.. what you had in mind?"

Aisha walked around the desk and knelt between his legs. "What do you want me to have in mind huh?", she asked biting the corner of her bottom lip with raised eyebrows as she unzipped his pants. "Show this dick some of that police brutality."

"Lol! Boy you are crazy."

Aisha stroked his dick in once hand while massaging his balls in the other. It never ceased to amaze her that this niggas meat was almost the size of her forearm. Dullah relaxed, laid his head back and allowed Aisha to work her magic. She brought his sack up to her mouth and gently sucked and licked all over them while double fisting him above her head. Her tiny feminine hands could barely wrap around his girth but she worked that shit like a pro. Dullah was getting super horny so he grabbed a fist full of her hair, snatched his dick out of her grasp and slid in between her soft jaws. Saliva instantly ran down the corner of Aisha's mouth as she sucked as hard as she could. With every thrust, Dullah's dick went deeper and deeper down her throat, which would almost double in size every time he went down there.

Aisha was a submissive lover and that turned him on the most. Whatever he brought her way, she would take it like a champ, even if it was too much. Feeling his already massive dick begin to swell, she knew Dullah was about to blow her face off. She quickly stood up, turned around, pulled her dress up and crawled on top of the desk. Face down ass up, she wiggled that soft booty from side to side as she looked back at him with lust in her eyes. Dullah came fully out of his pants, parted her ass cheeks and slid all 11 ½ inches inside of Aisha's guts. Her walls flexed around him in reaction to being stretched so wide and penetrated so deeply. Her head shook from side to side as she lowered it on the desk. This nigga just be ramming his dick up in her like that shit was average.

"Dam Aisha.", he sighed in ecstacy. "Your pussy so fuckin tight." "Yo dick just too dam big!"

Dullah gripped her hips and slow stroked that kitty at a steady pace. He leaned forward, spit on her asshole and stuck a finger in it. In return, Aisha wiggled on that dick then started throwing it back. She loved it when he did that and it always transformed her into a whole different type of freak. White thick nut coated his meat in no time and he was now drilling her back out. And she loved it. Nicolle walked into the office, saw all that dick and her mouth hit the floor. Karen walked in behind her covered her mouth as her eyes grew wide in amazement. She had only seen a dick that size on the internet.

Dullah was so deep in the pussy that he didn't realize that they were not alone. Karen pulled out her office in an attempt to get some footage for a hard night alone but Nicole snatched her cell with that "bitch really?" look. Karen just hunched her shoulders and crossed her arms with a smirk. Nicole felt that they were violating her man's office and decided to interrupt their little fuck session by slamming the door hard as hell. Dullah spun around and Karen dam near caught a heart attack seeing all that dick up close.

Nicole busted a silent nut. Aisha dam near fell off

of the desk and quickly got herself together. Dullah found it more difficult than usual to fix his clothes with a fresh erection but managed to get it done. Nicole wore a scowl on her face but Karen had the goofiest grin ever and have him the double eyebrow lift twice.

"What the hell are y'all doing here?", Dullah asked.

"Didn't you tell us to pull up not even twenty minutes ago?", Nicole sassed. "You could've fuckin knocked."

"Looks like you've been ah knocking enough for the both of us.", Karen joked. "Bitch chill.", Nicole hissed, giggling but trying to be serious.

Aisha fixed her clothes and walked to the office bathroom like she didn't just get caught taking all that dick. Nicole and Karen took a seat and waited on Dullah to get his life together.

"So what was on thet phone?", Dullah asked. "Karen was looking through it on the way over."

"Well", Karen smiled, clearly with the shits and giggles but did her best to get serious. "This dumb bitch got one of the numbers saved as "plug", and another saved as MexDingo..... Sounds like a Mexican with a big dick to me but anywayssssss. They both got the same area code so obviously it's the connect and wherever drops the shit off. I was looking at the footage from her camera...."

"The car has a camera?", Dullah asked suspiciously, cutting her off. "AND IT caught the license plate plus driver, nigga you rude as fuck!" "Was he Hispanic?"

Nicole just stared at him and Karen just rolled her

eyes.

"That gotta be who we're looking for! Write them plate numbers down. When was the last time she talked to him?"

"Lemme see….", Karen said. "Like two weeks ago."

"When was the last time they met?

"The clip on this app says a week ago."

"Ok, so that meet up a week after making the order. .."

Just then, Aisha walked out of the bathroom all smiles popping gum. "What's up y'all?"

"Heeyyy giirrrll!", Karen sang making Aisha blush.

"Yo Aisha," Dullah began, grabbing a piece of paper from Karen. "Run these plate numbers and see who is this vehicle registered to. Text that info to me asap. Nicole, set up a play with whoever's the plug. From that phone, act like Trina. You already know that numbers so make an order of fifty of em. Aye Karen, cam you tell from the location exactly where they met up at?"

Karen reviewed the footage once more and her mouth went dry. "Y'all ain't gonna believe this shit…"

"Why? Where they at?", Nicole asks sitting up. "They're meeting up right here."

Nechelle had been so busy with north the sex store and gym, she barely had time to handle anything else. She found herself grocery shopping because she hadn't bought food in weeks. Ever since Friday came up missing, her whole routine had been thrown off. She surely couldn't depend on Nicole because the bitch couldn't cook. As she finished up selecting her items, she made her way to checkout and bumped into a pain in her ass.

"Well, well… what's up Ms. Hollywood?"

"Evening Detecting Fuck Nigga.", Nechelle spat while rolling her eyes.

"Come on. We don't have to go down that road. I'm not here to harass you. Hell, I'm not even on the clock."

"Then why exactly are you here?"

"It's a fuckin grocery store.", Griggs said with a wave of his arm. "Well I'm done. Excuse me and have a nice day detective."

"Hey Nechelle", Griggs called out softly. "How did you get here?" "The fuck? I drove!"

"No Hollywood.. I mean how did you get caught up in this mess? I can tell that this ain't your style."

"Oh, so you know me now?", she asked

"As much as I'd like to get to know you, I never said that I did. For some funny reason, I feel like I should help you."

Nicole stood straight and face him at eye level. "Help me how? If I wanna be handcuffed, I'd be with my bitch and a bedpost. And if I wanna see a judge, I can go kick it with thee Almighty. Some help me…fuck outta here. Corny ass nigga!"

"Listen to me Nechelle", Griggs snapped. "Sharif is wanted for murdering numerous police officers in a bank robbery which civilians were gunned down also. He's wanted in connection with three home invasions where more people were murdered. The same type of guns that were used in these crimes were found in a storage unit rented out in his name. And what do you think would be discovered when that hospital footage is finally viewed? Huh? Your whole gang will never make it to the local county jail because their gonna shoot yalls asses dead on sight!"

Nechelle was silent as she let it all sink in. This fucking detective was on point like a decimal. He knew every fucking thing so she thought it would be wise to not play with his intelligence. A lone tear fell down her face.

"What do you want from me?", she sighed.

Griggs stepped so close that she could count the hairs on his chin. "Tell me that I'm right and I'll walk away.", he said calmly.

Nechelle didn't say anything. Just continued to stare with watery eyes. "I like tacit. Your time is running out."

"Wait!", she called out as her spun to leave. "Tell me…. What do I have to do? What will it take to make this go away?", Nechelle asked desperately.

"You can turn yourself in, confess your role, and testify against those involved." "You know that I can't do that!"

"Pack light and move fast." "Griggs! Please!"

"Griggs?", he chuckled. "I thought that it was Detective Fuck Nigga!" She rolled her eyes. "There's gotta be another way.", she pleaded.

"Once this footage is recovered, your ass better be looking gone Hollywood.", he warned as her walked away.

Nechelle knew that her time was short and she

needed a plan fast. At the end of the day, she needed that footage by any means necessary. And that was the mission.

Friday sat at the kitchen table reading folders of information that was obtained on the crew of double crossers. He noticed that they all had police records, except for once. A Nicole Scotch. So he wondered, why would he pick a bunch of common criminals to work directly under him in a cartel like Amelio's? It just didn't add up. These individuals were never in the streets heavy enough to even be considered being a part of this. His gut was telling him that something wasn't right but until her figured it out, he was sticking with the mission.

"There you are Eric.", Calynda said as she walked into the kitchen. "What are you up to my love?" She had just gotten out of the shower and wearing a silk rob and nothing else.

"Just going over this info that I asked for. What's up? What's on your mind ?"

"You.", she said kissing his nose. "How much more longer will you be?" "Not much longer. I'm almost done actually."

"Well, by the time your done, I'll most likely be sleep. Take care my love."

Calynda leaned over and kissed him lightly on the forehead. Friday reached up, grabbed the back of her neck and tongued her down. She hadn't been kissed like that in so long Calynda clutched her pussy because it damn near jumped out of her rob. Friday picked her up and roughly placed her on the counter. He shoved her legs open and Calynda's eyes grew wide as fuck as she looked around for spectators. "Baby, we can't do this right…..uh-oohhh shit!"

Her words were cut short when Friday placed his face between her thighs and sucked on her clit. Calynda gripped his head and bit her lip. She was no virgin but she has never experienced oral sex before. She was a killer. She never had time for foreplay. It was always a quick dick and she's disappear. Never the same person twice. Friday was giving her a feeling that she'd never had and when he eased a finger in her ass, she completely lost sight of the mission…

"Shit Eric. Yes! Y-y-y suck this pussy daddy. Suck get dry!"

Friday continued to finger stroke her ass while sucking on her clit, moving his head in a circular motion.

"I'm cumming my love! Eric! Eric, ooooo suck this pussy just right!", she panted.

While his middle finger rested in her ass and his index in her pussy, Calynda gushed all over this nigga's chin.

"Mmmmm Damm Eric!"

Friday gave that pussy one last suck, went to the sink. He washed his hands and face then walked out leaving her sitting on the counter.

"What the fuck just happened?", she thought silently. He forgot a lot of things but not how to eat that pussy!

Tyler and Tonia sat in the OBGYN's office, waiting to be seen. Tonia kept denying that she was pregnant but Tyler was no dam fool. Never in their relationship had Tyler ever witnessed Tonia throwing up, or even getting sick at all. And for no apparent reason, just spilling her guts. Tyler has a suspicion about how all this came about but decided that it was best that she found out what if she was pregnant first before revealing what she thought. Forty minutes after checking in, an assistant called them to the back and set them up in an examination room. A short while later, an elderly woman came in and introduced herself. After she confirmed Tonia's info, she then prepped her for an ultrasound. Once the cold jelly was placed on her belly, Tonia became even more nervous. Soon as the monitor touched the jelly, a heartbeat echoed throughout the entire room. Tyler's mouth dropped to her kneecaps.

"What the fuck is that noise?", Tonia frowned, looking at the screen. "It's a baby!", the old woman beamed.

"That ain't no dam baby!"

"It is dear. That noise is its heart beating."

"How the fuck did this happen?", Tonia whispered aloud.

"Well I can't tell you 'HOW' it happened, but maybe I can tell you around 'WHEN' it happened.", the lady said. "And judging by what I'm looking at, I'd say your around 6 months. Maybe more.'

"Can we have a moment please?", Tyler asked as her patience ran thin. "Sure. I'll leave something to clean with.", the nurse offered then left. "Nechelle and Nicole are gonna fuck you up Tonia!

"Nechelle and Nicole? What do they have to do with this?" "Bitch you fucked Friday! Or did you forget?"

Tonia took a split second to recollect and dropped

her head, rubbing her hands down her face.

"How could you Tonia?"

"I was drunk! And he was too! And don't act like I did this shit all on my own either."

"Well, it's too late now. ", Tyler said as she gathered her things. "Let's go. I got shit to do."

"Go? Bitch we ain't going nowhere yet!", Tonia snapped.

"The fuck you mean? There ain't shit left to do but pay the bill!"

"I'm aborting this shit. I'm not about to have no dam baby. I hate babies!"

"News flash bitch!", Tyler spat. "You're dam near six months or better, ain't no dam abortion! Too late for that shit, you better start getting shit together."

The nurse returned with photo copies of the ultra sound and gave them to Tonia. "Congratulations young lady.", she beamed. "It's a girl."

"Mm,mm,mm…", Tyler mumbled, shaking her head. "Chiiilld, I tell you. This shit is one messy ass mess. Bitch come on. I'm ret ta go."

CHAPTER 6

D ullah stood in the club's office looking out the window that gave a view I'd the front of the building. The call had been made for the cocaine so 3-T and Pepp waited on the delivery to pull up. Whomever that came to make the transaction was getting snatched the fuck up. Twenty minutes later, a black Cadillac SUV pulled up with only one Hispanic. They must've made so many drops that went good that they had gotten comfortable enough to ride solo. Stupid. Soon as the truck was parked, Pepp and 3-T pointed carbon 15's at the vehicle and motioned for the guy to step out of the truck.

Thinking that it was just a lame robbery, he calmly got out with his hands up. His thoughts shifted when 3-T popped him in the nose with the butt of the rifle. Pepp snatched the man up and 3-T popped him again.

"Ma nigga. Chill.", Pepp advised. "This ain't the time for that."

3-T walked up to the man and hawk spit a glob of mucus right on his lip and chin. "Alright! Let's go!", Pepp said, dragging the dude by his collar into the club.

He wasn't too fond of 3-T's foreplay. Once they got inside of the office, Pepp tied the guy to a chair and Dullah hauled off and smacked the shit out of the guy.

"Y'all niggas is wild yo, for real.", Pepp said shaking his head.

"Get Penny and Aisha over here.", Dullah told 3-T. He then turned his attention back to the Hispanic. "Who do you work for?"

He said nothing. 3-T bitch slapped him and Dullah kicked him in the chest, causing his chair to fall backwards. Pepp just sighed and picked the guy up. Fifteen minutes later Penny and Aisha walked through the door just in time to see Dullah punch the guy in the mouth.

"Oh my gosh!", Penny hollered. "Who the hell is this man? What did he do?" She then looked at the man. "What did you do sweety?"

"He dropped off the coc.", Pepp answered with a hunch of his shoulders. "Oh.", Penny said dryly. "Did he say anything?"

"Duh! Obviously not.", Aisha spoke up, rolling her eyes.

"Well what do y'all wanna know? Maybe I can help.", Penny suggested.

"Ain't shit that you can do that'll be any worse than what has already been done.", Dullah said.

"Oh you think?", Penny asked. She walked up to the man with an unopened bottle of water. She cracked the top and held it to his busted lip. "Drink.", she said flatly.

The guy slowly opened his mouth and drank. "Seeee!", Penny beamed. "I'm making progress."

"Bitch you are too goofy, you know that?", Aisha said rolling her eyes.

"Watch and learn motherfucker.", she spat then turned back to the guy. "Hi there pumpkin. My name is Penny, and you are?"

The man said nothing.

"Ok. I understand that you're a little upset about the kidnapping, ass kicking, and not to mention that your drugs are on the house. Thanks for that by the way. Anyways, all we want are a few simple answers and you can be in your way." She turned to Dullah, "What do you want to know?"

Dullah was highly frustrated but decided to see where this would go. "Who does he work for?"

"Who do you work for?", Penny asked. The man still said nothing. "I'm glad that you're giving me the silent treatment. Now I can show these rookies how to really extract information. Tony baby, grab me a scissors please."

3-T found it weird but did what was asked of him. Penny cut away the man's pants and underwear exposing his little dick and tiny nuts.

"Oh my gosh lol! Tony, I love you baby but if you were that small, you had no chance lol!" 3-T looked away. He did not want to see that shit. "Aisha, hold his legs open."

Aisha grabbed the man's ankles from behind and pulled them up the sides of the chair, causing his thighs to spread. Penny took the butt of her gun and rocked it back and forth like she was trying to hit his nuts with precision.

"Now answer the fucking question or I turn into the nutcracker!", Penny threatened. "No! No! No! Please don't do this!"

"Wrong answer buster!", Penny snapped and slammed the butt of her glock on his left testicle.

The way this man screamed, you would think that he was set on fire. Aisha was having a hard time holding his legs back plus she was looking over his shoulder trying to get a peek.

"Hooo shit! Penny!", Dullah panicked. "What?!"

"You're taking shit too far!"

"Too far? Too far?!!" Penny stood up and walked to Dullah slowly as she spoke. "I was in that hospital giving it all that I had, fighting for my life with my bare fucking hands! I watched J.J. get slaughtered like a fucking pig! That BITCH stabbed me in the back and I dam near lost Nechelle! I was in a fucking full blown dog fight while y'all were able to have each other's backs, not to mention Officer Aisha Brown was too busy wiping her ass to do anything about it. Yea, how fucking convenient!"

Penny's eyes were wild and she was waving her gun around like it wasn't loaded.

"Point made. Point taken.", 3-T said. "But we need to find out what he knows. So just calm down and…."

"FUCK calming down! Whoever that bitch was, she will have to answer to me and only me!" Penny then walked back over to the prisoner and raised her gun. Poor guy. "Who! The fuck! Do you work for?!"

"Amelio! Amelio Diaz!", the guy confessed.

"Where the fuck is he?", Penny gritted through clenched teeth. "Please…. Please. They'll kill me."

"Wrong answer motherfucker!", Penny snapped and squashed the last testicle. His sack exploded and Pepp freaked out.

"No! I didn't sign up for this shit!"

Penny chambered a round and blew the captive's head wide open. Blood splashed all over Aisha's face and she went nutts.

"Bitch really?!", Aisha hollered.

"I'm going downstairs.", Pepp mumbled walking off. Aisha went to the sink and washed her face off.

"Who the hell is Amelio Diaz?", Dullah asked.

"A pain in the FBI's ass.", Penny sighed. "When I was active in the field, Amelio was flooding the south east coast with cocaine. A RICO indictment encouraged him to go ghost. Hasn't been on the radar for some years now. Even when I…." Penny paused midsentence with a look of deep thought etched on her face.

"What's on your mind?", 3-T asked.

"Jesus Christ! Now this shit is making perfect sense!"

"What makes perfect sense Penny?" asked Dullah impatiently.

"Amelio has a daughter that was under surveillance when he was being investigated. If my intuition is right, his daughter was the bitch at the hospital."

"So we robbed a cocaine kingpin named Amelio?", Dullah asked. "Shit!", Penny snapped.

"Who has Friday as well?" "Fuck!"

"What's this bitch's name?", 3-T asked.

"Calynda.", Penny sighed. "Calynda Diaz. A

ruthless little bitch!" "You think she took the homie out?"

"Can't say babe. But it's something that she's after if she took him from the hospital instead of killing him."

"Well if this Amelio is a kingpin line you say he is, ain't no way he's holding Friday for some white."

"Could be gold.", Dullah said. "Gold? What gold?", Penny asked.

"When we jacked all the spots, Nicole came back with some gold bars. A lot of them."

"But it's been months since we took that gold.", 3-T said. "If he hasn't come for it then Friday never told him where it's at."

"Or he could've took it to his grave.", Dullah said.

"Well I'll say this.", Penny said standing up. "Whether Friday is dead or not, Amelio's coming for that gold. So you either go at him or wait for him to come for you."

"How can we go at him if he's been missing for ever?"

"His daughter. She's not wanted so there's something in her name that will lead us to her.", Penny assured.

"How are you gonna get that type of info?", 3-T asked. "You know what 3-T?", Dullah chuckled. "You stupid."

"Fuck you mean nigga?" Penny pinched him. "Sorry babe. Fuck you mean bruh?" "Penny and Aisha is the fuckin law! They can get that kind of shit."

"Oh…I knew that."

"Anyway.", Penny said rolling her eyes and gathering her things. "I'll have that info for you as soon as I can. Ask Aisha to search as well. She may come up with something that I didn't."

"That's what's up.", Dullah said.

Aisha returned with a scowl on her face, grilling Penny who just gave her a fingerly wave walking out. They put her up on game as well and she promised to do what she could. When she left, 3-T got up to leave next.

"Hold up ma nigga. Help me with this body bruh.", Dullah demanded.

"Nigga you got me fucked up! You better roll him up in carpet and have Pepp burn his ass."

"Where the fuck you see some damn carpet at dumbass?! The floor is glass. " "A mirror.... Two way.", 3-T slick talked.

Dullah just stared at his homie with a blank expression. Their friendship definitely required patience and toleration.

Boogey sat behind the wheel of his Audi a7 in deep thought. He had been doing his own investigation on finding out who were the Hispanics at the hospital that day they went to take 3-T out. Now back in the states, in the passenger seat of his ride sat one of his many hood boogers he fucked with when he visited. He needed information and this bitch has no issues breaking her water.

"So I'm thinking that these bitches want some work or whatever, man babe these hoes kicked my ass and took my phone!"

"Now why dem wan do dat gal?"

"Because them hating ass bitches wanted my connect! I know that you don't fuck with it but my people got the rawest shit moving out this bitch and muthafuckas can't stand to see a bitch win.", Trina capped.

"So wha ya gwan do bout it?"

"I don't know the bitch that jumped on me but that bitch Karen, the one that took my phone, I promise I'm gonna dog walk here ass on sight!"

Hearing Karen's name got Boogey's full attention. He knew that she rolled with the crew and he has a thing for her too. But he had no idea that she was fuckin with the coc. But what made him wonder was why did Karen go to the extreme to get the connect, THIS connect in particular.

"Me no blame ya fa seeking revenge, ya know. Do wha ya gotta do. But why ya tink she wan ya connect out of all da connects outchea?"

"Man babe, these Puerto Ricans got the best cheapest shit ever sold! Like I'm telling you, there's nothing like it. The crew used to buy from them until a guy named Friday that rolled with them got shot the fuck up then came up missing. He was like the boss or some shit but when that happened, they just stopped moving work. So my man did his research and found they plug they had and it's been on and poppin ever since."

Boogey couldn't do a better job at keeping his composure. From what Trina was saying, he was able to put the puzzle together somewhat. The crew robbed since Puerto Ricans and got into a war behind the it. Somehow, the war ended up at the hospital where he found himself in the fight for his life with the same Puerto Ricans. He was about to turn the fuck up, but he had to play it cool and be patient so he could kill two birds with one stone.

"Dam! Dat sound crazy gal. But if me wan get coc, could ya help me?" "You don't fuck with that shit babe lol! Cut it out."

"Fa real gal. Me wan ta make mo money and me know people dat fuck wit it. So ya gon help me or no?", Boogey pressed.

Trina's greedy ass started seeing dollar signs and took the bait. "Mmmmm…. What's in it for me daddy?", she asked all sultry. "Tell me wha ya want."

"Welll…I did see a cute Chanel pose the other day…."

Boogey pulled out a bank roll and extended it to her. Trina's dog ass reached for the cash and Boogey snatched it back.

"When me get wha me wan?"

Trina sucked her teeth and rolled her eyes. "I'll give my man your info and he will put you on babe now stop playingggg."

"Dat not enough.", Boogey pressed.

"Give me your phone!", Trina snapped. She took it and put her boyfriend's number in then threw it in his lap. "His name is DuPree. I'll tell him that we met through a friend and gave you the number. You're on your own from there. Now, is there anything else, sir, before I can get my purse?"

Boogey sparked a blunt and gave Trina that familiar look. In return, she gave him a devilish smirk as she looked around. "Lean your seat back nigga.", was all she said as she pulled his zipper down and cheated on her man the best way she knew how.

C2

Friday sat alone on a huge rock watching the waves crash on the shore. He was having trouble grasping the reality of his life and not remembering anything from his past. But from what he was told by Calynda, he came to the conclusion that a lot of people had to die for crossing him. He was betrayed, crossed, and left to die a slow death. But he survived. And he vowed that his enemies would not. Even though he was set out for blood, something about this whole situation didn't sit right with him. He couldn't put his finger on it but it was something about his wife that made him think that it was more going on than he was privy of. But figuring that out would have to wait because he was ready to get active.

"There you are my love! I've been looking all over for you."

Friday looked up to see Calynda standing beside him. To him, this woman was drop dead gorgeous, one of the most beautiful women he had ever seen. Her full breast sat up perfectly without a bra and her ass looked like she paid a Rolex for it. Tall, butter tanned skin and long wavy hair falling down her back. But her eyes held evil, even though she was smiling. Friday was big on energy and something about this bitch's vibe was way off.

"Ain't like I could've went far, this whole place it's surrounded by water.", Friday said, taking a look around.

"Well, that's for our protection. Anyone trying to harm us will not have an easy time doing so. It is a must that…"

"Get me back to the states.", he said cutting get off. "What? Why, what's wrong my love?"

"I just want to go to the states. Too much shit need to be done for me to be sitting on a fuckin hill top catching a tan."

"But your health! What about your memory? What's your plan when you get there?" Calynda was worried because she did not know if he knew anything or what he planned on doing.

"Check it chica. You're asking all the wrong shit at the wrong time. You gave me info on the muthafuckas that did me dirty, so I'm taking it and running with it. You want your gold and I want blood. Get me $50,000 and a passport so that I can get the fuck off of this island by tomorrow night. I can handle the rest and I'll keep you posted if anything happens."

"My love, I don't think…"

"Bitch! I don't need you to think!", he snapped, cutting her off once again. "I need you to do what the fuck I asked you to do so I can blow this bitch. Even if I gotta swim to Miami, I'm getting the fuck off of this rock."

One look in his eyes and Calynda knew that this nigga wasn't bullshiting. This is exactly the state if mind that she needed him in to get the job done. But he was rogue. Unwilling to listen to anyone and uncompromising. Which was not good on her behalf because now she could not figure him out or calculate his moves. Calynda could feel this whole situation staring to take a turn for the worst. She just needed the gold located and everyone would die. So she figured it was best to let this pitbull off of the leash and follow the trail of death.

"Ok my love. If this is the easy that you want it, I'll help you. Everything that you need will be ready by night fall. A flight to the states will be ready in the morning. Is there anything else you will need before you leave?"

Friday looked down at Eric, the 86 pound pitbull that roamed the estate. During his stay, Friday grew really fond of the dog and they ate the best of friends.

"Yea, Eric is coming with me.", he responded.

Calynda's face twisted in confusion. "Are you serious? You're taking the dog with you?" She crossed her arms slightly pissed. "Why not me?"

Friday gave her ass a nice smack as he walked pass her. "Make that shit happen.", was all he said headed to the mansion with Eric on his heels.

"Girl! What the fuck is your problem? For the past few days ya ass been quiet as hell acting like you're ready to lay down and die or some shit.", Nicole spat.

"Just a lot on my mind, nun serious.", Nechelle responded like she was mentally preoccupied.

Which she was. Ever since her last run in with Griggs, Nechelle had been on edge. She knew that once that footage got reviewed by the jakes, all their asses were done!

"Yeah, I bet. Well, I'm gonna swing by the club then grocery store. You need me to get you anything?", Nicole asked.

"Naw, I'm good babe. Just be careful."

"Bitch whatever. You acting real funny.", Nicole said waving her off as she gathered her things. "See you later tonight and I hope that you're in a better mood. A bitch needs a nut!"

Once Nechelle was all alone, her mind took the fuck off. She needed a plan and one quick. She had to get that footage of the hospital before it could be reviewed.

Otherwise, her and the crew were on borrowed time. Not one bright idea came to mind and it was killing her. She knew that Aisha couldn't get close to it because she was a patrol officer who was not assigned to the case anyway. Penny was FBI. She couldn't get close without raising suspicion. After a while of zoning out, a light bulb went off in her head. The idea that she has was a far cry from solid, but she had nothing to lose. It would take plenty of hard work and sacrifices, but it was worth a shot because at this point, she was all in.

As quickly as possible, Nechelle took a shower, found some sexy shirts and thin shirt, then took off on her mission. Thirty minutes later, she pulled up a block away from her destination and waited for her mark to exit. After another hour, her mark got onto a vehicle and pulled off. Following four to five cars behind, she ended up at the city mall, watching her mark casually walk inside without a clue of being stalked. Nechelle checked her makeup and briskly walked into the mall. Lingering outside of a few department stores, she made sure that her mark saw her as he excited a sporting goods store.

"I'm starting to think that I'm the one under investigation because I just keep bumping into you. Or is it a coincidence?"

Nechelle looked beside her and soaked her pantie liner on both sides and ends. This nigga was so dam fine that she almost lost sight of the mission and was two minutes from dragging his ass by the balls to the Marriott. But she was on a mission and ready to do whatever.

"What the hell do you want? If your weird ass don't stop following me I'll report you for harassment."

"Harassment? This is a public place and I had no idea I would see you. But don't worry, won't be long before I put this wrist jewelry on your ass and book you into the county jail!"

Nechelle walked up on Detective Griggs slowly, watching his gaze roam all over her body. She knew that her sex appeal would be the only thing to get him out of detective mode and into dumb ass mode as all men so when they smell pussy.

"You gonna lock me up detective fuck nigga?", she asked low and sexy. "Dam right I will!", he responded, trying his best to hide his lust.

"You gonna cuff me too?", she pouted, batting her eyelashes. Griggs didn't respond but Nechelle noticed his breathing changed. "You want me in your backseat detective?", she asked biting her bottom lip.

Without so much as a glance around, Nechelle slyly

rubbed her palm against his crotch and felt his body stiffened. The detective's eyes began to dart around but never once did he resist her touch. Nechelle gave his wood a nice squeeze, turned on her heels with much action in her hips and left him stiff. Never looking back, she made it halfway to her car when Griggs called out to her.

"Hollywood! Hey Hollywood!", he called out to her.

Nechelle slowed her fuck me strut to a stand still, but never turning around. Griggs was soon standing face to face shocked and confused of what he saw. Nechelle was crying silent tears with eye liner running her cheeks in a charcoal mess. She just stared.

"Dam Hollywood.... What the fuck is going on?", he spoke softly. Nechelle just crossed her arms and looked away. "Ok listen, let's do this. I'm not Detective Griggs as of right now, I'm just Larry." Griggs removed his badge from his hip and pocketed it. "I'm off duty and off the record. We don't have to talk about no hot shit, alright? But talk to me Hollywood. Tell me what's the problem."

Nechelle broke eye contact. She played her role a little more then rolled the dice. "Can we speak some place private?"

"Ok ok. That's not an issue. Let's just get something to eat and a drink. No pressure.", Griggs offered.

Nechelle just shook her head in agreement. "Can I ride with you?"

Griggs looked at his cruiser and hunched his shoulders. "If you don't mind, then I don't."

Nechelle just took the lead and walked towards the

unmarked. Not even checking her surroundings, she got sat in the car with no hesitation. Riding the interstate, the ride was a quiet one, minus the dispatcher radio. Nothing but crime everywhere. Soon they pulled into a low key tavern where a bunch of nobodies came to unwind. Even when the drinks and food came, Griggs remained calm, saying nothing. He didn't want to initiate conversation, hoping she'd open up on her own. And not even a few drinks later,

Nechelle felt comfortable enough to speak. "I'm tired.", she sighed.

Griggs looked up mid gulp and shook is head empathetically. "I get tired sometimes too Hollywood."

"What exactly are you tired off?", she pressed calmly.

Griggs wiped his hands and mouth then sat back in his chair. "Being the man of reason. Being in control, being controlled, if that makes sense. I get tired of…of being stagnant. I mean, my life is so routine you know. No change. No feeling. Everything is just fuckin automated."

"I see. So why do you do it?"

"It's a job. I do enjoy the thrill it brings at times. And other times it's depressing being the one to drag my people towards a harsh discipline."

"In some ways, I can relate.", Nechelle agreed. "But I was raised to think that it's not cool to be a cop."

"Shit I came up the same way.", he admitted. "But as I got older, my mentality shifted and I gave up those street ways."

"Yea I know. Listen, I think it's time to go. This is

getting a little awkward." "Well, let's not speak on uncomfortable topics."

"At this point, I don't even care anymore. I just wanna spend my last days of freedom in the clouds because soon, the judge is gonna put me in the ground lol."

"That's not funny Hollywood." "Well it's the truth."

"To a degree.", Griggs slick talked. "Nothing I can do about it now."

"Bullshit. It's plenty that you can do about this Hollywood and you know it!" "Like?", Nechelle asked rhetorically with a roll of her eyes.

"I've told you, I can help. Testify against those involved and I can get you a very small sentence doing your time at a low level security prison."

"I'm not gonna rat my people out and you know that!"

'Well my fucking hands are tied and forced! I can tell that the shit that you're caught up in is not what you planned out to be and I want to help. But you and this corny ass street code are gonna leave me no choice but to treat you as the cold blooded, heartless criminal that the media has painted you to be." "Well fuck it! It is what it is!", Nechelle snapped, slamming her palms on the table.

She stood up so abruptly that her chair fell backwards as she stormed towards the tavern's exit. When she stepped outside, Nechelle was drenched instantly because it had began to pour down mercilessly "Hollywood! Hollywood, it's fucking storming. Get back inside here!"

"Fuck you pig!", Nechelle spat over her shoulder as she walked off to nowhere in particular.

She had no clue where she was but she knew that she had to get away from Griggs. The detective said fuck it and went after her, getting soaked from head to toe as well.

"Stop it Hollywood! Just stop!", he pleaded grabbing her by the arm.

Nechelle spun around with her hair a wet mess over her face with a scowl of death. "Don't fuckin touch me!", she hissed, pulling her arm away. "Next time you see me, you better have a warrant and some back up because when I see you, it's on sight." Nechelle turned away to walk off again but Griggs grabbed her arm once more. Huge mistake....

WOP!

Nechelle spun around and popped Griggs on the chin with a clean right cross hook, landing him on his ass. Then she lost it. Nechelle dove on Griggs and tried to rip his face off. Clawing, punching, biting, whatever it took. She was out for blood, at wicks end and spiraling out of control.

"Hollywood! Calm the fuck down!", Griggs pleaded as he tried his best to restrain her. But she wasn't having it. Her figured that the only way to calm her was to give her a dose of her own medicine.

POP!

Griggs punched Nechelle on the forehead, causing her to roll off of him. As he struggled to his feet, he was dumbfounded to see Nechelle already on her feet with her guard up. He approached her with his hand out.

"Ok. Listen. I'm sorry Hollywood. Let's just get out of this rain so that we can talk about…."

"WOP! BAM! BAM!!

Griggs found himself on his ass once again in this rain. He never saw them hands greeting him until they were leaving him. He now had a serious headache and was having a hard time standing up. Nechelle stood over him for a second then dropped her hands in defeat. Sticking out a palm, she offered to help him up. A bit hesitant at first, he took her hand and got up on his feet. Holding his head, Griggs walked off to his car, head down in the rain. Nechelle stood in the road watching him walk the walk of shame. She then turned to walk in the other direction when she heard him call her name.

"Hollywood!" Nechelle looked back. "Get your ass on the car."

He moved to the cruiser without waiting for a response. Nechelle just sighed heavily and made her way to the vehicle. Once inside, the two sat in silence as the rain continued to assault the windshield. Griggs looked over at Nechelle and gave a snorted chuckle.

"What the fuck is so funny?" she asked with much attitude.

"You look like a unicorn lol!", he cracked pointing to the lump on her forehead.

Nechelle lowered the visor to take a look at herself and her mouth fell in her lap. She punched him on the thigh as he continued to laugh. "This shit is not funny Larry!"

"Larry?", Griggs asked surprised.

"That's your name right?", she said crossing her

arms, leaning back in the seat. She then gave a smirk herself. "That's why it looks like you got a mouth full of nuts! Punk ass!", she barked, giving him the finger.

Griggs stopped laughing and took a look in the rearview mirror. "You ugly bitch! You swole my shit up!"

"Guess we're even.", she joked with her long tongue out, eyes crossed.

"I guess we are.", he sighed sitting back. "Well, guess I'll take you back to your car huh?"

Nechelle was quiet for a moment staring out of the window. "Can you take me with you?"

Griggs' head snapped in her direction at her request. This was not what he had expected. "With me where Hollywood?"

"Whatever….I just don't wanna be alone."

CHAPTER 7

"I understand why you feel that way el jefe, but if you interfere with her plans, we may find ourselves clashing with our own men.", Cheewaus tried to reason.

"The little bitch is incompetent! I want my fucking gold!", Amelio growled, slamming a fist on the desk. He had no patience for Calynda's plan and wanted to do everything his way.

"Well, Friday is on his way to the states as we speak el jefe. He plans to eliminate his own people, which will only help us out. I think we should not get directly involved, but oversee from afar cabron.", Cheewaus advised.

Cheewaus was Amelio's most trusted henchman and confidante. He was Amelio's voice of reason, second opinion, as well as his personal assassin. Calynda was bad, but Cheewaus was terrible. He was as ruthless as they came, having killed enemies, families, even villages in a blink of an eye without hesitation or reservation.

"Ok. Well we'll do this. We send our men to shadow Friday without him knowing. Every friend that he watches from afar, we'll double back and kill them.

Soon, the gold will end up with the last man standing. That's when we fully eradicate the pirates and him as well."

With that, Amelio sat back in his chair with a sly smirk on his face locking his fingers behind his head. Cheewaus has to admit, the old guy was slick in the game. The plan would force the remaining survivors of the crew to protect the gold until it was one line soldier left who would be eaten alive.

"Well thought of el jefe. I will gather some men and give the orders. They will land before Friday does and will be ready to carry out your orders.", Cheewaus assured.

Amelio just stroked his beard and nodded his head in agreement.

C2

Dullah cruised through the city streets towards 3-T's crib with a lot in his mind. It's been months and there still was no clues leading to Friday and it was eating him alive. Even though the crew was on the ups and the businesses were running smoothly, shit just wasn't the same without his boy. No more ball on Sunday, kick backs at the club, he hadn't even played Madden online since he last saw the homie. But he vowed to never give up his search all the way to the grave. Pulling up at 3-T's crib, he tried to push his thoughts to the back of his mind and kick it with his other homie. When the door opened, 3-T stood there dressed in just a pamper and air force 1's! The surgery in his dick made it difficult for him to piss regularly so he needed to use a diaper in order to catch any accidents.

"Bruhhh!! You look goofy as hell!!", Dullah laughed.

"Fuck you nigga…", 3-T said sucking his teeth. When he walked off, the pamper made a crispy crackle as he moved down the hall. Dullah was closed to tears.

"How long you gotta strap that muthafucka on ma nigga?", Dullah asked, hold back his laugh.

"IDK and mind yo business…what you want anyway?"

"Ain't hear from you so I just rolled through to see what's up. How you living homie?" 3-T took a seat and the diaper crackle forced Dullah to look away to save a straight face. "To be real ma night, I don't know what to call it. Like, what the fuck happened? Just the other day life was regular, now we on some mob shit."

"I know.', Dullah agreed. "But we gotta get this shit together though. At least find out if the homie is alive or not.

"Man, I don't wanna think like that. Because if he ain't breathing, then that crazy bitch shouldn't be either."

"Are you talking about me or this crazy bitch?", Penny said as she walked into the living room. She wore loose sweats that still gripped that ass and a wife beater. In her arms were a laptop and a glock. 33 with an extended 34 round clip. Since the hospital war, she never detached from the monster. When she ate, slept, showered and shit, that spitter was with her. She placed the laptop on the coffee table and a virtual file was displayed on the monitor.

"Calynda Diaz.", Penny began. "Daughter of Amelio Diaz. She's 35 years old, 6'1, 165 pounds. Solid bitch. Mixed martial artist, degree in Bio Engineering and culinary arts, sniper rifle, assault rifle, and semiautomatic handgun specialist, one tour in Iraq and demolition in Afghanistan, pretty handy with the stiletto, and assumed cocaine queen pin. Sponsored by Amelio. No criminal history at all, not even a fucking parking ticket."

"She ain't no joke!", Dullah admitted. "She can do all of this shit? How the fuck are we supposed to do her dirty and she's like this?"

"I kicked this bitch's ass! By myself! I don't give a roach's ball sack what she's qualified for…"

"Roaches ain't got no balls girl."

"Shut your fucking mouth Tony! This hooker and everyone with her are gonna have to answer to me. Anyways, it says here that she has a beach front property in Miami as well as an inland estate. Vehicles registered to her are a Rolls Royce Cullinan, Lamborghini Aventador, Corvette Stingray, and a Dodge Challenger Demon. All of them black on black on black."

"What's all those blacks for?", 3-T asked.

Penny shook her head while squinting at the love of her life. Dullah rubbed his forehead with the heel of his palm. "Black car, black rims, black head and tail lights, and black tint 3-T."

"Whatever.", Penny spoke up. "This bitch in Miami or will be there a time or another. If we want her then that's where we'll have to be."

"What's the plan if we spot her?", Dullah asked.

"We gather up as many armed men as possible and wait until she's most vulnerable then take her out.

That bitch is slick like hair grease."

"Well, Tyler has to run the club, Nechelle has to run the gym, Pepp will stick out in any crowd, Ariel, Aisha and Penny obviously can't go, and Karen is not active like that. So that leaves me, Nicole, Tonia and you 3-T.", Dullah advised. "I say we go down the like two couples on vacation and blend in. Track this bitch and trail her to where she lay, squad up and smash her."

"Not until we find Friday though.", 3-T added. "You're right ma nigga, we gotta find the homie."

"And don't forget, I wanna level with that bitch myself!", Penny spoke up.

"Well, it's a go. We get it together tonight and we ride out big tomorrow. I'll get with Iggy and the girls and y'all two…. Y'all just do what y'all do best lol. Just be ready when the time comes bruh." "Fa sure!", 3-T said walking him to the door, diaper crackling.

Friday sat behind tint in a smoke gray Mustang GT, waiting on his first target.

According to the file that Calynda gave him, this chick was some type of care taker. The only one without a criminal record. This is what made shit seem funny. Why would these regular ass people be knee deep in shit with the cartel? No entourage, security team, nothing. It just didn't look right. But that was not a big concern at this point. It was time for somebody to die. After about an hour of waiting, Friday saw a sexy ass chick in nurse scrubs exit a nursing home and headed to its parking lot. This bitch had hips and ass for days with a bomb ass face. He was having trouble getting a grip on the reality that this woman was behind his assassination attempt. The woman must have been waiting for someone because once she made it to the parking lot, she looked around disappointingly then pulled out her cell phone. The woman was facing the curb so Friday could get a good look at her face and something went off in his sub conscience. This woman felt so familiar to him that he could feel it in his heart. Her remembered Calynda saying that he picked these people himself to be on his team so he guess that it was all a part of his post confronting his present.

Still stuck in wonder, he witnessed a police cruiser pull up in front of his target and the woman got in. Now, what the fuck! So his opps are fucking with the jakes? Ain't no fucking way, he thought. Maybe the cop was in on it all. Well, cop , nurse or whatever. These two bitches were about to get it. As the police cruiser pulled away, Friday reached into the backseat grabbing a micro mini draco with a 50 round drum and placed out in the passenger seat as he pulled off in traffic as well…..

C2

"Oh my GOD! I hate this fuckin job. One day, I'm gonna poison all of them old muthafuckas!", Nicole capped.

"Um…Nicole…"

"Bitch what? Because you're late." "I am a police officer, you know."

Nicole looked over at Aisha and rolled her eyes.

"Bitch please! You with the mob!" The girls burst out in laughter because Aisha was as crooked as the devil's dick. "Thanks for the ride girl. I don't know why them muthafuckas taking so long to paint my dam car. It's been two whole weeks."

"Anytime love. So where are you going again?", Aisha asked.

"Take me to the gym. Nechelle left out when I was gone yesterday and never brought her ass back home. Ain't answer her phone or nothing. That bitch has been acting real funny lately."

"She's probably just missing her man."

"Shit, I miss him too!", Nicole said. "But I'm not being all weird and shit!" Nicole dropped back in the seat and banged her head against something above. "Dam bitch! What the fuck is this?"

"What it look like?", Aisha asked, cutting her eyes. "It's riot pump shotgun. Every cruiser got one."

"Ooohhhh. I like this big muthafucka. And it got all the bullets on the side." "Those are shells…"

"Whatever!"

The girls were so engrossed in conversation, they never noticed the two SUV's pulling along the side of them….

C2

Friday drove a half of a block behind the police cruiser with the submachine gun on his lap for almost fifteen minutes when he noticed some odd shit unfold before his eyes. Two black SUV's sped pass him and traveled three cars behind the cruiser for about five blocks. Then all of a sudden, all hell broke loose and he slammed on brakes….

"So when are you coming back to the club so that we can get fucked up?", Nicole asked as she scrolled on her phone.

"I really can't say.", Aisha sighed. "I've been working extra hours trying to get my money up, you know." "Girl I hear that. Well, wherever you ready to…"

POOOOOSSSHH!

The left rear windows shattered and something hit the tail end of the cruiser, causing it to spin out of control.

"What in the fuck!!", Aisha screamed as the car spun to a halt.

An SUV in the front and one in the back trapped then in and they both witnessed Hispanics jumping out with assault rifles. Aisha was no slouch and went into action in a split second. With the engine still running, Aisha threw the car in reverse ramming the SUV, causing the rear assault squad to scatter. Bullets came crashing through the windshield as the front squad lit it up. Pulling her glock.45, Aisha popped the trunk to provide s little protection from the rear gunfire and emptied the clip through the front windshield as she ducked down in the seat.

Nicole's scary ass stuck her whole body down in the leg space of the passenger seat covering her head. She looked up and saw the riot pump and a smirk grew on her face. Snatching the shotgun off of the hinges, Nicole pumped one in the head and waited for the reloading silence in gunfire. As Aisha popped in another clip, the air held a temporary quietness signaling to Nicole that she has a green light to get active. Before she could rise up from her crouch the passenger door flew open and she popped the top off of the first goofy of the day with a shot to the face. Before the dead body could hit the ground, Nicole rolled out of the cruiser and under the car. Now she would see the feet of anyone that approaches.

Aisha saw Nicole slide out of the car with the pump and kicked into overdrive. The moment she exited the driverside, Aisha caught three slugs to the chest and one whizzed pass her head. Luckily she had on a vest but the impact felt like a sledgehammer to the ribs, slightly lifting her off of her feet and slamming her into the car door. But she was in survival mode and before her feet touched the ground, Aisha was raising her glock when the man's right ankle disintegrated. Nicole shot from under the cruiser causing the man to fall to his knees screaming as Aisha gave him three to the face. And if using some unspoken language, the girls worked as a team because every time Nicole saw feet that weren't Aisha's, she shot it. And in return, Aisha would finish the job.

But this couldn't go on forever because they didn't have much ammo and Aisha was so deep in the mud that she forgot to call back up. Nicole felt a pair of hands wrap around her ankles and dragged her from under the cruiser. Rolling on her back, she blessed the hitman with a load to the gut, sending him flying to the pavement. Now with an empty shotgun, Nicole attempted to reload when the roar of an engine came barreling up the street. Sliding to a halt beside the rear SUV, a man with a mask covering the bottom half of his face jumped out of the coupe with a small machinegun and that little shit started spitting! The element of surprise allowed the mystery man to drop a few hitman without notice. Aisha saw what was happening and asked no questions. She didn't know who this nigga was but she surely wasn't giving a fuck because he was shooting at the right people.

Reloading her glock once again, she made her way over to Nicole who was reloading the pump and the girls joined the party. Another SUV pulled up with more Hispanics and everything went crazy. A smoke canister exploded in front of the police cruiser and more gunfire erupted. Aisha was not having it and took no prisoners. This bitch just started shooting everything moving! She couldn't see shit and really didn't give a fuck. She was having a flashback from the bank robbery and this shit just looked too familiar. Nicole did her best to stay active but the smoke made it so difficult to see to the point that beer vision was totally impaired by her own tears. She could make out Aisha moving in a crouch holding her ribs, doing the best she could to stay in the fight. But she could tell that her girl was losing strength. Seeing that Aisha was to her left, Nicole shot at everything to the right.

Then her shotgun clicked empty. She held the pump like a baseball bat, wacked the first muthafucka she saw and caught a bullet in the back and another to the hip. Aisha saw Nicole go down and the hitman creeping to finish her off. She attempted to shoot but her glock clicked empty. Once again, in a fucking gun fight, she was put off ammo. Quickly pulling her taser, Aisha sprinted in aim and zapped the hitman before he could finish Nicole off. Aisha kicked the man in the face, knocking him out cold then dragged Nicole behind the front SUV. The masked man shot the last of his bullets from the mini AK and pulled a 9mm Beretta. Only a few Hispanics were left and he spared none. Seeing the officer drag the nurse around the truck, he made his way to earn the kill that he came for. Creeping around the back of the truck, the masked man took aim at the cop, ready to blow her brains out.

Aisha saw Nicole's eyes widen in horror and spun around to see the masked man taking aim. With a millisecond to spare, Aisha cocked her head to the side and lunged forward as the bullet whizzed pass her head. Holding onto the gun for dear life, Aisha put up her best struggle and was met with more power than one human alone should possess. The masked man gave her a swift knee to the lower gut under the vest that felt like a mule kick, and followed up with an uppercut to the chin, knocking her out cold.

Nicole crawled away sideways from the masked man as he approached her with his gun drawn. He then snatched her up by her scalp and came dam near nose to nose with her as he placed the smoking barrel to her temple. Nicole would fight until her last breath and pushed the gun from her head only to be smacked viciously across the jaw with it. Coming again face to face, Nicole looked into the eyes of her killer and her heart stopped beating. The loss of blood had to have been playing tricks on her mental. This man couldn't be who she thought it was. Her heart came back alive and started beating a mile a second. She tried to speak but he jaw was broken. So she attempted to snatch the mask and had the hairs on her upper lip jacked off with another smack to the grill with the gun. Barely holding into consciousness, Nicole felt the warm steel pressed against her forehead, and saw the finger pull the trigger....

When Nechelle woke, her eyes landed on a glass of ice water and a bottle of aspirin sitting on a nightstand. Looking around, she didn't know where the hell she was at and the bed that she was in wasn't hers. The room was very neat and a bit dusty, like it hadn't been lived in for a while. The other side of the bed was undisturbed but had a set of sweats t-shirt, and bathing instruments atop of it. Nechelle looked around for a few more seconds and it hit her. Griggs! She tossed the covers back and was relieved that she was still fully dressed minus her footwear. As her heart calmed, she noticed that the room had a bathroom in it and hurried to take a shower. Twenty minutes later she walked out drying her hair and her nose was greeted by the smell of melting butter. Walking through the home in search of the kitchen, she had to admit that it was very nice for a bachelor, IF, he was a bachelor. Glossy hardwood floors and a few walls allowing each living space to invade the other. The kitchen was very spacious with a huge island in the middle.

But when her eyes landed on Detective Larry

Griggs, her pussy did a somersault, triple axle handstand without disturbing her panty liner. This sexy motherfucker was built like a compact Dwayne Johnson big dick having ass. Wearing nothing but some gym shorts and Nike flip flops Nechelle was able to take in every inch of this fuck nigga. His shoulders were very broad with bulging muscles connecting to his neck. Chest fully developed with a chiseled six pack across his belly. Think veiny arms and thick muscular thighs had him looking like he was created by a magical potter. But when this man turned to fully face Nechelle, her mind went into hoe-verdrive!

Those gym shorts did not a dam thing to hide the massive bulge between his legs. Not only could she see his dick print, but this niggas nuts were bouncing around like he wore no underwear beneath. She regained her composure and tiptoed barefoot into the kitchen and sat on a stool at the island. Griggs felt a presence and smelled shampoo. When he turned to see Nechelle staring at him, he froze. No make up, no hair weave, all natural, this woman was gorgeous. Her eyes and lips gave her a ton of sex appeal and her wet wavy hair gave her an exotic look. His lower desires went into a rage causing his manhood to grow towards its full potential. Nechelle noticed the shift in his shorts and locked in on that missile. He noticed her stare. She looked up and saw him looking at her. "Well", he said, killing the moment. "Are you hungry?"

"I can eat it. I mean, yeah, I can eat.", she stuttered.

He raised an eyebrow and shook his head as he turned to fix their plates. He placed before her some home fries, waffles, and egg whites. Then poured a glass of cranberry juice.

"Thank you Larry. But um, where's the bacon? The…. Sausage?", she tried not to look at his dick while asking the last part of the question.

"Vegetarian. Sorry Hollywood. No meat in this house."

You tell a dam lie!, she thought to herself thinking about all that tube steak dangling between his kneecaps. "Oh well, thank you anyway. She began to eat her food, but all the questions and concerns that occupied her mind gave her trouble holding an appetite.

"It's this even legal?"

"What? Egg whites?", he asked jokingly.

"No! Lol! I mean this. Us. Here, together."

"You're not a wanted woman Hollywood. Well, at least not by law enforcement. But unless there is a warrant out for your arrest, this causal meeting is perfectly legal."

"Understood. Well, let's cut the bullshit. What do you want from me?" "A confession."

"Don't fuck this vibe up Larry…" "You asked."

"And I been answered that!", Nechelle snapped dropping her fork on the plate. "Well what do you want from me?"

"To take me to my fuckin car!", she demanded, rising from the stool. "Hollywood, come on. Calm down. Please."

Nechelle began to walk past him and he reached out grabbing her elbow….

BAM!!

Nechelle popped him in the mouth and was reciprocated with a swift backhand across the cheek. She was not expecting to get pimp smacked and the blow spun her around, causing her to brace up against the countertop. Looking over her shoulder with a face full of wild hair, she wiped the trickle of blood from her lip and smoothly tied her hair into a messy bun. Cracking her neck and knuckles, she sprinted towards Griggs at full speed ready to let him have it only to be met with a swift punch to the gut, bringing her to her knees. Griggs grabbed her scalp by the roots and lifted her to her feet.

Nechelle winced in pain clawing at his wrist but it was no use. That ponytail was in a death grip. "Let my hair go you fuckin pussy!"

SMACK!!

Griggs peanut slapped her in the back of the head, still gripping her scalp. Nechelle reached out and grabbed both of his ears and dug her nails deep into the back side of them, causing him to release her and holler out in pain. She then yanked his head down so that they were face to face.

"You just put your hands on the wrong bitch!"

Nechelle spit in his face and headed butted him across the bridge of his nose. Griggs fell back on one knee holding his face and Nechelle gave him a flying knee to the chin. She knew that it wouldn't be long before his rage took over and she'd be in deep shit so she looked around for a weapon and spotted a kitchen knife near the stove. Griggs peeped the move and they both took off towards the knife but Nechelle wrapped her fingers around it first and wildly swung her arm around in an attempt to slice him open. Griggs jumped back just in time to have Nechelle continue to swing and jab at his face and chest.

"Hollywood! Calm the fuck down!"

"Suck my dick bitch! One of us is about to die and I got a hair appointment that I ain't trying to miss nigga!"

"I really don't wanna hurt you but you're gonna make me fuck you up!", Griggs threatened.

Nechelle responded by hammering swimming the knife, trying to bring it down in his belly. On the third swing, she stuck him good in the thigh and he gripped hare wrist for dear life. Nechelle held onto the blade and slammed her other palm on top of the handle, driving the knife deeper inside of his leg.

Griggs latched onto Nechelle's throat with all of his might and tried to squeeze the life out of her.

Nechelle released her grip on the knife and clawed at her neck. Griggs snatched the blade from his thigh, tossed it, and choke slammed Nechelle on the kitchen counter, dragging her from one end to the other, knocking everything to the floor. He then picked her up and tossed her through the air, causing geese to crash through the glass kitchen table. Nechelle landed on her back and hopped up like she was jacked up on meth. Griggs could not believe the tenacity and durability of this woman. Nechelle picked up a wooden chair and smashed it against the wall, creating a thick, solid batting stick out of its leg.

"Awe come the fuck on!", Griggs pouted in disbelief. "Hollywood!"

Nechelle twirled the stick as she wiped her nose

walking towards him. Griggs opened the kitchen drawer and pulled out an 8 millimeter pistol. Nechelle froze.

"Don't make me Hollywood!"

"You're bluffing!" Nechelle took one step and Griggs shot her in the arm, barely grazing her. "Son of a bitch! You shot me!"

"And you fucked up my chair! I loved that chair!"

Griggs suddenly felt dizzy and fell to one knee. The wound on his leg was bleeding profusely. Nechelle dropped the stick and rushed over to him.

"Dammit Larry! Look what you made me do!"

"I'm fine Hollywood.", Griggs lied, trying to brush her off. "I just need s seat." "Come on, let's get you cleaned up."

She then threw his arm around her shoulder and limped beside him up to the master bathroom. And that shit was huge! Jacuzzi sized tub and a 12 x 12 foot walk in shower. She sat him on the edge of the tub and ran the hot water. She then tore a towel and wrapped it around his leg wound to stop the bleeding. She then helped him out of his clothing and my gawd my gawd. This nigga was so dam sexy! And when them briefs came off..... nothing could prepare her for what she saw. This niggas dick was thick!

Thick like a bottle of water! Ten inches and pretty too. A set of big ass bull nuts sat between his legs and he was clean shaven. Once the tub was full, she helped him ease his way inside. A remote was beside the tub and Griggs had a sly idea.

"Hey Hollywood.", Nechelle turned to see Griggs holding out the remote. "Can you please put this somewhere. Don't need this getting wet."

Nechelle walked back over reaching for the remote and Griggs pulled her on the jacuzzi, fully submerging her. She popped up gasping for air as he laughed at her shock.

"Larry! You stupid muthafucka! What the hell is your problem?", she asked now standing in the tub.

The t- shirt stuck to her breast revealing erect nipples and the sweats now sagged at the waist, exposing the V in her abs leading to her crotch area. Nechelle saw the lust in Griggs eyes and moved to get out of the water but Griggs yanked her down between his legs. "You still haven't learned you're lesson about grabbing on me?"

"All you gonna do is hit me. I hit back though.", he said as he cautiously lifted the shirt over her head. Nechelle's full perky breast looked right back at him as he licked his lips then wrapped them around her right breast. The warm softness of his mouth made her melt as she cupped his face and threw her head back. With the slickness of a fox, he slid the sweats off of her and gripped her ass that felt soft as cotton. Hooking her legs into his elbows and holding onto her hips, Griggs lifted Nechelle up to his lips and sucked her clitoris with passion and purpose. Nechelle did her best to control the butterflies in her stomach as she floated in midair while this officer of the law arrested that pussy.

Gripping his head, she grinded and rocked up and down his face as she chased a climax that she thought she'd never experience. Suddenly, she don't know how it was possible, but Griggs thought that it would be a good idea to place his mouth over her whole pussy and suck the juices right from her belly and Nechelle literally passed out while cumming. Griggs heard her scream then go limp in his arms as she leaned forward on his upper body. Lowering her in his lap, he took a wet rag and squeezed the water over her face and she stirred to life. Once she regained her composure, Nechelle stuck her tongue straight into his mouth as she wrapped her arms and legs around him.

Raising her back out of the water again, Griggs slowly lowered her down on his dick and once that fat head penetrated her, Nechelle held on for dear life. Slowly, inch by thick ass inch, Griggs raised and lowered her into him until he was completely inside of her.

Nechelle's vaginal area felt like it was packed with cement. He filled her beyond capacity and the pain felt like heaven.

"Larry...", Nechelle moaned, looking him in the eyes as she rode him. "What are you doing to me?"

"Baby, I don't know."

"Oooh Larry, you fuckin me so dam good.... Please baby don't stop."

Griggs stood up with her still on that dick and walked them to the shower. Nechelle held on while turning on the water and they fucked as the steamy spray flowed over their bodies. Griggs had Nechelle pinned to the wall, slowly giving her the business. He buried his face in the crook of her neck while continuously touching the bottom of her cervix. By now, Nechelle had already came twice and had no energy to put up a fight. Lifting his face up, Griggs looked into Nechelle's eyes and almost fell in love. She stared back into his soul as he dug deep into her love. Something began to change within him and all he wanted to do was keep this woman.

Turning off the water, Griggs carried Nechelle to the bedroom and laid her down on the softest bed ever. This bitch's feet had never touched the floor ever since her pulled her into the tub. Without touching himself, Griggs guided that missile to her bunker and slid down in that thang balls deep, had this bitch clawing the skin off of his back. Slow, deep and steady, this nigga showed that pussy some grade A police brutality in its most gentlest form. After a few more organ shifting strokes, Griggs flipped her on her stomach and slid in from behind and Nechelle might as well had been a snake the way she slithered on her belly trying to get away from all that dick. He gripped her left shoulder and braced his other hand on her lower back and began to drill for oil wells pulling her back. Thick white nut began to coat his piece the more her dove in her juice box.

Nechelle looked back at Griggs biting her bottom lip with tears in her eyes. "Please Larry….. please love me. Love deep inside of me."

"Dam Hollywood…. What the fuck are you doing to me?"

Nechelle began to hump back causing him to penetrate deeper, feeling a new depth of warmth and wetness. Feeling his grind getting more intense and stiff, she knew that he was close to shooting up in her club and wanted to feel him release. Reaching behind her and pulling him in, Nechelle grinded back on all that dick until he pushed everything he had inside of her then came long and hard. She continued to milk him skiing kegels on that dick as she rotated in a circular motion, rocking back and forth. Once he spent his last drop, Nechelle rolled over still under him, looking him in the eyes.

"I fucking love you Hollywood." "I love you too daddy...."

CHAPTER 8

Iggy was spending the beginning of his day chasing his rottweiler around the backyard.

Tank was refusing to take a shower and was fleeing and eluding at all cost. Boogie walked into the yard all smiles at the sight of his bro covered in grass and mud. Tank spotted Boogie and sprinted towards him as if he would be protected.

"Looks like ya loosing da fight mon lol! Tank no go fa anytin.", Boogey joked. "Him smell like shit! And if him not take bath, he be homeless!"

Boogie knelt down to show the dog some love. "Not worry Tank. Me love ya and take care ya."

"Take em den!", Iggy capped as he sprayed himself with the water hose. "What on ya mind? Ya come ta watch me die a slow death?"

"Got some crazy tings ta tell ya."

"Eh? Come, let's sit on da porch.", Iggy offered. Giving Tank the evil eye, he led then away from the wet lawn. "Wha gwan?"

Boogey gave him the run down of what took place with what Trina told him, except for the part about her slurping him up.

"Me don't know mon. Cocaine izza risky bidnis ya

no. And we don't know dem people."

"Well wha tink we ta do, huh? Tis da only way fa us ta get close ta da devil incase Dullah dem can't.", Boogey reasoned.

Iggy remained silent to give it some thought. He knew that the Puerto Ricans were stronger and richer which meant that had more resources. A lot more than he possessed. And the only way to get close to an enemy of that caliber was to get in bed with them.

"Ok. I hear ya out. So what ya plan?"

"Da gal Trina gimme her nigga number, tells me ta set up a meeting to buy some cocaine.

I say we watch em close tah see how he come tah contact wit dem then follow the contact back to the Puerto Ricans. Den we gather many men and take dem lives."

Again, Iggy pondered on the idea and couldn't find a more simpler way to get the job done. "Ok. Set up few buys den find tis connect. But bet patient Boogey. We don't wanna fuck tis up eh." "Me won't rest till all involved is dead mon."

C2

Dullah sat in his barber shop on his lunch break going over the shops numbers. Even though the crew was at war, he still has to oversee the daily operations. His phone forced him to take a break and as he answered it, he looked up at the T.V. screen to see breaking news.

"Whaddup fool?"

"Ma nigga! Shit is crazy! The fuck you at?", 3-T panicked. "The shop, why?"

"Aisha and Nicole got flipped!"

"What! The fuck you mean they got flipped?"

As he asked the last question, the news showed the carnage from the gun battle between Aisha, Nicole and the Puerto Ricans. He recognized Aisha's squad car by the pink ribbons on the antenna and it looked like it traveled through a warzone. Yellow tape surrounded the police cruiser along with a few SUV's. Bullet shells and dead bodies were everywhere in the street. His mouth went dry.

"Bruh! You there?", 3-T yelled into the receiver, bringing him back.

"Yea...um yea. So where are they? Are they alive? What?", he asked add he grabbed his keys and headed to his ride.

"I don't know bruh. Penny said that she was at her job even the call came through for all available officers to report to assist and she went along to find Aisha's car at the scene. Nicole's purse was inside of the cruiser but there were no bodies."

"FUCK!" Dullah pulled out in traffic doing 65 mph in three seconds. "I'm headed to the hospital right now. Hit me up if you hear something."

Dullah tried Nechelle four times and got no answer. Tonia, Tyler, and Karen were on their way as well. When he got there, the hospital staff had no info on Aisha or Nicole which pissed him off even more. 3-T entered the waiting room ten minutes later. After all questions went unanswered, the obvious need to be addressed.

"Penny said that those bodies were Puerto Ricans. At least over a dozen. Now with assault rifles and greater numbers, I find it hard to believe that just Aisha and Nicole did all that damage.", 3-T admitted. "You're right. You think that Iggy's squad was closed by? That's who could've snatched the girls up before the jakes came.", Dullah thought.

"But why?", Tyler asked. "Aisha's city police and they did nothing wrong. It looks like an ambush."

"It does.", Dullah groaned. "Contact then Jamaicans bruh. See what they got going on and if they got the girls.", he told 3-T. Her then turned to Tonia. "Me, you, 3-T and Nicole were supposed to go to Miami to track this Puerto Rican bitch. Her name is Calynda Diaz and she pushing hella coc up the coast. The same coc that we snatched a few months ago and she was the bitch that got at us at the hospital. I don't know why she still coming for us even though Friday's not here but I assume she's trying to smoke all of us. So we gotta sneak up on that bitch and knock her off first."

"What you need me down there for though?", Tonia asked.

"If we go down there looking like we're in something, they'll spot us a mile away.", 3-T said. "But if we go down there looking like couples on vacation, it'll be easier to follow close by, you know."

"A couple? I don't look like no fuckin pillow princess nigaa! Or are you blind?"

"None of the other girls can make it because the businesses still needs to be managed. And now that

Nicole is missing, we're short a girl."

"So we're stuck?", Karen asked, knowing the answer.

"Not exactly…", 3-T said in deep thought. "What about Samantha?"

"Sam? Hell no!", Dullah objected. "She don't know the first thing about this game."

"And she don't have to know. Have her and Adrian think that they're on vacation with us and their ignorance will have them acting normal. You and Tonia take them and just stay in character."

Dullah thought about what 3-T said and couldn't deny that it was a nice plan.

"So I guess nobody's fuckin hearing me?", Tonia snapped. Everyone gave her the questionable look. "Why the fuck y'all need me?"

"We gotta look like two couples on vacation and none of the other girls are available.", Dullah explained again.

"Nigga I got more swag than you! How the fuck we're gonna look like a couple?"

"Bitch put some fuckin heels on then!", Dullah snapped. "Get with the program alright! We're all targets and we have to turn the heat up. So we do what we gotta do. That means that you needs to get in character." He reached in his pocket and gave Tonia a wad of cash. "Go shopping, like right now. Take Tyler and Karen with you since all you know is jeans and Timbs."

"I don't need these bitches.", Tonia spat. Karen's mouth hit the floor and Tyler just rolled her eyes.

"Well, it's settled. Anyone heard from Nechelle?" Nobody said anything. "Well we need to find her. And call around to every care center to see where Aisha and Nicole is at!"

C2

Before he left Miami, Friday rented an Airbnb outside of the city that he had to visit to find his targets. He sat in the living room deep on thought, thinking about what he'd just did. Seeing those Puerto Ricans go at his targets let him know that Calynda and Amelio were behind it. Calynda knew his plans and had to have had him followed and he was pissed. Those targets were rightfully his and no one else had the right or power to take that from him. So he flipped the script and knocked off every last one that tried to step in his way. He suddenly heard a noise coming from the rear of the rented home.

Grabbing his pistol, he went to check it out. That loud noise came from an empty room and he entered it with a mission.

"HEEEELLLLLLPP!HEEELLLPPPP!! Somebody please help me!!"

Friday rolled his eyes at the screaming woman. She had been yelling for the past two hours, ever since she has regained consciousness. Somehow she had wiggled the gag from over her mouth. When he couldn't shoot these bitches because he ran out of bullets, he thought it was smarter to just take them with him to see if he could find some answers. This police bitch was getting on his last nerves. But the other woman who was shot, he has found a nurse leaving the hospital and offers hard $10k to 'quietly service' a friend of his who in turn patched Nicole up and has her sedated. Nicole laid on a futon hooked to an I.V. Her jaw was swollen from being fractured and had a wrap around her head going under her chin to keep her mouth from hanging open. "Hey! Hey! You son of a bitch! I heard you walk in here!", Aisha snapped.

Friday had blind folded her as well as tied her a chair. He walked over and stood in front of her. Kneeling down, he snatched the blind fold off of Aisha and she bugged thee fuck out!

"Friday! Oh my God! Friday, hurry up! Untie me before somebody comes and finds us!"

Friday didn't budge and Aisha couldn't keep still, wiggling and looking at the restraints as if to choose which one he should untie first. When he didn't move, Aisha stared at him like her had lost his mind.

"Friday?! Take this shit off of me before whoever comes back. We gotta get outta here. Everyone is looking for you. We miss y…."

SMACK!

Friday bitch slapped her lashes crooked! Aisha sat frozen with her head turned in disbelief. Her mouth hung open as she slowly turned to face him and couldn't seem to grasp what was happening.

"Boooyyyy!! Have you lost your fuckin mind! Friday! What the fuck is your problem?" "How much are they paying you?", he asked a little too calmly.

"Huh? Paying me? Who? What the fuck are you

talking about?" "Who shot me?"

"Who shot you? Really nigga?! You know who shot you. You were the one that told us who shot you."

"You think I'm stupid huh? You think I won't smoke a pig? A crooked pig at that!"

"Nigga fuck you! I've been down for your ass since day one! Even when y'all were the ones who crossed me out first. You're acting like you've lost your memory or something!"

Friday took a step back and held a blank stare. This stranger spoke with so much conviction, so much convincing rage. The look in her eyes held more hurt than fear. Something was totally off about his understanding but he refused to go for anything. This bitch knew that she was on her death bed and would say anything to survive.

Calynda said that it was his own people that crossed him out so this woman was possibly playing on his mental. But when she said he was acting like he'd lost his memory, she hit home. He was more confused and conflicted now than ever before.

"Friday!" The women's voice brought him out of his daze. He looked up and saw tears in her eyes. "What the hell is going on man? Why do you have me tied to this chair? Why is Nicole over the instead of a hospital? That is your fuckin woman. We have both been there for you. Let me the fuck go!"

This lady was saying more than he could digest. Her truth and Calynda's truth eye at war on the battle field of his mental. He turned and began to walk out of the room.

"Friday! Friday! You let me the fuck go! You crazy son of a bitch. I swear to God I'm gonna shoot you my fuckin self!"

He just shut the door and stood with his back against it. He was lost. But he would have to address that later. Until he found out the real truth, his truth was to get at every member of the crew until he found whatever he was looking for. And with that, he strapped up and headed out to stalk his next target.

Amelio stared out at the ocean waves from his office window. His face held a calm expression but on the inside, he was a raging bull. The hit on the first two members of that crew was fumbled. How the fuck could two regular bitches eliminate a twelve man hit squad? And what's crazy is that the two women could not be found. Hospitals, police stations, morgues, nowhere had any record of the two. But he had no worries because that was child's play. That was just the first wave. Next time he sent his goons on a mission, the place of initiated contact will turn into a war zone. The sounds of high heels click clacking, angrily approaching from his rear advised him that he was about to deal with a whole new set of issues.

Calynda came around and stood in front of him, blocking his view. She remained silent but that look on her face plus the flames dancing in her eyes let him know that she was beyond pissed about him putting the hit on Friday's crew. The mission was to follow them until they were to lead them to the gold as well as allow Friday to do his own investigation. But she saw that Amelio obviously had other plans that were never discussed with her.

"Good morning princess. What has you with the upset face?"

Calynda took a step back out of arms reach before speaking her peace. "Good morning my ass! What the hell popa? We had an agreement."

"We had a discussion! You assumed that what we discussed was agreed upon. I never gave the ok to shit that was discussed either!", Amelio snapped.

"We lost over a dozen men all because you would rather ambush a few civilians rather than stick to the plan.", Calynda responded.

"My men! My cartel! My operation! Now which one of these properties negates the fact that you don't have a say so on how the fuck I operate?"

"Popa! You're making this more difficult than it has to be. We just have to be patient and follow Friday and he will lead us to the gold."

"WE don't have to do shit! I will do whatever the fuck I want and you will follow my orders. If you have a got dam problem with the way that I run my shit, then bitch I got a place for you! Are we clear?"

Calynda kept a blank poker face as she thought long and hard on her next response. "Yes popa.", she responded calmly, slowly walking away. "We are very clear."

As Calynda left, she came to the conclusion that she'd had enough of Amelio's bullshit. The threats, physical abuse, condescending attitude, and disrespect now held a price that she would make him pay in full. She was done with following his orders, being his puppet, his blood hound. She was now gonna be a fuckin headache. Pulling Chepae and Solas down into the estate's garden area, she approached her henchmen with a new objective.

"Listen carefully cabrones. I need to know where your loyalty lies. With me or Amelio?" "What exactly are you asking la jefa?", Solas asked suspiciously.

"Exactly how it sounds!", she snapped. "Popa has gone rogue. He is putting our men in danger, losing their lives, all because he is not patient and I refuse to become a sacrifice. Not another day. I'm ready to move at my own pace, follow my own rules, but only for this mission. I'm not going against the familia, but I will no longer play in the shadows of this operation. I'm ready to gather my own personal team and go after the gold. And those vatos. Following my own plans, not Amelio's. I need to know if you two are with me?

Chepae and Solas gave each other a quick glance then shot Calynda the head nod of approval.

"Put only a few highly trained men on notice. We don't want to move a lot of people to raise Amelio's suspicion. Continue operations as normal and I will give you the objective very soon."

After a quick shower at the crib and a bite to eat, Nechelle made her way to the gym to see what the deal was. She had left her phone in dnd the whole time that she was with Griggs and once she took it off, her notifications went crazy! The whole crew was calling and texting her all night and day. Something has to be wrong but she had a lot on her mind at the time and did not want to deal with any new problems. She has just been fucked into a coma by the detective that was out to bring the whole crew to its knees and had know explanation as to her whereabouts. She knew that the crew would want answers that she was not prepared to give but she would deal with that when the time came. Right now, she just wanted to be left alone with her thoughts. When she entered the gym, Adrian and Samantha were doing whatever it was that they got paid to do so she quickly made he way to the office. As soon as she entered the office, she saw Penny sitting atop of her desk reading through one of the many magazines she ordered. Oddly dressed in spandex shorts, shorts bra and Jordan 7's, Penny held a 'don't bullshit me' stare as Nechelle froze at the sight of her.

"Close the door." Nechelle let the door shut. "Where were you?", Penny asked as she stood up to face Nechelle.

Nechelle sagged her shoulders and attempted to walk around her desk but Penny moved to stand in her way. Nechelle stopped in her tracks looking up at Penny, giving her a raised eyebrow. Penny raised one back and stepped up on her grill.

"What? What the fuck is your problem Penny?" "Answer the got dam question!"

"I was wherever the fuck I wanted to be!"

"You know what Nechelle? No. Not today. I'm not with the back and forth bullshit. So if you don't tell me where you were, I will beat your ass. Right now!"

"Something wrong with your ass bitter bitch?" WOP!

Penny smashed her fist in Nechelle's grill and they began to turn that little office upside the fuck down! Gym equipment and paperwork scattered everywhere as the two tried to knock each other's heads off. I'm talking a hair pulling, face smashing, belly kicking, body slamming brawl! They were in closer quarters so Penny couldn't use all that crazy Kung-Fu bullshit and Nechelle took full advantage. Both women had long hair but Nechelle's was braided as where Penny's was not. Nechelle kept a fist full of Penny's hair and tossed her around that office, painting the dam walls. Penny's feet were off of the ground for the first fifty seconds of the fight because Nechelle was flinging her ass around by her scalp. "I never did like you, you pale ass cracker bitch!" WOP! WOP!!

Nechelle served her proper as Penny struggled to get up off of the floor. Samantha was walking pass the office and saw Penny's back slide down the window with the blinds half way off the wall. Nechelle had no plans on letting up and continued to yank Penny's brains out.

"Oh my God!", Samantha panicked. "Adrian! Adrian!"

She opened the door and witnessed Penny tackle Nechelle like she was a defensive lineman. Penny dug her fingers under Nechelle's single French braid and rammed her kneecap into Nechelle's face.

"Now let me show you how it's done bitch!", Penny growled.

Twisting Nechelle's neck to get her to stand back to back, Penny bent forward with Nechelle over her shoulder holding onto that braid by the root and flipped Nechelle onto her head. Coming down on Nechelle's face with a hammer punch, Penny knocked a speed not under Nechelle's eye.

"Penny!", Adrian panicked. "What the fuck are you doing?" "You weren't here for the beginning of this shit Adrian!"

"Huh? Man fuck all that. You need to chill the fuck out! "

Penny looked down at Nechelle once more and....

BAM!!

"Penny!", Samantha screamed.

"Consider is even bitch!", Penny snapped at Nechelle.

"Penny, you bugging the fuck out right now homie.", Adrian signed.

Nechelle stood slowly and sat behind the desk. Her hair was wild and the left side of her face was swollen. She spat out a glob of blood and blew the rest out of her nose.

"So one of you wanna tell me what the fuck just happened?"

Everyone turned to see Dullah looking around the office as if a bomb just went off inside of it.

"Penny and Nechelle were having a disagreement.", Samantha chuckled.

Dullah looked at Nechelle all busted then gave Penny the 'what the fuck' look. "Ask this bitch where was she yesterday!", Penny snapped.

"That's a good dam question. So what's the deal Nechelle? Where were you?", Dullah asked.

"Minding my own dam business!"

"Well while you were minding your own dam business, Nicole and Aisha are missing.", Penny sassed.

144

"What?", Nechelle gasped.

"After a crazy shootout, that made the news by the way, only thing left at the scene was Aisha's squad car and Nicole's purse."

"What about hospitals? Police stations? Stuff like that?"

"We've tried them all.", Dullah sighed, taking a seat. "Cellphones are off and nobody knows nothing. But if you had answered your dam phone you would've known this!"

"Oh my God…. I'm so sorry…."

"Dam right you are!", Penny interrupted.

"Penny, chill the fuck out!", Dullah snapped. "We gotta get this shit together. Like ASAP! First Friday, now Nicole and Aisha. From now on, none of us travel alone until we're home. If we're coming up missing instead of dead, then somebody's collecting us. I say it's the Puerto Ricans. I'll get with Iggy and see if he can have one of his goons roll with each of us. Until then, stay on point." He then looked to Nechelle. "Sooner or later, you're gonna explain to me what the fuck you got going on."

Penny walked up to Nechelle and bent over to become eye to eye with her. "You might can fool many but you can't fool me. I may not know exactly what you're doing, but I know it's some sneaky shit."

"How the fuck would you know?", Nechelle spat.

"Because I hate shopping online for heels. I'd rather walk in the mall and get them myself."

The women stared each other down and while everyone was clueless to what Penny meant, Nechelle knew exactly what she was talking about. Penny was at the mall yesterday and had to have seen her talking to Griggs. But Penny didn't take it any further, she just looked Nechelle up and down then walked out of the office. Samantha gave Nechelle an ice pack and left without a word.

"Me, Adrian, Tonia and Samantha are going down to Miami to see if we can trap this Calynda bitch. Only easy to find Friday is to find her first.", Dullah said.

"Why would you take those two on a mission? They're practically kids.", Nechelle questioned.

"We're just trying to locate her, nothing serious. Once we can see where she's hiding at, then we can make our next move."

"But why them?"

"Was gonna be Nicole and 3-T but we can't find her so it is what it is." "I could've went!"

"You couldn't have done shit!", Dullah snapped. "Nobody could've contacted you." "Ok. Ok. So what do you need me to do?"

"Step in my place and cover the gym while I'm gone. Normal operations are still a go." "I can handle that. Anything else?"

"Don't make me have to look for your ass again."

"Why the fuck would you agree to go on a mission Tonia?", Tyler snapped in frustration.

Tonia was walking around the room packing the clothes that she had just bought and Tyler was on her heels with every step.

"It's not an active mission. We're just trying to locate

her.", Tonia tried to explain. "Bullshit! Plus you're pregnant!"

"Please don't fuckin remind me." "But you are, stupid!"

"I'm not even showing Tyler."

"I can just punch you in the fuckin face. Bitch you sound dumb!"

"Nobody else was left Tyler!", Tonia snapped. "All we're doing is trying to find where this bitch is at and then it's done."

"What if something happens to you? Or the baby?"

Tonia sat Tyler on the bed, held her hand and looked into her eyes. "Listen baby, please don't worry about me, ok. We are not going down there on bullshit. It's gonna be more like a vacation, you know. So don't trip, I wouldn't want anything to happen to this baby either."

"You promise you'll be careful?", Tyler pouted. "I promise baby."

"And if shit gets crazy, you'll haul ass instead of acting like a fuckin super hero?" "Yea Tyler lol. That too. Anything else?"

Tyler grew a smirk. "Let me fix your hair!" "The fuck! Naw. No, I'm good."

"But you bought all this diva shit and you plan on rocking braids?"

Tonia dragged her palms down her face and Tyler grew this big goofy ass smile. She was gonna be the first to see Tonia transformed into a straight woman.

"Fuck! Ok. Ok. But no pictures bitch!"

CHAPTER 9

"So tell me again why you never notified us if the drop never making it to you?" "For the third time, I never made a fuckin order!", Trina cried.

Chepae had snatched her up from a salon's parking lot and had her tied to a chair in a room somewhere. "Well the call came from your phone and my delivery guy went to the usual drop off spot. So tell me why this shit isn't adding up." "I can't tell you shit because I don't know shit!"

SMACK!!

Solas slapped that lace front half way off Trina's scalp. A lot of cocaine and a crew member of his was missing and the call came from this bitch's phone. She had better come up with something.

"Wait! Wait! My phone! Yea, my phone was stolen. I got jumped by these two bitches and they stole my phone."

Chepae chuckled. "So how would a thief know to call my guy and make an order?"

Trina shook her head and took a deep breath. "Listen, some chick that I dealt with a while back came looking for a connect and when I refused to give you up, they jumped on me."

"So how did they know to call us?" "I told them....", she sighed.

"You did what?", Solas snapped.

"I didn't know they'd rob you! They used to sell to me back in the day so I thought that they would just buy from you guys."

SMACK!!

That lace front went flying one way and Trina fell over the other way. Chepae knelt down while she lay on her side still tied down. "The GPS in the truck said that he was at the drop of spot."

"They own the fuckin club man!", she cried. "The girls who jumped me, their crew own that club that I pick up on front of! I swear!"

"Well, it's no longer your problem.", Chepae said standing up.

"Thank you! Thank you so much. I'll help you. I'll help you catch these muthafuckas!" "No need. Your services are no longer needed."

Chepae turned to walk away as Solas walked up with a ratchet grin. Reaching on his waist line, Solas pulled out one of the ugliest knife a set of eyes has ever seen. Trina's eyes widen in horror as he raised it above his head.

"No! No, please! I'll do whatever it takes just please don't kill me!"

Solas paid her no mind and began to slam the knife in her ribs over and over until her cries became gurgles.

Friday cruised the streets with Eric riding shotgun. Seems like the hound was the only one he felt that he could trust. Calynda's story made sense but the cop's story made him feel something. It was like she was honestly being straight up with him but he couldn't be sure because he didn't remember none of that shit. Calynda was the one who nursed him back to health so that's who he would remain loyal to until something comes up to negate her story.

He decided to go to his last known address in the city. A small house on the quiet side of town, nothing major and certainly nothing someone of cartel status would live in. This didn't make sense either. He realized that there were so many things that didn't add up that maybe he should consider the cops story. Just consider. Turning on a street two roads behind the address he was to come to, he parked the mustang, cracked the window and left Eric inside as he made his way to his destination. It was around noon when most people were at work so be chose a house without a vehicle in its driveway and made his way to the backyard. After jumping a few fences, he came to an alley behind his last home. A high fence made it so that he couldn't see in the backyard, so he pulled his .45 Luger and quietly hopped the seven foot wooden fence....

C2

Nechelle pulled up to the crib beaten, bruised and exhausted. The physical encounter with Penny was one thing, but having her AND Dullah up her ass about where she'd been was another. Not to mention Penny acting as if she knew what the fuck was going on between her and Griggs. Just thinking about the way that that man had fucked her gave her butterflies. But she has to stay focused and low key because a lot was on the line with no room for error. Stepping out of her ride, she kept her glock. 17 tucked because shit was real. They were coming up missing without a trace and she was not ready to become another statistic. Entering the house, she noticed Danny and Danielle growing at something through the sliding glass door leading to the backyard. She figured that they needed to relieve themselves but once she saw them take off outside before she could even slide the door open completely, she knew that something was up....

C2

Friday was on the side of the house looking from window to window but saw no signs of life so he figured that no one was home. Pushing the windows, he had no luck. They were all locked. Deciding to pull the car around to sit and wait for someone to pull up, he tucked his strap and started walking towards the gate when he heard a door slam from inside of the home. Peeking back through the window, he saw a female walk through the living room towards the back glass door and a vision flashed in his mind of this woman in boxing gear...what the fuck, he thought. He froze staring off in the distance trying to figure out where that vision came from.

First it was the nurse chick that he kidnapped, which the cop lady called his woman, now this lady seemed familiar. But again, Calynda had already schooled him about his old crew being close to him. With that, everything changed and he was back in kill mode.

Before he could pull the pistol back off of his hip, he froze at the sight of two huge ass pitbulls rushing into the backyard. They were looking around frantically but couldn't seem to spot what they were looking for. Then the big brown one froze and started sniffing the air. A few sniffs later he began to whine and pout. Then the other dog must've smelled what the brown one smelled and they both went into a frenzy. The big one began to howl and cry uncontrollably because he was smelling a familiar smell. Dogs could be away from their owners for years and would pick up their scent from a great distance. Danny and Danielle had just smelled Friday....

"What the hell is y'all problem?", Nechelle asked as she walked out into the backyard. She witnessed both dogs crying and unable to stand still. But she had no idea what the issue was. "Come on! Danny,

Danielle. In the house, now!"

As soon as the dogs came up the patio steps, a man made dash from the side of the house to the rear gate.

"Hey! What the hell after you doing in my fuckin yard!" POW!

Nechelle squeezed off a round at the trespasser and the dogs took off after him. The intruder hopped the gate with ease but Danny had a better idea and rammed a loose board head first and came flying through the fence. Danny was on Friday's ass, Danielle was on Danny's ass, and Nechelle took up the rear. Danny was two seconds off Friday's ass when he swan dove over a neighboring fence, dropping his pistol in the process.

Looking behind him, Friday saw Danny scrambling over the fence then got back up running.

POW! POW!

Nechelle let off more shots at the intruder, barely missing him. "Shit!", she growled.

She was trying to knock his head off. She picked up the gun that fell out of his pants and ran behind the dogs. She knew that the Puerto Ricans had sent someone to snatch her up but she was gonna send a message loud and clear by the time this chase was over with. Friday was now dog tired and could barely clear the last gate. He fell over it out of breath and began to crawl towards his ride. Danny and Danielle leaped over that fucking fence with grace and was on Friday's ass like a dog in heat. He rolled onto his back just ass both dogs became face to face with him as he threw his hands up on surrender. To his surprise, they both licked him all over and cried doggy squeals. Walking on him, rolling and laying on him, his heart calmed a bit, until he saw the lady approaching with a gun.

"Why the fuck are you two stupid dogs playing when you should be eating his ass alive!", Nechelle snapped as she walked up. "Who the fuck are you? And why the hell are you...."

Nechelle paused at the sight of his face. She couldn't believe what she was seeing and her knees went weak. She never heard the pistol fall from her hands.

"Baby..", she whispered. "Oh my God baby...how'd you...where did you come from?" She looked around with every question in disbelief. "Oh shit!" She threw her arms around him, cranking Danny and Danielle back up.

"Where the fuck were you?!", she snapped. Once

she realized what was going on, she flipped. "Why are you sneaking around the house, acting all creepy and shit! Why did you run? We were looking all over for you! Why the hell did you leave the hospital?"

Friday was speechless. He knew nothing of what this woman was talking about. But he did noticing one thing. Just as he recognized in the lady cop's voice, this woman really seemed to be on his side.

Police sirens could be heard in the distance, coming because Nechelle thought it was cool to start shooting in a residential area.

"Come on baby, we gotta get outta here.", Nechelle warned.

"Naw, come with me.", he suggested and they headed to the mustang.

C2

"You wanna join for lunch pal?"

"Naw, I'm ok, got a lot to catch up on. Thanks though.", Griggs replied.

With Lee out of the way, he finally had some time for himself. Nechelle had been on his mind heavy lately and he feared that it will all be short lived. He really liked her and thought that she was a really cool chick. She was just tied up in the street bullshit. Just as he got really lost in his thoughts, a knock came at the door.

"Come in."

"Morning Detective Griggs.", Brittany greeted. "Hey what you got for me?"

"Well, Lt. Pines said for you to take this master copy

and make duplicates after you review it. Then file the copies in their proper places.", she informed him as she passed him a mini harddrive.

"Um, sure. But what is it?"

"The St. Lilly's Hospital footage."

Griggs' mouth went dry as he took the device. He quickly left the office and headed home for privacy. Powering up his laptop and inserting the device, Griggs braced himself for what was to come and was he surprised. At first, it was normal operations in a multi squared camera screen. All squares showed nothing unusual that would go on in a hospital. Then all hell broke loose at the front entrance as men with locs shot everyone in their sight. Then at another entrance, the same thing was happening, but the shooters were Hispanic.

This went on for a while until the two parties crossed paths and started shooting at each other. He remembered from his own investigation when Friday was housed and focused on that square. Moments later his heart sank as he witnessed Nechelle and her crew shoot it out with both of the other crews. Nechelle's crew soon scrambled around the hospital fighting for that lives, trying to find a way out. The end of it all was heartbreaking watching some Hispanic bitch drive a knife into Nechelle as she lay beaten and helpless. But seeing her drag herself to safety was the most refreshing scene that this footage had to offer. He knew that once the right people saw this tape, careful analyzing and evaluations will lead them exactly where to look to lift fingerprints from weapons used and surfaces touched. Meaning that every last one on this camera that was in the police database would be issued a warrant to be arrested for some type of connection with this crime. That meant Nechelle's ass was done. He took a while to ponder on this situation. Everything in his heart wanted to help her out of this situation but the only way to do that was to get a confession from her...

"I'm hungry as shit yo!", Tonia stressed as they cruised down Ocean Drive in Miami.

Her, Dullah, Adrian and Samantha rode in a Cadillac SUV in search of Calynda. Only Tonia and Dullah knew the real reason that they were there and that was cool. They didn't need Adrian and Samantha looking all goofy while they searched the city.

Pulling over to park so that they could walk, Dullah cuffed a 9mm. and hopped out of the truck. When Tonia came around the front, Dullah couldn't believe his eyes.

Dressed in n.v; I 889 inch heels, skin tight Prada jeans and Prada tube top, long silky hair flowing down her back, plus her ass looked thick, wide and heavy. Never would be have imagined that under all that baggy clothing, was a stallion. Not to mention the stone gray contacts made her look exotic.

"Gooott dam Tonia!", Dullah capped. "You thicker than a muthafucka. Lil gay ass!" "Lol! Fuck you yo. I'm ready to eat, where we going?"

"Let's go to Johnny Rockets.", Adrian suggested.

"And how do you know about some dam Johnny Rockets?", Samantha asked suspiciously. "Chill out babe, I looked up places to eat on the way down here." "Mmhm."

Walking up Ocean Drive, Adrian and Samantha

were like two kids in a candy store.

They've never been this far from the city and everything about Miami was brand new. But Dullah and Tonia were on high alert. Tonia was in her phone looking like most chicks do but was really looking for exit routes from Calynda's property incase things got ugly. Dullah kept his vision on their surroundings because even though they were there for one thing, a tourist was always lunch meat to the inner city thugs and he wasn't going for nothing. While they all ate, Sam and Adrian were in their own little world as Dullah and Tonia got strategic.

"So the only plan is to check out where this bitch stays at and head out?", Tonia asked. "Pretty much.", Dullah responded.

"This shit does not take all of us to do! And I didn't have to dress up like some punk bitch!"

"Lol! Yo, you wild. But you look good though homie." "Keep all that gay shit to yourself ma nigga."

"Gay shit? The fuck you talking about? You're a woman ain't you?"

"I fuck women just like you playa! I use my dick just as good as you use yours so two dicks is some real gay shit!", Tonia pressed.

"Tonia…I got man meat, not that rubber shit you like to strap around ya waist. No way in hell you can use that shit as good as I use mine! "

"Bend over nigga, I'll show you."

Dullah stared at Tonia with a blank face and she burst out laughing. Dullah had to admit, those pretty teeth and exotic eyes made her vibe contagious and he gave in to laughter himself.

"No but seriously.", Dullah tightened up. "One man in the wrong area is an accident looking for a place to happen. Because if I'm by myself and Calynda is up in an area where nobody belongs but the people that lives there, then that's my ass. Especially if I'm strapped. But we look more like a family unit this way, so hypothetically, if we bump into her, we'll use the family card and wiggle out of the situation."

"Never thought of it like that. Well from what Google map is showing, this bitch's property sits almost a mile off of the main road on an estate. We can maybe case the place out from afar, but that's only the perimeter. We will have to trespass on her property in order to get a good look at the layout and that could get us in a fucked up situation."

"Well we gotta do something because just knowing a location alone without intimate details it's futile. We got to get in there somehow."

"Listen", Tonia reasoned. "We just carry on with the rest of the day like normal for the sake of these two. They're not old enough to club so later tonight, we roll out like we're going out drinking. Change into all black in the truck and then freestyle our way around that property into we figure out what we need to know."

"You sound like you've done this before lol.", Dullah tripped. "Nigga I'm a crook if you ever seen one!"

The crew carried on like a normal family for the remainder of the evening. Once the night life came alive, Dullah and Tonia headed out as if they were going to a club, but actually was to change clothes and see about Calynda's estate. Cruising pass the front entrance to the estate a few times, Dullah could not find an inconspicuous spot to park the ride so they had to park almost a fifteen minute walk away and made their way on foot. There were no road lights leading to their destination but a full moon that hang low gave then just enough light to find their way.

"Check it, we're not on some James Bond shit tonight alright.", Dullah said. "Let's just find our way around the property and bring some sort of blueprint back to the crew."

"Lemme ask you this.", Tonia quizzed. "If this bitch is the cartel boss' daughter, won't this place have some type of security that wouldn't allow two average muthafuckas to just waltz on in to do as they please? "

"That's a possibility."

"That you failed to mention!"

"What the fuck do you want me to do?", Dullah snapped, stopping in his tracks. "I'm just trying to get the homie back alright. I'm not used to this shit, got a lot of pressure on me. So if you got a better idea then please speak the fuck up. Otherwise, walk your gay ass up this road and do what the fuck I tell you to do!"

"Yooo…just chill, alright…. I'm in this shit with you and I got a lot going on too.", Tonia admitted.

"Yeah, aight. Let's just get this shit over with."

They began walking again towards the estate and once they got there, it looked like a black sky beyond the entrance. Literally nothing as far as the eye could see and that was dangerous. There was no telling what awaited beyond the point if entry and that shit scared the fuck out of them. But the job had to be done and they were here so it was time to move forward. The brick wall was only five feet which was an easy jump then they walked along the edge of the property that was lined with woods. About a half mile away from the mansion, the lights could be seen at the beginning of a long driveway.

Expensive foreign cars sat on front of the house which every room was lit up brightly on the inside.

Once they got close, a very obvious guard could be seen on the roof as well as two patrolling the front of the house. Dullah figured it would be better to make their way to the rear of the property and sneak up close from there. No armed men were on plain sight at the back of the house but a huge pool, that was lit up from its depths, set at the end of a concrete walkway that led from the mansion. A woman could be seen pacing back and forth in front of the pool, talking on her cellphone. Dullah and Tonia crawled in the dark towards the home to get as close as they could without being seen....

After a short flight from Cuba, Calynda headed to her Miami estate to clear her head of her family's bullshit and to find Friday. She knew that he'd rather work alone but with Amelio interfering with the original plans by sending troops after the crew, it will only start a war within the operation because obviously Friday was not having it. He wanted his rightful kills and anyone standing in his way would be met with fatal aggression. She traveled to the states with a few good men along with Chepae and Solas. She would just find the gold and hunt down the crew on her own. But if

Amelio's men got in the way causing Friday to oppose, she had a trick for her father. And Amelio would never know what hit him.

"What do you mean you can't find him?!", Calynda screamed into her phone. After a short pause, she continued. "Because he is not using the name Sharif Smalls idiot! He believes that he is Eric Snipes. I've told you this before. Now find him before morning or I'm gonna rip your fucking head off!"

She slammed her phone down and sat to sip her drink. Finding Friday and staying two steps ahead of Amelio was becoming more of a challenge than she thought. Staring out into the dark, she was trying to get lost in her thoughts when she spotted movements in the shadows. Thinking about the hounds that roamed the grounds, it couldn't be because they were in the kennel by now. She never imagined that someone was foolish enough to trespass into her property but that was they only conclusion that she came to. Acting as if she was unaware, she texted one of her men to release a few hounds into the rear of the estate....

C2

"Did you hear what the fuck I just heard?"

"If you're talking about the name change, I surely did.", Dullah admitted.

"Why the hell would he think that his name was Eric Snipes though?", Tonia whispered.

"Only thing that I can think of is that he lost his memory while in that coma and was brainwashed. And no telling what this bitch has done to the homie already."

"Plus she was on the phone giving orders to find him, meaning Friday must've gotten ghost. He's alive Dullah! That means that…."

"Sshhh!", Dullah hissed, cutting Tonia off. "You hear that?" "Here what? I don't hear shit."

"Sounds like….like chains." "Chains? Yo, you buggin ma nig…" "Listen!", he cut her off once more.

As they looked around, Tonia began to hear what he heard and they both zeroed in on a small fleet of about seven doberman pinschers roaming the yard on high alert. A few sniffed the air and let their vision lingered the Tonia and Dullah's direction.

"We gotta get the fuck outta here. Like now!", Dullah whispered pulling the 9mm. He looked beside him and Tonia was already hauling ass through the dark. She took thee fuck off at the sight of the first hound. By the time Dullah turned back around, he was met with a set of teeth the seconds off his ass.

BOW!!

Dullah dropped the mutt but caused the rest to rush on his direction. A bright spot

light shined right next to him and he took off after Tonia who was nowhere in sight. He was no match for the four legged beast that were sprinting after him and he decided that he'd rather face his match than get bit in the ass.

BOW! B-B-BOW!!

Two more dogs twisted and wiggled with some hot shit pumped in their chest causing the rest to halt but continue to bark in his direction.

C2

Calynda saw the intruder took off shooting her dogs and grew another head. One of her man walked up to her and she took the gun right off of his hip then shot him in the face. The price to pay for allowing an armed trespasser on the property. Sprinting through the home, she barked orders to not let the trespasser off of the property as she barreled through the front door. Spotting a four wheeler, she hopped on and spun up the driveway. In the distance as she approached the front entrance, she spotted an intruder almost to the gate and let off shots in that direction....

Dullah saw the four wheeler hauling ass up the driveway headed straight for Tonia, who was dam near to the front gate. The lady on the four wheeler began to shoot at Tonia, causing Dullah to shoot at the lady to buy Tonia some time....

C2

Closing in on the front entrance, Calynda raised her pistol to shoot again when shots rang out to her left, striking her front tire. The Mongoose lost control and ejected her over the handle bars. But her training allowed her to tuck and roll on impact, which she rolled into a sprint towards the front gate still. Even though she was getting shot at, the objective was to not let anyone of off the property. One intruder was in front of her and the other behind...

C2

Tonia heard the gunshots and saw the bullets strike the fence on front of her but she never slowed her sprint. She was not about to get trapped on this muthafucka! Plus she was scared for her baby. For the first time she felt a connection to the child and her survival instincts kicked into overdrive. Running full speed, she leaped over the gate and hit the ground running. Yea, Dullah was back there but there was nothing that she could do to help him, plus the was no use for both of them to get captured. She ran full speed up the road and didn't slow until she reached the truck. And once she was there, she feared the worst for Dullah. He was nowhere on sight…

CHAPTER 10

Tyler was happy that happy hour was finally over for the day at the club. What was meant to be a small everyday after work crowd turned into a weekday midday party spot. People ordered just as much shit as they did on the weekend. Penny sat at the bar while Pepp helped clean up the common area.

"You do a really great job Tyler. Like, you really do.", Penny said.

"Fuck this job!"

"Lol! What? Why would you say that?"

"Because I need more help! Yea, the pay is good but I'm management, not supposed to be taking and running orders and shit."

"Well if the job doesn't get done, shit rolls down hill.", Penny advised. "Yea, I know right."

The front door chimed and in walked Boogey. He wore so much jewelry that you would think that he was a rapper, locs flowing freely everywhere, dressed in Gucci from head to toe. A short skinny man that looked to be in his early twenties strolled in behind him. The young man held the look of death in his face with dark energy. Anyone could see that he was Boogey's shooter. Both men took a seat at the bar but the young boy sat farther down towards the end alone, watching the whole club.

"Heard bout ya friend.", Boogey said.

"What the fuck do you want?", Penny snapped. Even though the crew was teaming with them, she never forgot what they did to 3-T and it was forever fuck them.

"Me wan know wha cha plan tah do. Tree of ya men are gone and dey still comin for ya. Soon won't be no mo crew, me er' to help. Me wan dem dead so wha ya wan do?"

"Well Dullah is not here at the moment and that's something that you would need to discuss with him.", Tyler said.

"Make sho ya tell em' ta get at me soon. Tis shit gettin outta hand."

Pepper had went upstairs for trash bags and peeped movement on the monitor.

Taking a closer look, he witnessed three SUV's pull up and Hispanics hopped out with assault rifles and formed a semicircle around the front of the building. Spotting the chrome AK47, twin glock 33's, and twin desert eagle .357's mounted on the office wall, Pepp snatched up the weapons and flew down the steps….

C2

Amelio had once again grew impatient waiting for the gold to turn up. Not only did he lose a dozen man on his last failed attempt to knock off members of the crew, but his daughter Calynda seemed to think it to be a wise idea to go rogue and deal within his operation the way she deemed proper. But she has no clue that he was on to her antics and would deal with her with the same iron fist that he dealt with with everyone else. He gave Cheewaus the greenlight to fly to the states and let it be known that he was coming for what was rightfully his. Serving through traffic, Cheewaus and his goons made it to The Boulevard and hopped out ready to fuck shit up…..

C2

Pepp made it down the steps taking them two at a time, rushing to the bar and threw all of the guns on the counter. The young boy jumped up and slid a folding AR15 from under his shirt and Boogey did the same.

"What the hell is all of this for?", Penny gasped at the sight of all the shiny guns.

"I don't know what the fuck is going on but peep the monitors, shit is about to get ugly out front!", Pepp warned.

Tyler grabbed a remote and turned on the monitors on all TV screens across the room and I'll be dam. Puerto Ricans were attempting to surround the club armed with rifles.

Pepp snatched up the AK and a .357 and started barking orders.

"Penny, Tyler, go upstairs in the office." He reached for a mallet under the bar used to break up ice and handed it to Tyler. "Go up to the office and knock out the floor square in the far corner. Penny, you do the same on the opposite side of the room. Lay flat on your belt and anything that comes through that door, you drop their ass off! Boogey, you take the far right corner." He tossed Boogey the other .357 and gave Tyler and Penny the glock 33's before they ran upstairs. He then looked to the young fella that came in with Boogey.

"What's your name lil bruh?" "B.J.", he said with his chest out.

"Aight B.J., lay flat on your belly in that far left corner and aim that cannon at that door. No matter what comes through that entrance, you burn that ass up. I'll lay in the middle. Nobody shoots until a few of them come through the door."

Just as he finished his sentence, he saw glass shattered from the left side of the ceiling. Moments later, glass shattered from the other side. The girls were in position and ready for whatever. Suddenly, it sounded as if rocks were being thrown at the building then the windows began to shatter. Pepp dropped down soon as a bullet flew pass his head and another took his hat off. Liquor bottles disintegrated and TV's exploded and jumped off of the wall. Cotton and feathers pooted out of the furniture and splinters of wood peppered the air as bullets riddled the place.

Previously, every television showed what was going on at the front entrance but as they looked up while the shooting took a pause, only two monitors remained functional and it showed Puerto Ricans reloading as they walked to the front door. Pepp could control the lights and music from his phone, so he turned the lights off and blasted the music. Coming into the club, you couldn't see anything but if you were already inside, your vision had adjusted to the dark and you would be able to see anything beyond the front door and shattered windows.

Tyler saw the first goon come into the club who looked around with caution. Penny waited until the seventh entered and popped his ass in the throat! Bullets came from everywhere and about ten Puerto Ricans made it in before they knew what was going on, but by then it was too late. Even though they shot back at the crew aimlessly, it was no use. The crew had the drop and it paid off. Cheewaus couldn't believe what was happening. Down to his last two men, he reached inside of the truck, grabbing two concussion grenades and threw them into the club. If there was any glass left after all that shooting, there dam sure wasn't any now. The grenades even blew the remaining monitors out. Pepp couldn't hear a dam thing as his ears rang him deaf. Penny and Tyler were barely affected by it but still felt the impact.

The remaining two goons rushed into the club shooting everywhere before the men downstairs could gather their wits. Luckily, they weren't immediately spotted. Penny jumped up and looked out the 'O' of the office window and spotted a mean looking Puerto Rican dressed on boots and fatigues. This motherfucker was muscled up too and she could tell from perception alone that this fella would be trouble. But he had no gun in hand, which she would use to her advantage. Against her better judgment, and seeing that she was almost out of ammo, she slowly opened the window. The muscled Puerto Rican was walking towards the entrance and his sunshades made it impossible to see her. Penny was about to stick one leg out of the window when Tyler stopped her. "Bitch! What the fuck are you doing?!"

"Headed to the corner store. The fuck do you think? I'm not about to sit in here and wait to die. I'd rather fight these motherfuckers...."

"But I can't fight like you!", Tyler whined.

"Well, keep your sorry ass still. I'll be back.... hopefully."

Penny tossed Tyler her own personal glock. 40 and slid out of the window. Walking the ledge, Penny waited until Cheewaus was directly under her and eased down so she would be able to hang low before she dropped down. Cheewaus stopped in his tracks because her oddly smelled perfume and once her spun around at the sound of something hitting the ground behind him...... BAM!!

Penny drew back and with all her might, threw her hips into a vicious eight cross hook to cheewaus' jaw. As he staggered, Penny shuffled two steps forward, leaping into the air and came down across the bridge of his nose with a sharp elbow. Penny gave Cheewaus no breathing room and kept it hot on his ass by wrapping his ponytail around one of her fist and bashed his face in with the other. Cheewaus remained his wits somewhat and grabbed a hold of Penny with the strength and grip of a silver back gorilla. Penny felt they power of four men when Cheewaus snatched her ass up off of her feet and slammed her on her back, knocking the wind from her lungs. He then brought his body down on top of her with a hammer punch towards the grill but Penny threw up her elbow over her face, which absorbed most of the blow. Wrapping Cheewaus' forearm in a headlock, Penny rolled sideways and attempted to snatch his shoulder out of its socket. Cheewaus felt all that pressure and panicked. Locking his elbow and grabbing Penny's hair with his free hand, he picked her up while she was still wrapped around his arm like a snake and slammed her onto the ground once again.

But see, Penny was one of those real white bitches, you know, the kind that could really take an ass whipping because she held onto that arm for two more slams before Cheewaus finally ran out of juice. She was bleeding from the back of her head and started to feel dizzy, but refused to give up. With all that she had left, Penny jammed her foot against Cheewaus' throat pulling back on his arm with all her might and felt that sucker pop! Cheewaus was sup fatigued and the pain was so severe that he passed out. Penny went limp and let out a deep breath, she could not have taken another one of those body slams.

The last two Puerto Ricans that entered the club got dropped off in no time. The crew didn't know how many there were so they waited patiently but none came. Seeing that the coast may be clear, Pepp got up cautiously, and walked towards the front entrance and he'll be dammed. He witnessed Penny tear drop from the ledge of the club behind this ugly ass Puerto Rican and when he spun around, Penny dug all in his ass!

Figuratively. Seeing it to be a fist fight, he decided to let them shoot the fair one and he had to admit, he was proud of the chick. The sexy little white bitch had a set of hands made for beating ass because ole boy never stood a chance. He slammed her a few times but his ass was grass from the start. When it was all over with, Penny was leaking from the head and ole boy looked like he had a broken nose AND arm. Penny looked over and saw Pepp standing to the side cradling a rifle and lost her mind.

"Seriously! You sorry asshole! Why didn't you help me?"

"I heard about you. Figured I see what the hype was about.", Pepp shrugged then stuck a hand out to help her up.

Penny smacked his palm away and hopped up with a scowl on her face ready to kick ass again. All this time he could've helped out but watched her get slammed like a rag doll. Pepp saw the anger boiling and gave his warning shot.

"This ain't that.", he said pointing down at Cheewaus. "I will seriously fuck ya lil white ass up.", he warned with a straight face.

"Whatever. Drag his ass inside.", Penny snapped as she walked towards the club. "Inside? We gotta get the fuck from around here! Twelve dam sure on the way."

"Look around!", Penny said, spinning in her tracks. "We're in the middle of fucking nowhere. Who is there to call the cops?"

"Yeah, I hear you. If they pull up, you better get me out of this shit." "Drag him in Pepp!"

Pepp sucked his teeth, grabbed Cheewaus by the ankles and dragged him inside. The club was a mess. It looked like a bomb has went off in there. Pepp found a chair and placed a slumped Cheewaus in it. Her peeped Tyler and BJ crouched in the back of the club and went to check it out.

"What's going on?", he asked as he walked up.

Tyler just stared down and BJ had tears in his eyes.

172

Boogey laid on his belly in a pool of blood. A hole was in the top of his head and it looked as if his left shoulder was barely attached to his body. BJ took off all of Boogey's jewelry, put it on then kissed his cheek.

"Love you father." BJ whispered.

Tyler gasped and Pepp looked away. Boogey was his pops, his name was BJ....Boogey jr.

"Holy fucking shit!", Penny said walking up. Then she looks towards Cheewaus and a look of death came over her face. "Pepp, find something to tie his ass to that chair. BJ, get me a tall bucket of ice water. Tyler, where's that gun I gave you?"

"What you got going on Penny? What're you about to do?", Tyler asked handing her the glock.

"Don't worry. I've done this before. He's gonna tell me everything that I wanna know."

Danny, Danielle, and Eric lounged in the backseat of the mustang like they knew each other like that.

Animals had their own way of communicating and somehow they all agreed that Friday was their owner. So for the sake of him they got along. Nechelle couldn't keep her eyes off of him. He had gained a little weight, but it was all muscle. His beard was thick and his hair was a nappy fro with no edge up. He was fucking sexy! But she could tell that something was off with him, like he was missing something. She didn't know where they were headed and didn't give one fuck! She would ride shotgun straight to hell as long as he drove them there.

Friday pulled up to the spot and without saying a word, he got out and let the dogs out as well. He headed top the house with the dogs on his heels and Nechelle just followed in shock. She almost shot this nigga for nothing! Letting the hounds linger in the front, they entered the home and immediately heard faint yelling coming from the rear of the home. Nechelle scrunched her face at him and he just rolled his eyes shaking his head. He led her to the room where Aisha and Nicole were at and all hell broke loose.

"Friday! You ignorant! Son of a bitch! Get me out of these fuckin ropes!", Aisha hollered.

Nechelle gasped and rushed over to untie Aisha. She couldn't get the restraints loose and looked up to Friday for help.

"Take these off of her! What the hell is your problem babe?", Nechelle asked in shock. "So you know this bitch?"

"Do I know her?!"

"Bitch?!", Aisha snapped. "Girrllll. Please! Just please untie me. I'm gonna fuck him up!" "Sharif Smalls! You take this shit off! What the hell is your problem?!", Nechelle growled.

Friday pulled his pistol and pointed it at Nechelle's face. "My problem is y'all muthafuckas think shit sweet. You think y'all gonna double cross me and I'll let it slide?"

"What in the fuck do you mean 'double cross' you? Nigga we almost died in that hospital protecting your ass.", Nechelle spat.

A faint moan came from the back of the back of the room and Nechelle spotted a woman laid out. As she walked closer, her mouth hit the floor.

"You have Nicole too? What the fuck is going on? I

will MAKE you shoot me you dumb son of a bitch I'll kick your ass myself if you don't explain this shit!"

Something wasn't right. Either these hoes were some good actresses or Calynda had spun him a dam good story for a hidden purpose. He kept his gun drawn but couldn't find the right words to say. Everything confused him but his heart was telling him that these women were his people. Nechelle went to help Nicole into a seated position and Nicole moaned out in pain.

"Careful, she's shot.", Aisha warned.

"He shot her?", Nechelle asked wide eyed. Then looked to Friday with slanted eyes. "You shot her?"

Aisha went to tell Nechelle the whole story from picking Nicole up from work to Friday saving then in the shoot out to waking up tied to a chair.

"So he saved your lives but turned around and kidnapped you too?" Nechelle then turned to Friday. "Babe. You gotta tell me what's going on.", she spoke softly.

It took Friday a second but he eventually told them everything that he could remember. From the time he awoke in Amelio's estate, Calynda reprogramming him, the memory flashes of Nicole and Nechelle, to the here and now. Nechelle was pissed. This crazy ass Puerto Rican bitch done fucked up her man. She took her time and gave Friday the history. The real history of the crew up until the point I'd the hospital shoot out. It was hard for him to process everything because none of this was familiar. But as he looked onto the eyes of his captives, he recognized one thing. It was love. They all loved him and was willing to die for him. Now he had to figure out what needed to be done to make things right with his family, the crew.

"Listen.", Friday said, staring back at the women. "I'm sorry. I really don't know what the fuck is going on but my gut tells me that this is where I'm supposed to be. And if what you're telling me is true, then we gotta down this bitch and her pops before we all get caught up. We need to…"

"We need to get me the fuck outta these ropes Friday!", Aisha snapped, cutting him off. She was patiently sitting in the chair as he came to realization. Friday walked over and untied her ankles first. Aisha gave Nechelle a sneaky eye and Nechelle gave her a slight nod back. As soon as Friday untied Aisha's wrist…

WHOP!!

Aisha popped him in the mouth and kneed him in the nuts. Friday doubled over grabbing both of her wrists and that's when Nechelle stepped up.

BAM!

Clean uppercut to the lower jaw…. BAM!! BAM!!

A two piece to the left eye dropped Friday on his back and the girls were on his ass like a dog in heat! Aisha had a fist full of his afro, holding his head down, beating the shit out of him as Nechelle sat on his chest choking him with the left and hammering his grill with her right. They were fucking his ass up! A loud noise brought everyone to a halt as they witnessed Nicole chambers in a round inside of the gun that fell out of Friday's waist line. She stood holding her hip but had the gun pointed steady at Friday. Her jaw was swollen but she snatched the head wrap off and attempted to speak. Her speech sounded as if she were talking through clenched jaws.

"Get off of him!", she screamed, waving the gun. "Nicole...", Nechelle spoke softly. "Calm down for..." "Bitch I said move!"

Aisha did not need to be told twice and hopped her ass right back in that chair that she was tied to.

"Ok. Ok.", Nechelle said with her hands up in surrender.

Nicole trained the gun on Friday and tears came flowing from her eyes. "Stand up.", she whispered. Friday must've taken too long for get liking...

POW!!

"I said stand the fuck up!!", she snapped, shooting by his head.

Friday stood up on shakey legs and peered over to Nicole. He has just pistol whip this woman after she'd gotten shot and now she had the gun.

"The only reason I haven't dropped your ass off is because of what I just heard. We are family. You hear me? We're Crew Friday! Look at us! If we were against you, we got the drop on you. We can kill you right now." She walked closer shoving the gun in his direction. "I can kill you right now!"

"I believe you...", Friday whispered. "Let's do whatever we have to do to get things back to where they were. I've heard everything y'all said and it sounds like this is where I should be instead of with Calynda."

Aisha got up and went over to Nicole. "First, we have to get her to a hospital."

"Bitch move, I'm good.", Nicole said shoving Aisha out of the way as she walked over to Friday. Nicole closed her eyes and cried her heart out as Friday nervously wrapped his arms around her. Nechelle could tell that he was a bit uneasy but joined the embrace anyway. He knew he had to get used to having two women as well as everything else. He just hoped to get his life back to where it was before.

C2

Griggs sat in his office trying to get some work done but his mind was not allowing him to focus on anything. After viewing that footage of what happened at the hospital, he found himself between a rock and a bigger rock. Any average person could see that Nechelle and her friends were clearly defending themselves but with all of those lives lost, the county prosecutor would give two shits about acting in self defense. All parties involved were gonna get slammed. End of story. There wasn't much that he could do to help Nechelle except buy her some time by warning her of what was to come, giving her a running head start. Other than that, she was on borrowed time. He hated that he would be the one to give her the bad news because he had grown to really like her. He knew that she was a really great person, just caught up in the wrong shit. But all of that was irrelevant now because once this footage was reviewed by the right people, her ass was hoping to jail. He has just build up enough courage to call her up when Detective Lee came into his office knocking and entering without permission. "Sup pal? How's it going?", Lee asked as he took a seat.

"Not much, you know. Usual shit. Paperwork."

"I see. Well, Brittany tells me that you have that footage from the hospital." "Yea, I surely do. She gave it to me yesterday.", Griggs admitted.

"Well, lemme see it!", Lee said, throwing up then slapping them on his thigh.

Griggs felt the hard drive burning a hole in his jacket pocket but knew that he could not allow Lee to view it unless he was ready to start serving warrants in the morning.

"I took it home with me and it's still in my laptop. I'll bring it by in the morning." "Uh-huh...I see.", Lee said suspiciously. "Did you make the copies at least?"

"As a matter of fact, I didn't.", Griggs responded. "I had so much going on that I let all of my assignments pull away from me."

"Mmhm...I see. Well pal.", Lee said as he stood. "Make sure you get it here in the morning. You know L.T Pines will have that industrial sized jar of vaseline on his desk waiting for us if you don't." Griggs chuckled and assured Lee that he would get things done.

C2

Nechelle sat in the hospital's waiting room with Friday while Nicole was getting patched up. Aisha hadn't heard from Dullah and decided to go home, take care of her life then try to contact her man. Nechelle spent most of the time telling Friday about his life before getting shot, but he just couldn't seem to remember any of it. But he had to admit, the story felt familiar for some reason. A different feeling than he got from when Calynda told her version of his past. He was anxious to meet his two best friends Dullah and 3-T, they seem like really good people from what he was told. Nechelle felt her phone vibrate and when she saw the caller, her mouth went dry. She knew that she had gotten in bed with the devil and the was a hefty price to pay. But at this point, she was all in. There mission was taken and she gave herself the green light. To not raise any suspicion, she answered the call without leaving the waiting room.

"Hello?"

"I need to see you.", Griggs said, getting straight to the point. "Is everything ok?"

"Not really, but we need to talk." "We're talking right…"

"In person Hollywood!", he snapped, cutting her off. "How soon and where?"

"My house around seven. And don't make me look for you Hollywood."

Griggs hung up without so much as a fuck you later. She felt uneasy about meeting up but not so much because it was at his home. Didn't think he would want to arrest her there. But an even bigger problem was, what was she to do with Friday? It was like having a baby, she couldn't just leave him alone. He might run off somewhere or worse. But she couldn't take him to Griggs' spot either. Somebody would die or go to jail for sure. It was only one in the evening so she had six hours to figure that shit out.

When Tonia made it back to the hotel without Dullah, Adrian was demanding answers that she honestly could not give. She knew that a number of things could've happened to him and none of them were good. So she just packed them up and left Miami. She tried calling Penny but got no answer, Nechelle wasn't picking up either. She tried Tyler at the club and got the same results, it seemed like no one was available. She dropped Adrian and Samantha off at their apartment then made her way to the club.

From a distance, she could see a few trucks in the road as she neared the building. But once she pulled up in front of it, she could not believe her eyes. It looked like the homeland to a warzone. Bullet shells peppered the front entrance and huge lemon sized holes were everywhere across the building. Everything in her told her to turn around and get the fuck out of there but she really had nowhere else to go. None of her friends were answering and she was afraid that this may be the reason. She didn't have a gun so she crept out of the truck and cautiously made her way into the club. The inside made her heart twist. So many dead bodies were laid out, she just knew that her people were dead in here somewhere.

Seeing am assault rifle laying next tip a body, she picked it up, figuring that the dead guy didn't need it anyway, and made her way up the steps. She was still in heels so she crept to the office door and heard a conversation. Quietly checking the clip for ammo, she readied her gun and swung the door open, finger on the trigger. Penny and Pepp stood in front of some random guy tied to a chair, Tyler was barking into her cell phone and a strange young man with locs sat on the office desk, face puffy with tears.

"What the fuck happened here?!", Tonia snapped, dropping the rifle and running to Tyler crying. Tyler hung up immediately and embraced her girlfriend.

"This clown and his friends thought it to be a bright idea to throw rocks at our building.", Penny said.

Tonia looked at the man, recognized him to be a Puerto Rican and put the pieces together. Without warning, she hauled off and smacked Cheewaus' mustache crooked. Penny raised an eyebrow and Pepp just shook his head in approval with a smirk.

"Where's Dullah?", Pepp asked.

Tonia just continued to stare at Cheewaus, breathing heavily. She had no solid answer to that question and just thinking about all the horrible possibilities brought tears to her eyes. Tyler saw the cloud coming over Tonia and grew concerned.

"Tonia...", Tyler whispered. "Baby, where's Dullah?"

Tonia let out a gut wrenching scream and took off on Cheewaus, raining blows to his face. She banged on him so much that his chair tipped over and she started kicking him in the face. Penny knew that if this continued, Tonia was gonna kill him. So she tried her best to restrain Tonia but she was just too much.

"Can you please help me with this bitch?!", Penny looked to Pepp. "It's like trying to hold back two people!"

"You are...", Tyler mumbled.

"What?", Penny asked, not understanding.

Tonia shot Tyler a nasty look who in turn just crossed her arms and popped her gum.

Pepp picked Cheewaus up off of the floor and turned back to Tonia. "Yo, where the fuck is Dullah?"

Tonia finally pulled herself together and told them about what happened in Miami. In turn, Penny put her up on game about what just went down at the club. They all were so caught up in the moment that young BJ was the only one who saw through the floor that some people were walking briskly through the front door of the club and making their way upstairs.

"Big problem. Moo Mo people tah come.", he panicked pointing to the floor.

The crew grabbed their weapons and positioned themselves around the office so if anything came through that door, it would get pushed right back out. When Nechelle burst through the door with Friday on her heels, time stood still. Penny cocked her head to the side and Pepp walked up slowly with a frown on his face. Tyler held her hands over her mouth crying and poor BJ didn't know what the fuck was going on.

"Eric!"

"Cheewaus?", Friday questioned unbelievingly. "Eric?", Tyler asked, face scrunched up.

"Who the fuck is Eric?", Penny asked looking around. "Cabron! Get me outta here!", Cheewaus panicked.

Friday looked around at his crew then back to Cheewaus and an expression of death grew over his face. He slowly walked over and knelt in front of the hostage and got straight to the point.

"My beef is not with you, but you can die. Makes me no difference. I'm gonna ask you some questions and you're gonna answer me. Simple shit. You don't answer me, you die. More simple shit."

"You really have let these motherfuckers fool you? Do you know who we are? Do you know what will happ… "

SMACK!!

"Shut your bitch ass up!", Friday said, smacking the shit out of him. "Now who shot me?"

Cheewaus looked into Friday's eyes and could detect no soul. He knew that him being tortured would be a sign of mercy. No, he was gonna die swiftly. He looked around at the other crew members and just knew that he was belly deep in coon piss.

"Amelio ordered the hit.", Cheewaus confessed with a straight face. "Calynda's father…", Friday whispered. "Why would he send a hit?" "You stole his gold cabron."

Friday took a second to let it all sink in. The same gold that Calynda fooled him to believe that it was theirs was actually Amelio's. He was a pawn, a puppet, the sacrificial lamb. Even though he had lost his memory, he hadn't lost his common sense. He was being used to recover the same gold that he was being accused of stealing. He had been played a fool.

"What gold is this nigga talking about?", Friday asked, looking around at the crew. At the time of the gold heist, the only person in the room that knew about the gold besides Friday was Nechelle.

184

"We flipped some local dope boys that ran cocaine for Calynda and one of them was stashing gold bars for Amelio.", Nechelle informed him.

"Where is the gold?", Friday asked her.

Nechelle looked around and all eyes were on her. "We got it…. Can't let everybody in our business.", she said, shaking her head with a tilt.

"Well this is what we're gonna do.", Friday said. "First, we have to get…"

The office door flew open and everyone with a gun pointed it at Aisha and 3-T. Aisha couldn't find Dullah so the next person to call was Tony. 3-T hadn't heard from Dullah since he left for Miami and tried calling everybody else in the crew and got no answer. Aisha had also told him the story about Friday and he couldn't believe it. After rushing to the hospital thinking that Friday and Nechelle was still with Nicole, but not there, they flew to the club. 3-T was his day one and tears came flooding. Friday had no clue who this man was that walked up and embraced him but he felt love. This was his family.

These were his people. Here was where he belonged. This was the crew. Aisha had put 3-T up on game about Friday losing his memory as well.

"I know that you don't remember me, but I'm your boy.", 3-T admitted. "I fuckin love you ma nigga and I'm riding with you for whatever cause, I don't care. Just say the word."

Friday gave him a reassuring nod and a shoulder squeeze then demanded everyone's attention. "First, I want to apologize to you.", he said to Aisha. "I was in a different place and I hope that you understand as well as forgive me. Even though y'all two fucked me up lol.", he grinned looking at Nechelle. "But priority, we have to get Dullah back. If he is one of us then there we'll be no man left behind. Next, we have to get this place back operational. No way we'll be able to get shit done with twelve sniffing up our asses over this shit. Sooo…. It's Tyler right?", he asked looking to Tyler.

"Uh-huh.", she beamed at him smiling hard.

"It's you who runs this place so get the job done. No excuses only results. Anyway, it's obvious that Calynda is not gonna be at that spot in Miami and you know she's taking Dullah with her. So Aisha and…. Penny right?", he said squinting at Penny. They acknowledged him.

"You both are the law so do whatever it takes to get all the info you can on Calynda and her crew. In the meantime, I'm gonna go back and play dumb like I don't know what the fuck is going on. Do not attempt to contact me. I'm gonna learn their operation inside and out and when the time is right, we're gonna smash that shit! We taking everything! Dope, money, jewelry, I don't give a fuck. It's coming with us. And they gonna die! Simple shit. 3-T and Pepp, y'all just gotta hold this shit down. It's kill or be killed and we're not taking any prisoners. They've came for us for the last time.

Nechelle, get them jamaicans on stand by and let them know that the beef is up and be ready for the green light."

"Wha bout me?", BJ asked. He had been quietly listening and waiting patiently for his turn to speak.

"Who the fuck is this?", Friday asked no one in

186

particular. "He came here with…"

"Boogey me father!", he spat, cutting Penny off who just rolled her eyes. "Him dead downstairs and me wan revenge. Me no scare of nuttin and shoot at er body wa wan rump!"

"Tonia and Tyler, y'all watch this lil nigga. And if he's a shooter like he claim to be then he'll be good to keep close.", Friday instructed. "Once Nicole is out of the hospital, I'm outta here. In the meantime…"

"This is some real live bullshit!", Penny growled. "What are you talking about?", Aisha asked.

Penny held the barrel of the gun like a hammer and pointed it at Cheewaus. "I had plans on busting this fuckers balls."

##

Everyone sat at the kitchen table as they ate breakfast. Nana always over do it when she had a new guest and this morning, she really showed off. Waffles, home fries, bacon, sausage, eggs, omelets, steak cubes and four different kinds of juice. Everyone was yelling Spanish around the table as if everything was normal except for the guest. Dullah hadn't said shit yet. Ever since they'd snatched him up the night before, he had no plans on speaking. And no time soon. Nana had fixed him a plate from the same dishes that everyone else ate from so he knew that the food was safe to eat. But he still didn't eat that shit. Then say never sleep with the enemy. I say if we're both asleep, fair game.

Never eat with the enemy. Lose your vision when

you look at the fork.

He knew Calynda by prior investigation but was none the wiser to the two kids, old lady, and two bodyguards that stood on opposite sides of the room. Every now andagain, Calynda would shoot him a look, but only got a brief moment and he couldn't identify what that look meant. It was completely impassive. The little boy who sat next to Dullah reached in his pocket and pulled out a small green frog and placed it on the table between him and Dullah.

"Adam! Get that shit off of the table!", Calynda snapped. "But LynLyn", Again whined.

"I said remove it before I…" SMASH!!

Adam's mouth dropped and his sister Lisa snickered covering her mouth. Dullah gave the little frog a heavy pound and guts went everywhere. Chepae gave a nod of approval and Nana gave Dullah a mean scowl through squinted eyes and he gave her a look of not giving a fuck.

"Go get ready for school kids, ok.", Calynda said with a tone that made it clear that this was not up for debate.

"Yes LynLyn.", they said in unison and left without complaining.

Once the kids were out of sight, all attention was on Dullah. "You don't have to starve yourself you know. The food is perfectly safe.", Calynda smirked. Dullah didn't say a word, just looked around at everyone. "Well, do you kind telling me who you are and why are you trespassing on my property? SHOOTING at me?"

Silence.

"You had an accomplice that got away. No idea who that might be either huh?" More silence.

Nana had begun to clean up the frog guts next to Dullah and was mumbling something in Spanish. He couldn't tell what she meant but knew that she was talking shit. He gave a light chuckle and a smirk. Nana looked up at the sound of Dullah's snort then stormed off.

"I really am doing my best to be patient with you cabron.", Calynda reasoned. "But you're making this…."

WHONG!!

Nana cracked Dullah upside his head with a skillet and was talking cash shit in Spanish a mile a minute. She pointed the pan at him and shoved it his way emphasizing certain phrases as Solas did his best to lead her away from the kitchen area. Chepae folded his arms across his chest and held a fist to his mouth, trying to hide his amusement.

Everyone knew that Nana was not too be fucked with and she will go head up with anybody. Once Nana was ushered away and Solas had returned, Calynda got down to business.

"Chepae!", she snapped and Chepae handed her a thin folder. She opened it and began placing documents in front of Dullah as she called them out.

"Abdullah Muhammed AKA Dullah." She slid a copy of his driver's license in front of him. "Address, blah blah blah blah. Owns Tender Heads," slid a building permit in front of him. "Here's a pic of your car, your girlfriend Aisha who is a city cop, crooked bitch, and here's photos of your little band of thieves."

She slid pics of the whole crew across the table for him to see. But one was missing.

Friday. But he didn't say shit. He just continued to remain silent.

"Now that you know that I know who you are, let me guess why you were on my property." She slid a pic of Dullah and Friday coming out of a real estate office, oblivious to being watched.

"Mr. Sharif Smalls. You came looking for your best friend huh? Well guess what? He's very much alive, and healthy too. But not quite the same vato as before. You see, he's lost a bit of his memory, well, mostly all of his memory. And doesn't remember shit before walking up from that coma. Not his name his age, family, nothing. So he was pretty much a blank page. MY black page, I might add.", she said with a toothy smile. "Now, he's Eric. And all Eric knows is that everyone on this table must die! You, the law, those other bitches, everyone! And until I find my gold, I will not call him off.", she snapped, pounding her fist on the table.

Seeing that Dullah was not reacting to her antics, her pistivity meter shot through the roof and she snapped her fingers. Suddenly, Solas wrapped a cake around Dullah's throat and began to strangle him. As Dullah fought against the pressure, Calynda got up and slowly walked around the table. She straddled Dullah's lap as to face him with the look of death in her eyes. She could see the blood vessels bursting in his eyeballs as the oxygen left his face.

"Enough of your games puto. This is what you

want? Then this is what you get. You will die a slow horrible death if I don't find my fucking gold! So either tell me what I need to hear or you will receive this very same treatment every hour until your body shuts down for good. I wish you would've eaten because that was your last meal cabron."

She lifted off of his lap and gave Solas slight nod, who in turn released the rope from around his neck. Dullah threw up instantly and fell top the floor gasping for air. He could barely see because the damaged vessels in his eyes impaired his vision. Calynda looked at her watch then back to Dullah.

"You have fifty- eight minutes Mr. Muhammed." She then looked to Chepae. "Secure him and we will continue as planned."

With that, she walked away while Dullah was escorted somewhere in the home.

C2

Friday drove Nechelle and the hounds back to the crib when they left the club. He had so much going through his mind at one time and he really need a place to take some time and think. Everything was brand new to him and he was doing his best to not let his emotions cloud his judgment but he started his day off as a lone wolf and ended up leading a wolf pack with the revelation that he was deceived by Calynda. As he cruised through the streets he never realized that he was talking his right hand and slid it between Nechelle's thighs right up against her pussy and had a flashback. He had numerous visions of him doing this very same gesture again and again while Nechelle squeezed her thighs together around his hand. Her pulled over quickly then looked at her, and Nechelle had a shocked expression with eyes full of tears.

"You remember…", she whispered, voice full of hope.

Friday shook his head in agreement and a big goofy grin grew across Nechelle's face as she threw her arms around him and stuck her tongue in his mouth.

"Baby please come back.", she whispered nose to nose, eyes closed as she cupped both of his cheeks. "Daddy I need you here. Please come back to me. You just gotta remember baby."

He grabbed both of her wrist and looked her in the eyes. "I may not remember everything just yet, but I know I'm supposed to be with you guys. My memory is coming back slowly and it's showing me the crew and never Calynda. That's how I know that it's real. I'm gonna figure this shit out and make it all right."

"WE!", she stressed. "We are gonna figure this shit out and make it right. One thing that the crew does is everything together."

Friday pulled off and she took his hand and jammed it between her legs and squeezed. They pulled up to the crib and the dogs raced to the door jumping on one another. Once inside, Friday didn't get any familiar feeling but felt right at home.

"Well, I have to make a run so do as you please, after all, this is your home. No one should pop up because nobody knows where we stay. Food is everywhere in the kitchen and take your time with the cable because we have crazy channels. Oh yea, your game is right over there. "

She walked up on him and rubbed the side of his face. "We never changed a thing because we knew that you were coming back." With that, she gave him a really nasty kiss and grabbed a fist fill of dick, eyes flying open feeling that rocked up log. She grinned then backed away towards the door. "And when I get back I'm gonna need to speed around that curve with no brakes.", she smiles pointing between his legs.

Once she was out of the door, her whole mood changed along with her facial expression. A scowl replaced her toothy smile and that killer instinct kicked in. She had business to take care of and needed to get her mind right.

Cruising the city streets, she came to grips that she had some serious decision making to do tonight and it was now or never. She had been ignoring this muthafuckas calls all day and knew that it was time to face the music. Pulling into the driveway of her destination, she tucked her compact . 40 cal and walked up to the door. Before she could ring the bell, the door flew open and Griggs snatched her in by the shirt collar. Slamming the door, he spun Nechelle around and towered over her breathing heavy like he was ready to beat that ass. But they both knew from the previous encounter that Nechelle had no issues ducking shit up so he stuck with his theatrics rather than getting physical.

"So I guess you don't have shit to say huh?!"

"Shit to say about what Larry?", Nechelle snapped, rolling her eyes. "I've been trying to reach you all fucking day!"

"Oh well nigga. I had shit to do. Plus I'm here now so what the fuck do you want?"

Griggs walked off heavy footed towards his living room area and powered on his laptop. Sticking the hard drive inside, he loaded the footage from the hospital security camera and motioned for her to take a look. Nechelle came around to view the footage and even though it looked like a normal day at the hospital, she knew what was to come.

"I take it that this will hold your attention until I get back.", Griggs said and left to get dressed.

As Nechelle watched the monitor, all of the events of that day unfolded and the shit looked like something out of a movie. Puerto Ricans killing innocent people, jamaicans killing innocent people, the crew fighting for their lives, the jakes popping everything that looked suspicious. It was pure hell on earth. A vibration brought her attention to Griggs phone receiving a text. She looked around then picked it up seeing a text from another jake asking did he make copies of the hospital footage. What the fuck? She thought to herself. So this was the only copy? Ain't no way! If she took this copy and hauled ass, her and the crew would be free.

"So you've seen enough or do you need more convincing that…" POW!

At the sound of his voice, Nechelle spun around with the 40. cal in hand and popped Griggs dead in the face. He immediately grabbed where his nose was and fell on his back, then allowing his arms to fall at his side as blood leaked from his head. Seeing him laying there motionless, Nechelle snatched the hard drive from the laptop, shot the monitor twice and shot his phone once and fled the scene.

CHAPTER 12

"Bitch, get the fuck up and let's go! That's what the fuck you get!" "Tyler, I can't. I'm sick as fuck babe."

"Babe my ass! You want dick right? Then this is what dick brings bitch, now let's go!"

Tonia's pregnancy was kicking her ass and the sickness was not helping. She was always weak and throwing up everywhere all day. She made her way to the car so that they could meet up with the contractors that were remodeling the club. Penny and 3-T agreed to wait for them and keep the contractors entertained until she showed up. Once there, Tyler left Tonia in the car to help herself out. She had begun to show in a major way and had been avoiding the crew but to no avail because she had to show her face as well as the baby's one day.

When she walked in, laborers were everywhere hauling out everything that was of no use. The walls and ceiling were being repaired and new light fixtures were being installed. A few men in business suits sat in they lounge area waiting for Tyler's arrival. Once the introductions have been made, out came the paperwork and discussion of payment method. When everything was over and done with, Tyler made her way to the office to make a few phone calls. Aisha had swung by they hospital to pick up Nicole and had walked in the club with her in a wheelchair. They all made their way to the office and was just making casual talk when in walked Tonia, big belly and all.

"No! Fucking! Way!", Penny yelled, eyes dam near bulging out of the sockets. "Bitch you pregnant?!", Aisha asked in disbelief.

Nicole bust out laughing and the girls began to crack up high fiving each other. Tyler was the only one not laughing because she knew that if she told everyone who the father was, shit would get really serious, really quick.

"Daaaammmmm!", Aisha chuckled. "Just when you finally decide to get some dick....BOOM! Ya ass get prego! Well ain't that a bitch." "So...who is the father?", Penny asked.

"None of your dam business!", Tonia spat.

"Come on girl, don't be like that. Let us know.", Aisha said. "Bitch ain't you worried about the wrong shit?"

""What the fuck is that supposed to mean?"

"You're so concerned about the dick between my legs when you need to be out there trying to find the dick that belongs between yours! "

"Come on now Tonia.", Nicole chimed on. "We're all trying to find Dullah, don't do her like that." "Oh bitch please. Miss me with that bullshit ok. Everybody need to just leave me the fuck alone!"

3-T sat in the corner quietly thinking that this shit was all hilarious...until the bomb was dropped.

"Well fuck you too bitch! We just asked a simple

fuckin question.", Nicole shot back. "You know what? Since yall wanna know so bad...."

"Tonia! Don't!", Tyler warned.

"Don't- my ass! It was Friday! Yup. I fucked Friday the night those Puerto Ricans bought the coc at the club. Now what bitches?!"

"Oh my gawd...",3-T whispered. Penny's mouth was locked open and Nicole was looking in Tonia's face for a hint of hate joking. There was none.

"We were drunk and we fucked in the office bathroom. And that nigga fucked me good too!"

"Bitch you fuckin lying!", Nicole snapped.

"Lol! Oh yea? Ask Tyler." Tonia then turned to Tyler. "Go ahead, tell em."

Tyler just shook her head at Tonia who in turn wore a smug look on her face. All of a sudden, Nicole went from crippled in a wheelchair to having the Teenage Mutant Ninja Turtle spirit the way she flew out of that chair trying to get to Tonia. 3-T dam near dove for her as well as Aisha and the three collided falling to the floor. Nicole was kicking and screaming trying her best to break free.

"You funky bitch! Ima kill you! I swear to fuckin gawd I'm gonna kill you!" "Yea, yea, yea...", Tonia yawned.

"Bitch really?", Tyler snapped at Tonia.

"They would've found out one day so fuck it!"

"And you know all along Tyler?", Penny asked. "Why didn't you say anything?" "Because it ain't my place to! I didn't fuck Friday and I'm not pregnant."

"Get off of me! I'm cool. I'm good!", Nicole snapped. "You sure?"

"3-T get the fuck off of me before I really lose my shit!"

Nechelle came through the door just a everyone was getting up off of the floor. Friday walked in behind her just s confused.

"What the hell yall got going on in here?", Nechelle asked. Everyone was looking at Tonia and when Nechelle saw her belly she bugged out. "Oh bitch! I know you ain't pregnant! Lol, get the fuck out of...."

WHOP!

"NICOLE!!",3-T snapped.

Nicole had eased her way next to Friday and popped him in the mouth. He had grown a little afro so Nicole was able to do her signature move by gripping his hair, throwing gin to the floor and dove on top of him raining blows. Friday was on shock because he didn't know what the hell was going on.

"Stop Nicole!", Nechelle yelled, trying to pull her off of Friday. "What the fuck is your problem?!"

"This no good son of a bitch ain't shit!"

"3-T, help me nigga!", Nechelle hollered. Once they peeled Nicole off of Friday, Nechelle got to grilling her. "Bitch have you lost your got dam mind? What the hell is wrong with you?"

"This goofy ass nigga ain't shit!", Nicole spat. "What? Where is all of this shit coming from?" "He got Tonia pregnant bitch!"

Nechelle grew a puzzled expression then looked

over to Tonia who refused to hold eye contact with her.

"Tonia…", Nechelle called out calmly. "You wanna tell me what's going on?"

"Bitch is you deaf or is you dumb?!", Tonia sassed. "The night before Friday got shot, we fucked in that very same bathroom over there and Tyler is my witness."

"Bitch you cappin!" Nechelle then looked over to Tyler. "Is this true? And if so, did you know about this shit the whole time?"

"This ain't none of my business aight. And ain't like I fucked him! So please get off of my dick."

Nechelle and Nicole looked to Friday and he could swear that they both grew an extra head each. Nicole began to pin her hair in a ponytail as Nechelle dropped her purse and removed her earrings.

"Hold up yall, just wait a got dam minute alright!", 3-T yelled, seeing the beat down coming.

"Naw, fuck that!", Nechelle snapped. This nigga gonna get it!"

"But he's not the same person!", Penny tried to reason. "So let's calm down and figure this out."

"Penny, stay out of this!", 3-T warned.

"No!" Penny made her way next to Friday. "He doesn't know! Ok? It wouldn't be right to hurt him when he can't even defend his own memory!"

"Well, you gonna take this ass cuttin for him or naw?", Nicole sassed. "Awe hell…", Tyler mumbled.

Aisha was silently watching and listening up until this point and thought it'd be cool to address the situation.

"Listen! Listen! Here me out, ok!" Aisha hoy the crew's attention and attempted to make some sense of this. "Yea, he was wrong and ain't no excuse for that shit. And Tonia was just as wrong...."

"Oh that bitch got it coming, trust me.."

"Girl, just chill the fuck out! ", Aisha snapped cutting Nicole off. "But right now is not the fucking time ok! We just got Friday back and now Dullah's gone. BJ is down at the gym with Adrian missing a whole father, died right in front of him. Like dam yall! Focus for once. Let's get these muthafuckas for what they've done, THEN, we can handle our in house shit."

"I think she's making perfect sense.", Friday stated calmly. "Right now, we gotta get our shit together and handle our business. Too much is at stake for us to be fighting each other while we got other people trying to kill us." He then walked up to Nicole and Nechelle and towered over them. "And when it's all said and done, if you two still got something yall wanna get off ya chest, then say that and we can dance. But try me like that again and I'm kill you...AND YOU!"

Penny wore a smug grin with her arms crossed.

"Bitch fix your face!" "Nechelle!", Aisha snapped.

C2

After arriving back in Miami at Calynda's estate, Friday was emotionally and mentally drained. His previous life before the coma had him currently in deep shit with both sides of the war. Calynda was trying to mind fuck him and as of now he was the funkiest piece of shit in a three way relationship where he obviously got another chick in the crew

pregnant. And this bitch was supposed to be a dike! Like what the fuck! But he had to push all of that to the back of his mind and get into character with these Puerto Ricans. He could not let them know that he was privy to their scheme or he was a dead man. The sun was setting so he knew that everyone was there. As he walked through the front door, a multitude of aromas came rushing up his nostrils. Nana was in the kitchen doing what she do best.

"Uncle Eric! Uncle Eric! Where have you been.", Adam shouted as him and his sister Lisa literally ran circles around Friday. They both each grabbed a hand of his and led him to the kitchen area.

"LynLyn's friend killed my frog today.", Adam pouted.

"Yea! He squashed it like BAM!", Lisa teased, pounding a fist in her palm. "LynLyn's friend?", Friday questioned. "He?"

"Yea! He's right in there at the kitchen table again!"

Friday was led into the kitchen where Nana was cooking over the stove. Chepae and Solas on opposites ends off the kitchen as usual, standing guard and a man with his back facing him was seated at the table. When Friday walked around the table to get a look at the man's face, he had trouble keeping his poker face on. Dullah sat at the table bruised and beaten. Two swollen eyes, busted lip, and his neck was scarred like he'd been strangled.

"Hey my love!", Calynda cooed as she walked into

the kitchen. "Are you hungry? Dinner is about ready."

"How would you know? You're not doing a dam thing to help!", Nana snapped.

Calynda just rolled her eyes and motioned to Dullah. "We have a guest for dinner as well. This is Dullah, he was caught on the property last night trying to sneak up on me. Had a friend with him to. Fucker got away though."

"Watch your dam mouth young lady!", Nana snapped.

"Anyways, do you recognize him?" Friday shook his head no as he looked down at his best friend. "He was part of your crew. The same crew that tried to take your life.", Calynda lied.

Friday looked from Calynda back to Dullah and took a knee in front of him. "Whaddup fool?", Friday asked.

Dullah froze and grew a slight grin. "Sheeed...Nunn." He was sort of relieved. He knew that Friday just greeted him in a way that only the two of them would know about, and everyone in the room would never catch on. Friday remembered him. And he let Friday know that he caught on by the response he gave back. He didn't know what his boy had up his sleeve but he knew to keep it cool and play along until a way was made.

Friday gave a slight smirk back then stood up to address Calynda. "Why is he still alive?"

Dullah now thought that this nigga was trippin.

"He might could lead us to the gold.", Calynda responded.

"Might? So after all this time yall been fuckin him up and he still ain't said shit?" "No, he has not. We haven't even found out why he was here."

Calynda then gave a slight head nod to Solas, who in turn wrapped a chord around Dullah's neck and began to strangle him. Friday did a dam good job at hiding his shock because he was not expecting to see this.

"See, every hour we bring this vato to the brink of death and he still won't speak.", Calynda said in amazement. "Tough motherfucker eh? Should've been one of ours."

Dullah's face was swelling and his eyes looked like they would pop out of its sockets any second. It broke Friday's heart to look his comrade in the face, suffering beyond measure, and could do nothing about it. Dullah held on to dear life until Solas released the chord and Chepae immediately punched Dullah in the face. He spat out blood and blew snot on the kitchen floor.

"Allahu Akbar!", Dullah spat in defiance.

"Yes, you're right cabron.", Calynda said as she walked up on Dullah. "God is the greatest. And at the rate that you're going, you gonna meet him really soon." Dullah just stared at her with a look of resistance.

"Take him wherever you usually take him.", Friday command. "And that's enough for tonight, we don't need him catching a heart attack before we find the 'gold."

Chepae looked to Calynda for the greenlight and she gave a slight nod. When her henchmen removed Dullah, Friday turned to Calynda.

"I need to speak to you in private.", was all he said

as he headed to their bedroom.

Friday stripped down and got right into the shower. He needed a plan and one quickly. He knew that she could flipped out at any minute and that would cost him his life. He made a decision in the shower that he would change things around immediately and shake some shit up. If he tried to leave killing anyone, he would never make it out alive. So he came up with a slick plan to turn this shit upside down once and for all. Calynda's phone rang and when she saw the caller, she immediately got the cotton mouth.

"Hello popa."

"We have a problem.", Amelio said flatly. "What's new?"

"Cheewaus is missing."

Calynda stopped pacing and froze. "Missing? How? What do you mean he's fucking missing?"

"I sent him to visit that club of your new husband and he never returned." "And why the hell was he at that club popa?"

"To send a message!", Amelio snapped. "What fucking message?!"

"To return my gold!"

"That's why I'm in the states popa! I'm here looking for the dam gold and you keep fucking shit up!"

"You watch your dam tone with me."

"No! You watch me do what the fuck needs to be done!" She hung up on Amelio and was ready to kill everything breathing until she was startled dam near out of her underwear.

"Everything ok?"

Calynda jumped and spun around and the breath was sucked right out of her lungs. Friday stood drying his hair butt ass naked with a full erection. When her eyes locked in on all that dick, she might as well have had a hunting knife to her throat because there bitch was terrified. He took a few steps forward…..she took a few steps back.

"I asked a question Calynda."

She clutched her pearls and swallowed not a dam thing. "Wh-what was it that you asked? I couldn't understand you my love.", she responded, looking up in his eyes and then back down at that hook over and over again.

"I asked….", he came so close that she was now against the dresser. "Is everything ok?"

Calynda felt his warm dick pressed up against her mid inner thigh and came in her panties as her eyes lowered in lust. She was not the type of woman that frequently have sex. Maybe twice a year. Maybe. She was an executioner. A hunter. A queen pin. She had no time for a social life. But she was a woman, none the less and her hormones began to override those killer instincts. Now, she felt like she was the one being hunted, stalked, and preyed upon by the way Friday towered over her. She'd been in gun fights, knife fights, fist fights, and even feet fights. But she could never train herself to get fucked.

She was now dam near sitting on top of the dresser and Friday had both of his palms planted on either side of her hips as he inhaled the scent on her neck. He eased his pelvis between her knee caps, forcing her to spread her legs and he could feel the heat radiating on his lower abs that came from her vagina.

Calynda wore a pea green cotton dress that buttoned up the middle and Friday slowly unbuttoned each button as he took in her perfectly shaped body. The way that her breast spilled out of the top and her ass spread out beneath her made his dick jump without being able to control it. He had no idea when was the last time he had sex but he dam sure knew when the next time would be. He peeled the dress from Calynda's shoulders and completely away from her body then in one swift motion, he gripped this bitch's throat in a choke hold and spun her around so that she was facing the mirror. She looked his reflection dead in the eyes as she felt him stretch her walls, letting the tip of his dick jab the bottom of her pussy. The pain felt so good that she was literally on the tip of her toes ballerina style while holding the edge of the dresser in a death grip. Still having her throat in a fuck hold with one hand, and holding Calynda's right breast in the other, Friday yanked her forcefully on his dick as he viciously drilled them cheeks from behind. Calynda was doing her best at being a soldier and refused to whimper, which made Friday choke tighter and pound harder until she let out a cry that you could tell was being held in for too long.

"Call my name bitch!"

Calynda shook her head in refusal and Friday wrapped her ponytail around his fist and yanked her head back.

"Uuuhhggghh!", she hollered out from the mixture if pain in her scalp and dick in her guts.

"I said say it!", he growled in her ear as he sucked on her neck. "Hooooo Eric!", she whimpered. "Eric baby, you're in too deep."

With a smirk on his face, Friday then mushed her face against the mirror causing her back to arch, ass cheeks to spread, and fucked Calynda like lights, camera, action! Just digging in the kitty. Visions of him playing basketball as a youngin, training in the gym with Hollywood, shooting at a cop, answering a door just to get shot, all came flooding his conscience as he came hard and deep inside of Calynda. His breathing was barbaric and drool was hanging from the corner of his mouth.

He looked down at Calynda and saw that he had applied so much pressure to the back of her head that her face had cracked the mirror. She just kept still as he regained his wits and allowed her to lean up a little off of the broken glass as blood trickled down her cheek. A small cut was over her left eye but that had no comparison to the throb between her legs. She had came twice from the penetration and didn't give two shits about the way he just assaulted her. She wanted more. When Friday finally slid out of her love box, Calynda slowly turned around and saw that his monster was very much still alive. Now it was her turn to be the aggressor as she placed both palms on his chest, pushing him backwards on the bed. Dropping to her knees, Calynda used no hands as she smacked on that curve and tasted herself for the first time and was not disappointed. Her pussy tasted like water and that dick felt like thunder in her mouth.

She gagged the first few times that she took him to

the back of her throat but after while she was slurping on the pole like it would give her extra lives. Friday never once let his guard down even though she was eating him alive. He never remembered how sex felt and thought that this shit felt amazing. He palmed the back of her skull and drove his dick in as far as it would go.

At the rate he was going she knew that it wouldn't take long for him to cum, so she quickly climbed on top of him and eased all the way down to his balls. Her belly felt full as she rose and fell on this foreign object. Looking up at Calynda, Friday had to fight his urge to fall for her beauty. She was the most beautiful woman he had ever seen and she gripped him like a hellcat on the race track. But he had seen his past and knew for sure that she was his enemy, and she was gonna pay.

Friday flipped Calynda on her back and entered her with ease. When he felt his balls rest in the crack of her ass, he brought her knees up inside of her armpits and dug in her cervix like it was gold somewhere in there. Calynda has never in her life felt so much good pain and power in her life and she never wanted him to stop. Why the hell was she fucking the enemy?, she thought. But she knew that she had to enjoy him while she could because when the mission was complete, he had to die. When Calynda creamed all over that magic stick, she pulled him to her face and kissed him like they exchanged vows. She was in love with the feeling that she was receiving and felt him cum deep inside of her. The hot cum gave her insides a warm invading feeling that she could get used to.

"Everything is fine my love."

"Huh?", Friday was confused. "What are you

talking about?", he panted.

"You asked was everything O.K.", she kissed him thrice across the chest. "Everything is all fine my love."

3-T was left alone with the construction workers who were remodeling the club because Tyler had to take Tonia to an appointment. He sat behind the bar on a laptop reviewing the footage from the Puerto Ricans that pulled up at the club looking for trouble. He noticed how the team spreads out and used tactics to win the battle, but he couldn't help but notice how trapped they were. They were fighting for their lives with nowhere to go. And even though it was only one casualty on their end, it could've easily have been them all. He sat back for a few moments and the brightest idea came to mind. There was a lake not too far behind the club that a city sewer pipe line that ran into it. He knew this because when the club was first being built, they were notified that their septic tank would be connected to that very same pipe line. He called up the contractor of construction and pulled him up on it.

"Sup Chip? My fault for the short notice."

"No problem. I'm here to work and you're here to pay." "Lol. You funny."

"Say, where's Mr. Smalls?", Chip asked. "I haven't seen him around lately."

"You know he stays in that gym of his."

"Oh yea, I was supposed to do some work over there too. But it was like he vanished off the face of the earth."

"I'll be sure to let him know the deal.", 3-T said. "But anyway, I need some work done here in the office. But I need this world some privately."

"Ok, no problem. I can have a few of my guys come up and map things out. What did you have in mind?"

"No Chip. I need YOU, ALONE, to do this work."

Chip took a while to study 3-T's expression and knew that this was a serious matter. "Ok, what kind of work are we talking about?"

"I need an escape route leading from this office, to the sewer that leads to the lake behind the club."

"Whoa Tony.", Chip said sitting up. "I can't do that kind of work without the owners consent."   3-T was ready for this and went in his designer bag and placed $60k on the desk.

"This is $60k. I got 40 more when the job is done. And this is excluding the expenses to make it"

Chip eyed the money then shook his head at 3-T. "But why can't my guys come up here to do the job?

I don't understand."

"I don't pay you to understand Chip. I pay you to hammer fucn nails. And because if only you do the job and someone finds out about it, then I'll it only you could've told. And you'll be the only one that'll have to die Chip."

Chip saw that he was dead serious. "I can't possibly do this job alone Tony, I'm only one man."

"Two more people!", 3-T said. "Make it happen."

Chip slowly shook his head grabbing the money and 3-T slammed his palm on top of Chip's, causing them to lock eyes.

"Don't fuck this up Chip."

"If you'll stop massaging my dick beaters, I can get

to work."

"OMG! Babe, I have to pee.", Tonia whined.
"Again?!", Tyler smacked.

"This little fucker is sitting on my bladder."

Tyler just shook her head resting it on one hand
while she drove Tonia to her appointment. Her left leg
was bouncing and her jaws were tight. Tonia's
pregnancy was botherin her more than it was bothering
Tonia. The constant nagging, sickness, mood swings,
eating, and raging hormones had Tyler ready to snatch
that baby out her dam self.

"Please pull into that gas station up there Tyler."
"Bitch, you are aggravating as fuck!"

Tonia squealed as they pulled up to the gas pump.
She was huge in the belly area and could barely get out
of the car. Tyler tried her best not to laugh. Tonia been
dyking all her life and this baby was kicking her ass.
Tonia waddled full stripes to the restroom while Tyler
paid for the gas. A random guy entered the store dressed
like he worked out in a gym with big muscles and it
reminded her of J.J. She really missed her man and the
short time that they were together, he was the best thing
that she had going on in her life. She always had her way
with him, true gentlemen, and one hell of a protector.
Her heart would be under lock and key until another
man was able to fill his shoes and more.

"Girl you on?"

Tonia had snuck up on Tyler and saw the mist in her
eyes. "Yea I'm cool. Just got a lot on my….."

"Aaahhoweee SHIT!", Tonia screamed holding her
belly. "Are you ok? Girl what happened?"

"Man that shit hurry! This baby already....AAAaahhh maannn! What the fuck!" "Oh shit!", Tyler gasped looking down.

"Oh shit? Oh shit what ?!", Tonia asked then followed Tyler's gaze and saw that her leggings were soaked at the crotch.

"Um excuse me!", Tyler yelled maneuvering to the front of the line. "I need $40 on pump six please. I have an emergency!"

"Um, excuse you!", a ratchet voice said from behind. "You need to wait in line like the rest of us."

Tyler continued to eye the cashier with the no bullshit look on her face, ignoring the woman. The cashier saw Tonia looking spooked holding her belly and just took the money, activating the pump.

"This is some straight up bullshit!", the woman smacked. "I didn't stand in this long ass fucn line for this bitch to just...."

WHOP!!

"Tyler, no!", Tonia panicked.

Tyler had popped the lady in the mouth midsentence, snatched a beer bottle from a near by customer and broke it over the counter.

"Today! Ain't the fucn day bitch!", Tyler barked holding the jagged glass up to the womans face. "I will gut you the fuck out and have you squealing like a got dam pig! Do NOT fuck with me!"

Tonia waddled up next to Tyler and looked at the lady holding her lip. "That's what the fuck you get."

She then turned to Tyler. "Bitch I'm having a baby.

We need to go!"

CHAPTER 13

Detective Lee had been trying to reach his partner all day but couldn't seem to catch him at all. Lt. Pines did that Griggs ever submitted the copies of the footage from the hospital. A job that was initially assigned to Lee but he was absent so the job was given to his partner. It was a simple task and he wondered what the hold up was. Lee decided to take s trip to Griggs home and see if he could catch him there. When he pulled in the driveway, Griggs car was there. Walking up to the door, he rang the bell then took a look around. The front yard could seriously use some attention and the home needed a new paint job. Focusing back to the door, no one had came and nothing could be heard coming from the inside. He looked through a few windows and couldn't make out much. But as he turned away from the last window, he noticed something strange. Peering in, he placed his face to the glass and saw a figure laid out on the floor resembling a torso.

"Griggs!", he yelled into the window. "Griggs! Everything ok pal?"

Lee decided to write it off as an emergency entry when he kicked in the front door,.44 bulldog drawn.

Right there 15ft from the door was Griggs body, unmoving with blood everywhere around it.

"Shit!", Lee snapped. Her knelt down and placed two fingers to Griggs neck and his partner slowly reached up and weakly grabbed his wrist.

"Hold on damit! You just hang the fuck in there!" Lee then pulled his cell and called it in. "Can you tell me what happened Larry? Anything? I swear the son of a bitch won't ever see a prison cell."

Blood just continued to leak from the wound in his face and Griggs was barely breathing.

"You bet not kick you son of a bitch! Don't do it!", Lee cried through tears. "What the fuck happened?", he whispered to himself.

In record time, the paramedics entered the home and rushed Griggs into the E.R. Lee stayed behind to oversee the investigation of the scene. Nothing was immediately turning up as far as clues but it was still early.

"Detective!", a C.S.I. called out. "You might wanna see this."

Lee was led to a backroom that was set up like an office with electronic equipment and file cabinets for decorations. The C.S.I. took Lee to a laptop like the one that was in the front area and what he saw blew his mind...

C2

Friday left the next morning with Calynda drooling in the bed after two more rounds of crazy sex. This was his first time back in some pussy since he came out of the coma and it was like driving a Ferrari! He couldn't get enough. But that pussy was the devil's pussy. She was clearly the enemy and even though he was thoroughly enjoying himself, he was just playing his role. First place he visited when he got back to the city was the club. Even though he had yet to become familiar with everyone in the Crew, someone was always there. But oddly, when he entered the building, only people that are there were the workers that were remodeling the place. With no one from the Crew in sight, he made his way upstairs to his office. He opened the door and noticed a really dark skinned man with long locs sitting at the desk, where HE was supposed to be sitting. He knew that someone of prestige who belonged to the Jamaicans had died downstairs the other day, but that blood was not in the Crew's hands. So he had no clue why this man was eyeballing him, sitting in his shit. He just closed the door and took a seat opposite of the man at the desk.

"Me not heah fo no long conversation mon. Me jus wan kno…"

"Why the fuck you behind my desk", Friday asked calmly, cutting the man off. "And who the fuck you supposed to be?"

Iggy cracked a small grin and leaned forward. "Me part da reason ya still breath." "Look bruh, rise up out my shit and…"

Boogey sucked his teeth and niggaz started appearing out of nowhere. Coming out of the restroom, the closet, even two were crouched behind the desk. They all were strapped and stood around the room with one man at the door.

"Tis wha gwan appin.", Iggy continued. "ya gwan tell me whea dat Mexican bitch iz at and we settle the score. You kill me lil brudda fa nun, den rob em. Only reason ya crew still alive iz because Dullah saved me life. I respect him. Only him. Me right hand died downstairs by da same Mexicans and dat was dey last straw."

Friday now remembered being told what happened at the hospital between the Puerto Ricans, Jamaicans and the Crew. They both came to take him and 3-T out. But it ended up the Crew and Jamaicans running for their lives. And the Puerto Ricans didn't stop there. Iggy didn't know that the reason was behind gold and Friday had no plans on telling him. That might give them a reason to double cross him so he let Iggy believe whatever he wanted.

"Check this out playboy.", Friday spoke up. "I don't care what Dullah did for, you and these goofy looking muthufuckas can suck my dick! Ain't no nigga breathing gonna tell me what the fuck to do in my own shit."

"Ya talk a nice game mon. Me don't tink…" "Ain't nobody ask you to think!"

One of Iggys goons thought it was a bright idea to smack Friday from the blindside for talking jazzy and all hell broke loose. When Friday jumped up, the other man began to move in on him but Iggy held up a hand telling them to stand down. By the time Iggy's hand was back on the table, Friday had already broke ole boys jaw and was locking him in a naked rear choke hold. Dudes eyes were bulging out the sockets and it felt like his neck was about to snap. Iggy came up beside Friday and drew his gun. Friday held on for a few more seconds then let him go, as the man fell to the floor in a coughing fit. Iggy looked Friday dead in the eyes as he shot his own goon twice in the face and once in the head. He stared

Friday in the eyes looking for a sign of fear. All he could find was death.

"No one does Nunn without me permission!", he snapped still looking at Friday. Friday looked around at the men in his office and saw that they all feared Iggy with every fiber in their souls. Friday just hunched his shoulders and took a seat behind his desk where he rightfully belonged.

"Calynda is her name. And she has Dullah.", Friday informed Iggy. "And we have one of her top men. I don't know her plans with my boy but I gotta get em back."

"Den we go witcha."

"And that's the plan. The more numbers the better our chances at survival. Calynda still thinks that my memory is gone and I'm still under the influence of her brainwashing me. Use that to our advantage. I'm gonna sit them down and come up with a plan, so she don't tear down my crew. But I'll obviously put y'all on point so when she pulls up, smash that bitch."

"And wha ya plans for da man of hers?" "I'm gonna kill em."

"Wha if she wan exchange? Dullah fa her mon?" "Then I'll kill him at the exchange.", Friday said.

"Dat will start a war right der moon. Dat no good." "Then what do you suggest?"

"Dat we surround her place and ambush."

"We don't know what she's working with at that place."

"You're there mon. Ya can find out if ya planning with her to kill ya crew." Iggy tapped his own temple.

"Tink mon."

Friday had to admit that Iggy did have a point. And a dam good one. Maybe the smart thing to do would be to investigate and give the crew Intel on what Calynda's strengths and weaknesses are. That would be his job when he returned to Miami.

"Well I'm going back soon and once I've figured everything out, I'll call you up then we can all sit down and come up with a plan."

"Yea mon, dat sounds like a good idea.", Iggy said standing up. "Me wan thank you for taking care me nephew."

"I don't know shit about what's going on with your nephew. I told the girls to keep him close but I never see him when they come around."

"He at ya gym. Wit ya youngin Adrian. Good kid. He teach me nephew how to box.", Iggy smirked proudly.

Friday stood to shake Iggy's hand and the two man made a silent agreement to pursue a common goal. Kill Calynda. "Well do me a favor and take ya man's with ya.", Friday said motioning to the floor.

Iggy sucked his teeth and his goons took off a few rasta crowns and wrapped up the leaking heads of the corpse and threw the body over the biggest shoulder. As the jamaicans made their way out of the office, Friday called out to Iggy.

"Aye yo, one more thing." "Wha ya want mon?"

"Next time you sit your ass behind my desk, I'm gonna teach *YOU* how to box."

C2

Aisha walked into work and the whole police station was in a frenzy. Officers were all moving and scrambling like their jobs depended on it and she couldn't imagine what could have happened. She saw one of her coworkers that was known for being nosey and figured that's where she'd get the 411.

"Hey Hattie!", Aisha hissed walking up briskly. "Girl what the hell is going on?" "So you haven't heard?", Hattie looked over in disbelief.

DUH! She thought. "No, nu-uh. What happened?" "Girl somebody shot detective Griggs!"

"Griggs? Who the hell is that?", Aisha asked.

"You know detective Lee? Bald, big bellied white guy? Been here like forever?" "Yea I know Lee."

"Well Griggs is Lee's partner!"

Aisha thought about it for a minute and it all came to her. "Ooohh! You mean that fine ass man, always got his hair cut with them waves?"

"Lawd yes, him girl.", Hattie lusted. "Somebody shot him in his home last night. Right in the face!"

"Oh hell no! Lt. Pines is gonna flip his shit! He don't take cop killings lightly." "But he ain't dead though!", Hattie said. "He's in critical, but very much alive."

"Ok, that's dam good! I hope we find the muthafuckas that did this shit too."

"Child me too. Come on, you know Lt. gets on his period when you late for briefing."

The two made their way to one of the many rooms in the station that were used for briefing prior to shifts. As the officers all took their seats, Aisha could tell that no once was in the mood for bullshit. She'd been in a few shootouts and had seen many officers lose their lives. And every time Lt. was ready to shoot some shit up.

"Ok everyone, straight to it. No secret that one of our own has been shot in his own dam home and is now in critical condition. We recovered footage from the home's security device and got the whole got dam thing on camera. Poor bastard never stood a chance, never saw it coming. I'll fill you in more after we view this recording."

The lights were cut and the footage was played on the big screen. It started off showing Griggs walking to his front door and when that shit opened, Aisha dam near fainted. Griggs snatched Nechelle by her collar and dragged her into the home. Some words were exchanged and he then led her to a laptop in the front room, punched a few keys, then left her alone to view whatever that was on the monitor. After a few more moments, the footage shows Griggs reentering the room and Nechelle abruptly standing up then shooting Griggs in the face. Gasps and profane language could be heard throughout the room as everyone witnessed Griggs falling to the floor holding his face then going limp. Nechelle then takes a small device from the computer and destroys the monitor as well as a cellphone before fleeing the scene. When the lights came back on, some faces were wet with tears, some were twisted in anger and some were just impassive.

"What was just witnessed was an attempted murder on one of our very own. It's obvious that Griggs knew the female who was highly invested in what was taken from the laptop, which was the footage from the hospital of that gang war. This female was willing to kill an officer in order to gain possession of that drive so it's likely that she was involved or hired to get the job done. C.S.I.'s have dusted the places got prints and when something turns up, so will the heat. We're gonna find this bloodless bitch and every known associate she has and fuck them in the ass! And if things look saucy, you better not hesitate to blow their asses to hell. Until then, stay safe and stay aware."

Everyone got up with a mission in mind. Aisha was floored and was having a hard time gathering her thoughts. She loved her crew but fuck that shit! This was about to get ugly and she didn't want a dam thing to do with it. But she had to give everyone a heads up, it was only right. And she still needed to find her man, and she was not gonna let a dam thing get in the way of that. She left the police precinct to put her crew on point and find a way to stay clear so as much to be a known associate.

C2

Tonia slept in the uncomfortable hospital bed while Tyler and Nicole watched the news. Nothing else was on and the two has slept through the night taking hourly turns. They were not safe no matter where they were and was not about to let anyone sneak up in them. A nurse came in and checked Tonia's vitals, then checked on the baby, and was out as quickly and quietly as she came. Nicole got up and walked over to where the baby slept peacefully and couldn't fight the jealousy. She wanted to be the one to have Friday's baby, she wanted to claim his first child. But she had fucked up long ago and was now living in regret as she stared at a beautiful baby girl who looked like Tonia's twin. Big oval eyes, little button nose and thick lips. Head fill hair with light brown eyes. This child was gorgeous and it broke her heart even more. She looked over to where Tonia lay and saw Tonia looking her right in the eyes.

"I'm sorry Nicole…", Tonia apologized. "I really didn't mean for this to happen. There is no excuse for what I've done, but I was drunk girl. And I know that…."

"It's cool, Tonia. What's done is done and all that matters is that this baby is taken care of."

Nicole's phone chime and saw that it was Aisha with a group text for the crew to meet up at the club and that it was an emergency.

"Well, I know y'all two just got that so I'm gonna head on over to see what the hype is.", Nicole said.

"Yea you go ahead.", Tyler said. "I'll stay here with these two." "Ok. Tx me if y'all need anything. I'll be back."

Nicole then brushed the baby's cheek smiling then slipped Tyler a glock 23 before walking out the door. When she pulled to the club, she could see that Friday was alone. It had seemed like forever since they were last alone and she got butterflies. Walking in the building, the place was now finished and it looked better than it did before. Even bigger T.V.'s were installed and ran the whole length of the wall, the D.J. booth sat above the bar and the ceiling was still mirrored. No one was around so she headed up to the office. When she stepped inside, Friday was on the couch with Eric trading a magazine. Eric looked up and gave a low growl until Friday cleared his throat, causing the hound to settle but keeping an eye on Nicole.

"Is it safe in here?", she asked nervously. "Last time I remember, you broke my jaw and kidnapped me."

Friday stare at her for a moment then snapped his fingers while pointing to the corner. Eric huffed and went to lay on his doggy pillow on the other side of the office.

"Come have a seat.", he told her as he smoothed out the spot beside him.

Nicole made her way over and when she sat beside him looking him in the eyes, she instantly forgave that nigga for smacking get up with that pistol in the middle of the street. She missed him and she missed him bad. She evaluated his features and had to admit, they has changed a little. More facial hair and lighter skin. But those eyes. This sexy brown eyes remained the same. She was having major trouble not jumping all over him and fuck his brains out right there on the couch.

"Listen Nicole.", he began. "I'm really sorry for the shit that I've done to you. Look, I know that I really fucked up but....."

He couldn't get another word out because all of Nicole's self control flew right out of the window. She locked her lips onto his and wrapped around that nigga like a snake. She hadn't been fucked in months and she needed that itch scratched before she made another move. Fumbling with his belt without breaking contact, Nicole then stood up and yanked this niggas pants off without taking off his dam boots! He had literally slid halfway off the couch, nuts dangling on the edge and Nicole wasted no time eating him alive.

When he felt them jaws lock around his piece, this nigga had another flashback slash stroke. Nicole knew exactly what he liked and was serving him properly. It hadn't been thirty second and so much spit was everywhere between his legs as he gripped Nicole's scalp and drilled her skull over and over again. This sex shit was still new to him and this was his second time.

226

But this head was amazing and has him in regret for doing her dirty. When he finally looked down at her, she was staring right back up at him while chewing that dick with ease. Nicole slowed her pace and released the cracken long enough to catch her breath.

"Fuck me daddy…." She stood and dropped them thongs on the spot. Turning around, she bent over the couch looking back at him. "Please…I wanna feel you inside of me."

Friday stood behind Nicole and couldn't believe his eyes. She had the smoothes, softest, plump ass with the smallest pussy he could imagine. He knew that judging by his thickness and how tiny he kitty was, he was gonna stretch her shit the fuck out! He took his time though, sliding the tip of his gift up and down the wet split of her love box and the heat from her under carriage alone almost crippled him. He tried to push his way inside but it just wouldn't fit.

"Come ooonnnn daddy! Shove it in me. Pleeaaasse…", Nicole whined.

Friday may not have been fucking like that lately but he knew that if he rammed his way into this tight pussy, this session was over! He took a deep breath and guided his tip back between her lips and pushed the head in and Nicole's head shot up as she reached back and grabbed his wrist. Her juices began to slide down the bottom side of his shaft as he slowly slid across her walls, watching her pussy lips puff out at the sides. Slowly strong deep in her belly, he could feel her tighten around him with every stroke. Whenever he pushed in, a low smacking sound filled the air.

Nicole dropped her head and arched her back and

felt his dick push against the bottom of her pussy. Gripping her throat from behind, he pulled her back against his abs causing her to whimper sexily and bite her button lip. She threw it back a little too hard a few times and when he saw that crazy fuck me face that she wore, he pushed in as deep as he could go and shot her club the fuck up! Nicole let out a low grunt sty the painful pleasure of having him stretch and dig her out and came hard herself.

"Doesn't look like he lost it all huh?"

Friday and Nicole looked back to see Penny standing in the doorway grinning as Tyler came in with her head down bumping into her.

"Bitch why you just standing here looking dumb and…." Tyler glanced at what Penny saw and burst out laughing. "Dayummmm bitch! Couldn't wait for that hook eh?" "Shit your ignorant ass up ok!", Nicole snapped trying to get dressed.

"Ok Friday, lol. I see you.", Tyler joked and he blushed.

"I'm gonna go grab a bottle from the bar.", Friday said and eased out if the office. "Sooo…", Penny beamed at Nicole. "How was it?"

"Really bitch?", Tyler squinted.

"What lol?! They both haven't seen each other in a while and quite frankly, I'd think it'd be magical."

"Please shut your corny ass up and help me find some air freshener.", Nicole said rolling her eyes.

"Yes please!", Tyler joked. "Because in her smell like nut."

"And you need to shut the fuck up!" Tyler just

waived Nicole off and walked away texting on her phone. In the next twenty minutes, the whole Crew was present and Aisha dropped the bomb.

"So…This bitch", she pointed to Nechelle who in turn gave her the stank face. "thought that it was cool to shoot a cop in the fucn face!"

Penny looked at Nechelle wide eyed like she had lost her mind. Friday's neck stiffened with raised eyebrows and Pepp turned down the corners of his mouth shaking his head in approval.

"The fuck you talking about?", 3-T asked.

"She shot a detective in the face in his own dam house!" "How the hell would you know this?", Nechelle smacked. "Because your dumb ass is on camera!"

"Camera?"

"Yes! Bitch! On camera!", Aisha just shook her head at Nechelle. "You're on a home recording device taking something from his laptop and shooting him in his shit!"

"Nechelle! What the fuck man?", Nicole snapped. "Bitch I had to!"

"What the fuck you mean that you had to?"

"That device was the footage from the hospital. I had to find a way to get it or we all were going to prison."

"How'd you get that close to him for him to trust you enough to let you in his home?", 3- T interrogated.

"Because she was fucking him!", Penny sassed crossing her arms in defiance. "I know you fucking lying…", Tyler gasped in disbelief.

"Yup!", Penny continued. "I've been following this bitch for a while now and she's been meeting up with him quite a bit."

"You wanna explain this shit?", Friday asked Nechelle.

Nechelle looked around the office at the Crew and saw that they all were looking for a valid explanation. She sank back in the chair and spilled her guts.

"Look, dude been on my ass trying to fuck for the longest but my loyalty was to my man." She looked Friday in the eyes. "And still is. And y'all know dam well that I gave his ass the boot every time he came sniffing around. But when he threatened to bring down the Crew with that footage, asking me to testify, I had to do something about it. So yea! I fucked him! And I got the footage!" She reached in her bra and threw the hard drive at Penny who caught it and observed it. "So what now? I took one for the team and what's done is done. He's dead and I left no prints so there's nothing to worry about."

"He's not dead Nechelle…", Aisha whispered.

Nechelle swung her head towards Aisha wide eyed. "What the fuck you mean he's not dead? I popped him point blank in the fucking face!"

"Well bitch he lived!", Aisha snapped. "And when he wakes up out of that coma you better hope that he don't remember shit or your ass is going on the dark side of moon."

"Well we'll make sure that he doesn't wake up.", Friday said like it was nothing. Everyone was silent. They all knew that he had lost his mind but this was a whole nother level.

"Ma nigga…", 3-T said getting up and walked over to Friday. "Do you realize what you're saying?"

"I know exactly what the fuck I'm saying. She just put her life on the line to save you and you and you and you.", Friday said pointing to everyone around the room. "So it's only right that we get down for her and do the same. Now if y'all ain't with this shit, then cool. Walk the fuck out of my shit and don't look back." Nobody said anything.

"What about Dullah?", 3-T asked.

Friday gave then the rundown on the home and how Dullah knew that Friday remembered him. "She still don't know that I'm hip to her' bullshit and I've been using that to my advantage. Her' estate is dam near a fortress now that they are in high alert ever since Dullah and Tonia snuck up on her."

"So how will we get the homie back though?", Pepp asked.

"Only way is to get the drop on them and light em up. We gotta go in there and get him. I know where they got him at and he's in pretty bad shape. Until they find that gold they're gonna keep torturing him until he dies."

"Well we got that fool that shot up the club. Can't we just swap them out?", Pepp asked.

Friday shook his head in disagreement. "Amelio wants that gold at all cost. Cheewaus might as well had went out shooting if he thought that his life was worth more than that gold."

"So what do we do with him?"

Friday stared off got a second and grew a slick grin.

231

"I got a nice roll for him to play. In the meantime, get Iggy on the line and let him know it's a green light. Time to go get my nigga back." Aisha clapped her hands once loudly with a fist pump and knee rise.

C2

Detective Lee sat in his office looking over the footage of Griggs home security system for the tenth time and nothing was sticking out to him. The woman had touched nothing inside or outside of the house so there were no fingerprints. No hair was left behind and the footage didn't even provide and audio to be able to know if Griggs had called her name. The clip was very short and precise. Woman enters home, woman is led to laptop, woman shoots Griggs and exit the premises. She grabbed the doorknob bit no prints were lifted. But her face was clear as a sunny sky. He stained her face in his memory and would forever remember her features. A knock came at the door, dragging his attention away from the monitor.

"Hey Lee.", Brittany greeted. "Lt. Pines would like to see you in his office. "

Lee sighed and dropped his head as Brittany gave an empathetic look and closed the door. It never failed. If Pines called for you, then it was your ass on the line. Lee just got up and walked the green mile. When he walked in, Pines sat reclined behind his desk reading today's paper and didn't even so much as look up at Lee as he entered the room. But what gave Lee butterflies was there open jar of vaseline that sat atop the desk. Pines noticed Lee froze at the sight of the lubricant and raised an eyebrow from over the newspaper. Lee looked from the petroleum jelly, then to Pines, back and forth a few times.

"You wanted to see…"

"Sit the fuck down Lee.", Pines interrupted.

Lee unbuttoned his suit jacket and took a seat. He was having trouble giving eye contact to Pine's and

Pines knew that he held him in fear. "You know what Lee…" "What's that si…"

"Shut the fuck up Lee!", Pines snapped. Lee remained right lipped. Pines took a long breath and continued. "I'm not even gonna yell Lee. Not this time. Because now is not the time. We almost lost a really good officer and a dam good friend. I know that the two of you are close so I can only imagine what you're going through. I don't have many words for this, you know. All I have to say is that when you find the bitch that did this, I really don't care about a court date."

And with that, Pines sat back in his chair, picked up the paper and resumed reading. On the way back to his office, Lee took some time to let what Lt. Pines said register. He was giving him the greenlight to kill whoever's responsible for the attempted murder on Griggs. And he was dam sure gonna.

C2

Nana say a plate of steak, broccoli and cheese omelet, home fries, and waffles in front of Dullah and walked off. He had watched her prepare the food so he knew that it was safe to eat but he was still like fuck it.

He'd learned to discipline his desires as a man of Islam and one of them were fasting. He could go for days without eating and that was his current situation. It had been three days and he was starving. He knew that he couldn't keep this up much longer but knowing that Friday was back in his right mind, he had high hopes of being out of there soon.

"If you don't eat, you have 36 hours to live.", Calynda said walking pass Dullah dropping an article on the table in front of him. The article explained how the bodies organs would shut down after a certain amount of time without food or water.

"Hi Mr. Doodah!", Lisa sang, pronouncing his name wrong, as her and her brother Adam ran into the kitchen. Adam was still pissed about Dullah for smashing his frog so he was not speaking to him. As they slid in their seats, Nana put their plates in front of them and they dug in. Dullah looked around the kitchen and saw Solas and Chepae in their usual spots, Calynda was speaking in Spanish on her phone, and Nana was doing the dishes. These muthafuckas were going about their fast like it was normal to have a fucking hostage just lounging around the crib. He looked down at his plate of food and almost farted because it smelled so good. He fought a good fight, a dam good one too, bit he just couldn't take It anymore.

Picking up his fork, he tried a corner of his omelet and it was murder she wrote. This nigga looked like a goblin the way he practically inhaled his food. Using fork and fingers, he was in action. He suddenly noticed how quiet it got and saw everyone frozen looking at him in shock. With a shoulder hunch, he continued to eat.

Calynda quickly made her way over to Dullah and smacked the plate from the table, and kicked him in the chest, causing him to fall backwards. Chepae was two seconds off of his ass choking the life out of him while dragging him back into the chair. Solas gave Dullah two rib rattling punches to the belly, forcing him to regurgitate but nothing would come up because of the rope around his neck.

"What the fuck were you thinking?", Calynda calmly spoke in Dullah's face. "That you would just be accommodated and pampered? Motherfucker you are gonna die a miserable death if I don't get that gold!" Calynda have a slight nod to Chepae who in turn released the grip from around Dullah's throat. He instantly puked up everything he had just eaten and realized that all of the meals were a setup from the beginning. They couldn't wait to catch him slipping and weak. Even the old bitch was in on it.

"Where the fuck is the gold cabron?"

Dullah spat on the floor and looked her in the eyes. "Allahu Akbar!"

BAM!!

Calynda punched him in the mouth and Chepae dragged him from the kitchen. Pissed off, she looked around the kitchen and saw that the kids looked terrified and Nana looking pisssed as well.

"What?"

Nana threw down her kitchen rag. "I'm not cleaning that shit up!", and walked out of the kitchen.

CHAPTER 14

The crew except for Tyler and Tonia, was with Iggy and his people were at The Boulevard. They had guns with ammunition, a few smoke grenades, a few concussion grenades, a couple of small mid grade explosives all laid out on the bar's countertop. Iggy had some vests, them Jamaicans keep a plug on the exclusives. With gloves on, everyone was cleaning, checking and loading up with ammunition. It was likely that anyone of them could lose their lives. Iggy was out for blood and Friday was bringing Dullah back by any means.

"Aight, it's looking like this", Friday spoke up. "We all know the deal so no need for the long speech. Kill everything breathing until we make it back. The ops, the jakes…anything breathing. With that said, **YOU**", get pointed to Aisha.

"You're sitting this one out."

"Huh? The fuck you mean, I'm sitting this one out?"

"You're a fucn jake Aisha! If shit hits the fan and 12 surrounds that place and catches you in this mix, ain't no deals on the table."

"He's got a point.", 3-T said.

"And you shut the fuck up!", she growled. "My man is in there! That bitch took my nigga and I'm gonna be the bitch to bring him back."

"No the fuck you're not!", Friday barked. "Fuck you nigga!"

"Chill sweetie. Just calm down…", Penny whispered.

"Chill my ass! When Tony was all shot the fuck being rolled into that hospital, I tried to calm you down. But no! No one. No one stopped you from having his back!"

"But we were being ambushed!", Nicole reasoned. "She had no choice."

"Bitch please!", Aisha smacked. "And you know your best move is to shut the fuck up because I still owe you something for what the fuck you did to my best friend at the bank."

"I mean you did taze her in the face.", Nechelle mumbled.

"And your nigga is the reason we're all in this shit in the first place! I mean come on, like what the fuck! I deserve this shit. I was taking a shit on the first one, don't deny me this one."

"She was a what?", Friday whispered to Pepp. "Long story."

He just hunched his shoulders and carry on. "You 21+ so move at your own risk.

Anyway, we gotta get the kid back home. They're doing him something dirty in there and he still hasn't given up the gold." "That's because he doesn't know.", Aisha said.

"Know what?" "Where the gold is."

Friday looked lost. "So who got the gold? Which one of you knows?" "*YOU!!*", the all said in unison. Friday looked lost.

"You don't remember where you put it, don't you?", Penny sighed.

"You will never be the sharpest tool in the box.", Nechelle said, face scrunched up. This nigga don't know shit but what we tell him." Penny rolled her eyes.

"So what's the plan chief?", Pepp asked.

"We got no choice but to surround the place and move in all at once. A few explosions with some shots fired should be enough to lessen the numbers while surprising them. Then we're on our own from there." "Once we penetrate the home, how do we know where to look for him?", Penny asked.

"I got a map of the property.", Friday said reaching in his pocket. He unfolded the paper and the shit hit the fan.

"What the fuck is this?", Penny asked.

"You serious right now ma nigga?", 3-T asked as well.

Friday looked down at the paper with the colorful lines drawn on it, then back at the crew.

"Is that crayon?", Nechelle cracked up. "Yea, so what?"

"Y'all laughing?", Pepp snapped. "Ain't no respawning in this shit! One and done! But we're going in blind?"

"Listen", Friday tried to explain. "What do you want me to do? It's two kids there and I stole the material from their backpacks. So if somebody was to come across it, it'll look like one of the kids drew it."

"Not a bad idea….um, I guess.", Penny said with a shoulder hunch.

"So look", he continued, "it's seven that's Crew, we each take two of Iggy's men with every two off us and do what we do. Me and Iggy gonna move together, Nicole and Nechelle, 3-T and Penny, Pepp and Aisha. That's four squads with four people each.

Move from all sides and close in. Dullah is here.", he pointed to a room on the map. "Its big ass basement and you can only get there from the middle of the home. It's a bookcase next to the fireplace. Pull the last book on the bottom left, push at the right and the bookcase spins open. Go straight down the steps and he's there.

"How much security dey got?", Iggy asked. Iggy had been silent this whole time and has now asked one of the most important questions.

Friday dropped his head then looked back at his comrades. "It's a small fucn army. It wasn't this heavy until Dullah and Tonia got caught creeping up on Calynda. What were they thinking, what were they even doing there?"

"Looking for you.", Aisha said with a broken heart. Friday could hear the hurt in her voice. He gave her a reassuring nod and continued planning.

"Security is crazy at night. No way in he'll we'll make it going at them during those hours."

"No fucking way!", Penny snapped. "What? No way what?", 3-T asked

"He's suggesting that we do this shit in broad day

light!"

"Yup! Broad fucn day." Friday confirmed. "If we go at night, it will be twice more guns and they got all kinds of shit like night vision and heat detectors in the woods that activate at sundown."

"This shit is crazy.", 3-T admitted.

"There's gotta be a better way Friday.", Nicole chimed in.

"Ya sound like a pussy bunch!", Iggy snapped, flicking his toothpick. "Tis er's ya general. No?", he said motioning to Friday. "Well act like it!"

"We're just consulting with him.", Penny hissed.

"Shut ya mouth gal. Me pledged cop killa. Tread lightly."

Penny's mouth was floored and she looked to 3-T who just crossed his arms and stared right back. This bitch just didn't know when to keep her mouth shut.

"So you're gonna do whatever the fuck he says?, Nechelle spat.

"He run da show eh? Em only one er' dats been in da house. Who I listen to? You?!" Silence. And Friday was giving Nechelle that same look that 3-T have Penny.

"Ok. Ok. Everybody let's cool out." Here then looked to Iggy. "You got any suggestions?" "No. But me bring few tings tah help deh journey."

Iggy passed out to everyone what looked like a bluetooth earpiece. "We communicate wit dis er. So tune on same channel." He then passed around tactical utility belts with extra clip holders, pistol holders, knife holders and grenades clips. "Load da belts wit ammunition so we can get the job done."

"What's this for?", Nicole asked.

"In case we get up close and personal and have to throw these hands.", Nechelle said flexing her knuckles. Iggy nodded his approval.

Friday continues. "So me and Iggy will take the south, Nicole and Nechelle take the east, Pepp and Aisha y'all take the west, and Penny....3-T, take the north. Shoot conservatively but don't hesitate. We're not trying saved lives, we taking em! Now load up, gotta get the homie."

"Yes please!", Aisha said. "Because I need some dick." "Bitch really?", Nechelle smacked rolling her eyes.

"Problem?", Aisha asked popping the mouthpiece in and throwing up her fist.

Friday shook his head. "Last thing. I need an old car, something we won't be missing.

And go grab Cheewaus, that nigga coming with us."

"And what's the plan with him and the car?", Pepp asked. "That's our way in."

C2

The pressure was on Calynda to find that gold like last week. She'd always wondered why Amelio was so pressed about getting the gold back and her recent conversation with him had let her know exactly why. Amelio had more millions than he could count and the gold was worth around $20 million, give or take. But Amelio promised the delivery of that gold to a very close business associate named Hessi Pollucci. Hessi was an Italian heroin monster with a reputation for wiping out whole families. She was a near middle aged drug lord that ran 87 percent of the dog food market in New York, Philly, and Jersey. Her beach front properties along with the shopping plazas and hotels she owned, was an easy way to wash and conceal her dirty money. But buying drugs with money was a very risky method of making a transaction. Especially an illegal one. So, she accepted other valuables like paintings, land, buildings, diamonds…. Gold.

She made a deal with a Cuban from down south and was to be paid in gold. Her dealings with Amelio made him a trusted candidate in her eyes to be the recipient of the payment and have it transported to her desired location for a small fee. Pusha had picked up the gold but never had a chance to deliver it to Calynda because Nicole had stamped his ass. Once Hessi was given the news of her gold, she was ready to eradicate Amelio AND whoever was responsible for taking her shit. Amelio offered to pay the equivalent to the gold in cash but Hessi wasn't hearing it. Cash money wasn't what we agreed upon, it was gold bars and that's what she wanted. Amelio promised her that he would get the gold back, so she had now all this time waited for him to keep his word and was now growing impatient. She gave him one month. That was three weeks ago. Amelio now had a little over a week to come up with that gold or Hessi was coming for his top. All of this was conveyed to Calynda and she now felt that same pressure. She knew that if Hessi came, they all were in some deep shit. Amelio had a strong team, but Hessi was in a whole nother league. She has politicians, government officials in her pocket. Amelio could find himself getting his melon popped during a bullshit traffic stop and no one would be the wiser that it was a hit. Or whole cartel could be swarmed all at once, at every location, and burned to the ground. That gold was either their ticket to salvation or hell.

Calynda was stressed out to the max and needed a drink. Her mind went to Friday and she agreed that she could've used some of that crooked dick as well. Something about the way that thang scraped her walls and pushed around her insides had her pussy pulsing out of control. She took a shot of 1800 and let the burn settle in. She had to think of a plan and fast. One week and shit was hitting the fan if she didn't find that gold. She poured another shot of liquor and before she could down the liquid fire, she heard a lot of screaming and yelling coming across her radio. Everyone in the house had one. She briskly marched over to the dresser where it was and could make out something being yelled along the lines of "front of the property" and "open fire". She sprinted through the house and stood on the second floor balcony that overlooks three front lawn to see an pick up truck barreling down the driveway at top speed headed for the front of the home.

Her security opened fire on the truck with a barrage of bullets but it kept coming until it rode up the steps, flying through the front door, and landing in the living room. Dashing out of the room, Calynda took the steps two at a time until she witnessed the truck on it's side with the engine still running. At a closer look, she realized that it was Cheewaus tied to the driver seat, shot the fuck up. Solas took the keys out of the ignition and pulled his fallen comrade out of the truck. All was silent but it only took a few seconds for Calynda to realize that this was wrong. Only one who could be responsible for this was the Crew. The very moment that she entertained that thought, gun shots could be heard coming from different areas of the estate. Calynda ran back upstairs to her room and tore off her dress and kicked off her heels. Pulling on a sports bra, crotch hugging spandex shorts and some balenciaga runners, Calynda strapped on a tactical belt loading it up with her glock. 40, extra clips and a hunting knife. Then pulling on some knee and elbow pads along with a vest, she tied her hair in a ponytail and made her way to her closet. Behind her coat was an arsenal. She picked up an AR-15 with 3 extra clips, flash bang grenades and pepper spray bombs. Radioing orders to take Nana and the kids to the safe room, she moved through the home looking for action.

C2

Once Iggy got the word that they were moving in on Calynda on her own mission, he knew that it was dam near a suicide mission. So he got three of his best shooters and placed them in the tree tops on the east, west, and south sides of the property.

"This shit better work!"

"Trust me. It will.", Friday assured Penny. They now had Cheewaus tied down to the front seat of the old

F-150 pick up truck. A brick was waiting to be placed on the gas peddle, turning the vehicle to a 1000lb battering ram.

"You'll never make it out puto!", Cheeawaus spat.

Friday gave him a squint and peeled a line of duct tape. "Neither will you". He then slapped the tape across that niggas mouth. Cheewaus started bucking and screaming.

"Poor guy", 3-T said shaking his head.

"I know right. He'll never make it to the front door.", Friday agreed. "WELP! Let's get this shit over with."

"You good?"

"The fuck you mean am I good?", 3-T asked Friday. "You ain't gotta shit ain't it?"

3-T went stoned face and Penny came up giggling caressing his face. "Awe calm down baby. We all get nervous every now and then."

"Fuck y'all, ain't nobody nervous.", he spat storming off.

Friday smirked then got serious. "Go with him Penny. The rest of y'all know what's up.

Penny, 3-T, send his ass up the driveway. Time to get active."

"La Jefa! La Jefa!", one of Calynda's men cried out. He ran up to her gun in hand. "Assassin's invade the property. We have to get you to safety."

"Negative cabron! I will never retreat! Tuck that pistol, go to my room's closet and get a bigger gun. Make it out alive cabron."

He gave a lingering look of respect then headed to

do what he was told. Only the grounds were being invaded, but the home had yet to have been breached.

"Come into the house! I repeat! Everyone come inside of the home and spread out!"

She figured that being out in the open while being ambushed from multiple angles would more than likely kill her men. But if they were to stand sentry at the entrances, the chances of survival is greater. But that idea was short lived when a man with locs came blindly walking through the living room, oblivious to her presence. Head cocked to the side with squinting eyes, she froze with the look of sudden death from the audacity of this fool strutting through her home. Then she almost lost her shit when she noticed him tracking mud on her fifty thousand dollar carpet. Her first thought was to just shoot him in the head and keep it moving. But this shit had just got personal because she spent two weeks in South Africa searching for the material and another week trying to get it shipped home.

She quietly walked towards her victim and pulled out her hunting knife. With all her might, she slammed the blade through his foot, nailing it to the floor. Before he could raise the pitch in his scream, Calynda stood with an uppercut to his com chin. He dam near had a heart attack before he landed on his ass, then looked up into the bottom of Calynda's sneakers. Before he could regain his vision, she snatched the knife out of his foot while straddling him and drove it down through the top of his skull. Twisting the knife for over kill, Calynda ripped it out and wiped it on his shirt. Pulling her. 40, she crept in the same direction that the dead man came from in search of some more action.

"You so dam big! Man I know they're gonna spot our ass a mile away!", Aisha complained. Her and Pepp were coming to the house from the west with nothing in between. They would be open targets as soon as they approached."

"Well, we'll make a distraction."

"Distraction? How? Everyone else is already shooting and we still got people watching this side. So please tell me what more can we do Sherlock."

Pepp just shook his head and pulled a concussion grenade. He pulled the pin, flicked the cap and threw it between two guards.

"Everything on the left, you shoot it. I got everything else.", Pepp ordered then ran out in a crouch. "What? Wait! What do you want me to do once we…."

BANG!

The majority of the windows blew out on the side of the home from the shock wave, causing a few guards to drop their rifles and cover their ears. Pepp wasted no time. Before the glass was done shattering he had 15 shots gone. Aisha flanked left and was trading shots with two men in the window. She got smart and threw a live grenade through that bitch and kept it hot, hearing "oh shit's" before the explosion. One of the men swan dived right out of the window before it detonated and Aisha spun around in time to have him stare down the barrel of her four nickel.

One glance at the window and she moved on forward to a lower window of the home. Seeing that the coast was clear, she crept inside the home and made her way to find that bookcase. She was not leaving without her man.

"I'm out of ammo!!"

"Seriously Tony!? What the hell do you mean you're out of ammo? We just fucking got here!", Penny hissed. They were pinned down outside the front door and those niggas were not letting up from the inside. It was like they had some type of cheat code because the bullets never stopped coming. Penny noticed his tactical belt had a glock in it and rolled her eyes.

"Use your handgun Tony. And don't start shooting crazy either!"

3-T tossed the rifle and pulled his glock. 23. Taking aim, he stepped out of cover and caught two in the vest. Penny stopped breathing as 3-T hit the deck gasping for air, grabbing his chest.

"You are so fucking stupid!", Penny snapped, dragging him back behind cover.

"Shit babe! We gotta stop the bleeding!", Tony panicked. He started shaking violently and his body began to lock up. Penny stuck her palm under his vest and rubbed his chest, shaking her head as she pulled her hand back.

"Get your sorry ass up Tony! It didn't go through!"

He stopped shaking. "It had better not!", he said struggling to get up. "Just stay behind me ok."

Penny peeked into the home and a smile crept across her face. Aisha was creeping from the side of the house on the men's blind side. The two women locked eyes and Penny shot twice where the opposition was held up at times give Aisha an idea of where the target was. Pulling and activating a concussion grenade, Aisha tossed it in the direction Penny shot at and everyone covered their ears. Being in closed quarters, the blast was so strong that it dam near knocked a few guards unconscious. Penny and Aisha lit their asses up and secured the front of the home. 3-T came an picking a rifle and a few clips from the dead as Aisha radioed that they had the front.

Friday has peeped Pepp shooting at everything moving, creating a major distraction. It seemed like Iggy's squad was doing whatever they wanted to do instead of what Friday had told them. But his only concern was his crew and their safety. As him and Iggy crept towards the rear of the home, he heard Aisha on the earpiece confirming that they had the front locked down. Just as it got silent, it sounded as if a helicopter machine gun went off in the house. Friday and Iggy hit the deck on the back patio as bullets that left lemon sized holes in the wall, went flying through out the property. At least 250 rounds went off before silence filled the air.

Iggy looked up to see Calynda throwing hands with one of his rastas and the poor guy never stood a chance as she punched and kicked him relentlessly. The rasta fell to one knee and Calynda wrapped the back of her leg around his neck then snapped it. She then looked down and locked eyes with Friday. The stare down was deadly as she realized that he was now hip to her deceit. She blew him a kiss then disappeared further into the house. Iggy attempted to run behind her but Friday clutched his shoulder.

"Keep calm Iggy. You're about to do exactly what

she wants you to do." "She devil murda me man in front me!"

"And she killed him with her bare hands for a reason.", Friday explained. "Don't you think that she could've just shot him? But she knew that we were watching and wanted to show off. Think! Don't act off of emotions."

Iggy gave the cri one more look then shook his head in agreement. "Let's juss get tis ova wit." Friday nodded and the two made their way into the home.

"Man where the fuck is this fireplace?", Nicole whispered.

Her and Nechelle had to kill only a few people, as they were the last ones to breach the home and most of the occupants gravitated to wherever the fight was. The place was like a huge palace and the fireplace could be anywhere. The sound of running footsteps could be heard approaching and Nechelle froze in her tracks. A Puerto Rican could be seen rushing to a door on the far side of the hallway and when he swung it open, at least thirty or more pitbulls came charging out of the room running in every direction. They all were familiar with the scent of the frequents of the home and if you didn't smell like you belonged there....lunch meat! Weren't your average size pitbulls either. No. They were at least 65lbs all muscle and trained to fight until the death.

"No! No! I'm not fuckin doing this.", Nicole panicked and turned on her heels.

Nechelle snatched her into a near by closet. "Bitch you need to get it together!" "You right! I'm gonna have to pull it ALL together if them dogs get a hold of my ass!." "Really? Like, you're really doing this right now Nicole?"

"Did you not just see what the fuck I just saw? Those are *NOT* normal dogs Nechelle!"

Nechell took a deep breath and tried the calm approach. She caressed the sides of Nicole's and gave her a soft firm kiss on the lips and Nicole jerked away with a twisted face.

"Get the fuck off of me! I'm not fuckin with you at a time like this. Right now I can't…"

"Just shut the fuck up! Ok?", Nechelle snapped. "I was trying to calm you but bitch you trying the fuck outta me right now. Now pull that knife out and if you have to, stab and shoot! Fuck it! But we're getting Dullah one way or another. You ready? You with me girl?"

Nicole took a few deep breaths them started wringing her fingers. "Man them shit is big as hell man…."

Nechelle chuckled and shook her head in agreement. "I know. But it's too late to run now Nicole. I'm here with you, ok?"

"Ok.", Nicole agreed. "Can I still have that kiss?"

Nechelle hurriedly locked lips with her lover and an instant calm came over Nicole. "Fuck it!", Nicole said hyped and ready. "Let's go get Dullah!"

"That's my bitch!", Nechelle said slapping her on the ass.

The two stepped out of the closet with Nechelle leading the way. Nicole had barely closed the door when a low menacing growl came from behind them. They froze looking at each other then slowly turned around.

Three of the ugliest pitbulls they had ever seen stood ready to kill or be killed. Nechelle heard a door slam and looked to see that Nicole had disappeared.

"Nicole!", Nechelle hide quietly. She didn't want to cause the hounds to panick. "Nicole!" "I'm not coming out!", she yelled from behind the door. "I can't do it."

"Nicole! You better bring your ass! Now!" "Nu-uhh....man I can't."

"Well let me in!", Nechelle demanded. The dogs began to slowly advance on her. "What?! So they can get in here too?"

"Nicole! You better open this fuckin door!" "Better run bitch!"

Calynda was running through the mansion having the time of her life. Even though she was under attack, she was bussing niggas up left to right, not even using her gun. It had been so long since she'd had the opportunity to really sharpen her skills and now couldn't have been a better time. She was disarming the opposition then breaking arms, ribs and jaws all ady the same time. Kneepads were cracking into bellies as elbows pads crushing foreheads. After running around cleaning up trespassers, she knew that Nana and the kids were in the basement with Dullah. She also knew that Friday would lead his folks straight to the basement if he got pass her security team. She made her way top the bookcase and adds she got near, she saw that it was being pushed back closed as if something had just went through.

"Shit!" She knew that it was Friday that just made his way to his friend but her family was down there as well and was no telling if they were safe after what they'd done to him. "Everyone report to the basement!", she yelled through her radio. "La familia in danger!"

She pulled her pistol and made her way through the bookshelf and down the basement steps.

C2

As Penny, Aisha, 3-T and Pepp waited in hiding throughout the front on the home, they could hear Calynda bark her orders over the dead man's radio.

"Somebody made it to Dullah!",Aisha said excitedly. "They found the bookcase." "Well that's the move. Let's find it too", 3-T said.

"Wait be careful.", Penny warned. "Obviously were not the only ones headed there."

The four of them moved swiftly through the home and was met by a pack of pitbulls on steroids." "Oh shit!", 3-T panicked.

"Man what the fu…"

BIM! BIM! BIM! POW! PO-PO-POW!

Gunfire cut Pepp off midsentence as Penny and Aisha opened fire. Two took off wounded northwest,and three lay dead or dying. Penny walked up and head shot the ones trying to hang on to life.

"Poor bastards are innocent.", Penny said sadly. "Just on the wrong team." She looked up see her team staring at her. "What?!", she asked. "Listen, we're don't have time for this shit. Let's get going!"

3-T was the first to step off giving Penny's ass a

squeeze on the way. She blushed batting her lashes and followed. As they navigated through the home, Pepp spotted a woman dragging another woman down the hallway and at closer inspection, he made out Nicole doing the dragging.

"Fuck!", he spat tucking his pistol. "What happened?", he asked as they all walked up on Nicole.

She did her best to explain what happened even though she was locked in the closet. When Nicole left Nechelle for dead and wouldn't open the door, the hounds looked at Nechelle as fresh meat. She knew that any sudden movements would trigger the dogs, and even though she was strapped, she wouldn't be able to down each dog before they tore her apart, judging by how close they were. Nechelle slowly reached for her belt and eased off a concussion grenade. Pulling the pin and flipping the cap, she took a gamble and dropped the live grenade at her feet between her and the dogs. Knowing she only had five seconds before detonation, she needed the dogs a little closer for maximum damage so she stomped her feet at them, causing the pack to charge at her. Eight inches away from her, the hounds moved over three grenades and a deafening *BANG!!* Erupted throughout the hallway blowing out windows and knocking the hounds as well as Nechelle out unconscious.

Nicole dam near passed out from the impact and thought that it was an explosive. She heard a heavy thud hit the floor and thought that Nechelle had went kamikaze out there and panicked. Opening the door, she had to shove a few times because a huge white devil of a dog along with the other two and Nechelle were knocked out in front of it. Nicole hooked Nechelle under the armpits and began dragging her away to nowhere in particular. One of the hounds began to groan and another stirred a little causing Nicole to drop Nechelle like a ball of lead on her head and started shooting each dog before they could fully wake. Putting in a fresh clip, Nicole looked around before picking Nechelle back up and dragging her away.

After hearing Nicole's story, Pepp threw Nechelle over his shoulder and the Crew continued to navigate their way through the home in search of this bookcase. It didn't take them long to find it either. Doing what they were told, they made their way through the bookcase and down a flight of stairs. Light fixtures were hanging from the ceiling as if it are a tunnel of a coal mine. The path was a simple narrow one, no turn offs or crazy maze like route. After a few minutes of cautious walking, am obvious argument could be heard in the distance. Everyone pulled their pistols and hurriedly made their way down the hallway until they spotted a few bodies in the distance. The hallway opened up into a huge room with a few couches, a fridge, bathtub, toilet, with Dullah in the middle of it all tied to a chair. Calynda stood behind Dullah, clutching him in a one arm chokehold with a gun to his head. Friday and Iggy had Nana and the kids at gun point, but Chepae and Solas had their guns trained on Friday and Iggy.

"I swear to God I'll smoke this old bitch! Let him go Calynda!", Friday demanded. "Fuck you and fuck her too!", Calynda smacked. "Where the fuck is the gold?!"

"It's in a safe place…. You give me my boy, I'll give you your family and your gold." "You don't get it so you?"

"What the fuck are you talking about?", Penny asked, clearly irritated.

"This is bigger than you think cabron. I'd that gold doesn't show up soon, we're all dead!"

"Speak fa yaself gal.", Iggy spat.

Calynda squinted her eyes at Iggy. "Hessi Pollucci!" Iggy's whole body stiffened and Penny's face showed recognition. "Yea! It's Pollucci's gold. We were to deliver it to her but you fucking retards stole it! So all parties involved heads are under the guillotine."

"Ya got ta give up deh gold mon.", Iggy advised. "Pollucci the devil she self." "Listen to the pot head ok. This is bigger than our beef."

Friday knew that Calynda was right. Wherever this Pollucci character is, was a big dog in the game for Calynda AND Iggy to hold fear behind her. And that meant that her better had cooperate.

"So if I hover you the gold back then what? All of this is supposed to go away?",

"I really don't give a fuck what happens between us. Priority number one is to get this bitch off of my back.", Calyndav said.

"Wha bout the death of me people?", Iggy asked. "Me not let it slide ya know."

"Casualties of war!", Calynda snapped

"Hey! Hey! Chill!", Friday spoke up. "I'll give you your gold, but I need your help first." "Are you fucking serious? You want me? To help you?!"

"You want the got dam gold right?"

Calynda shifted from one foot to the other. "What is it?"

Friday glanced at Nechelle then back to Calynda. "I need to kill a cop." Aisha's head snapped his way and Nicole already knew.

"A cop? That's easy, drop me the file."

"Not just any cop.", Friday said. "He's a top detective. Currently in the hospital in a coma and if he wakes up, he could wake up with information that could bury us all."

"What the fuck have I done to be worried about this corny ass detective?" Calynda asked.

Friday gave her a fabricated run down about Griggs holding the hospital footage and will turn it over with DNA evidence on all involved if he wakes. He also gave Nechelle credit for trying to get the job done. Calynda really could care less about what Friday was talking about but if it was going to get the gold back, then she was with it.

"Ok, so what do you need me for?", she asked.

"Griggs is heavily guarded at that hospital and when back up comes, all hell will break loose. That means we need to get this shit done as quickly as possible. So I need you and your fire power to combine with ours and get the job done. Simple shit."

"How do I know I can trust you cabron?"

"You don't know. But we're all we got. It's either this, prison, or the grave. You choose." Calynda thought on it briefly then sucked her teeth. "Fine! When do we move out?"

"Immediately!", Friday said. "Everyone grab up

some guns and whatever she has to offer. We surround the hospital then move in."

"Chepae! Solas!", Calynda barked. "Go get the…"

"Wait one fucking minute!"

Everyone looked to see Penny moving through the crowd to the front. "Babe…what you got going on?", 3-T whispered.

"Hold this.", was all she said as she passed him her jewelry. Calynda wore a slight smirk on her face as she watched Penny stop eight feet in front of her. "I want my round bitch!"

"Excuse me lol?", Calynda snickered.

"Bitch you used a knife on me when my back was turned! So before we do anything, me and you are gonna settle this shit!"

"What the hell is going on?", Friday asked looking around.

"Calynda stabbed Penny and Nechelle at the hospital the day we were protecting you from her and 3-T from Iggy.", Nicole said.

Friday looked at Penny. "Handle that shit."

"Wait!",3-T yelled. "Now is not the time to…"

"Fuck that Tony!", Penny snapped. "This bitch tried to ice me and she's about to get what's coming to her!"

"But we need her!"

"I don't give a fuck!" She then looked to Calynda. "I'm about to bare knuckle beat this bitch! Right here!

Right now!"

Calynda gave a head nod to Chepae who in turn took position behind Dullah. She then removed her knee and elbow pads along with her tactical belt. Penny removed her belt as well then cracked her knuckles.

"When I'm done with you.", Calynda began. "No one will be able to…" "Yea yea. Suck my dick bitch! Let's fight!", Penny said cutting her off.

The two women circled each other then squared off. Friday was so locked in on the becoming action, he barely noticed the blur fly pass in front of him. In slow motion, Nechelle had skipped as if she was about to throw a football, with her fist cocked back, attempting to deliver a cross hook from hell coming directly at Calynda.

"What the fuck? Nechelle! No!", Pepp screamed as he reached for her. But it was too late as Solas trained his weapon on Nechelle and Friday up his guns. All hell broke loose….

Here's a sneak peak of a new series *"She Ready"*

Chapter One

"Aye yo! Shorty! Lemme walk you home!"

"Nigga please! I'm good, I can see myself home.", Tiffany snapped.

Headed to the crib from a house party, she was too drunk and feeling herself, so her mouth was really jazzy right now. At the age of sixteen, she was built like a stallion. Standing 5'3, 152lbs, she was all hips and ass with fist sized breast. Natural wavy brown blonde hair that came pass her ass, thick full lips and stone blue eyes, thanks to a white and Hispanic mother, with skin the color of cocoa butter handed down by her Puerto Rican father, she was a man's dream come true. Trying her hardest to walk straight in six inch heels, she was in a hurry to make it home because she had snuck out of her bedroom window after knowing that her parents were asleep. If she was caught night walking these streets instead of sleeping between her sheets, her mother was going to beat that ass into a coma.

"Girl, stop tripping and bring ya lil fine ass here."

"Boy, fuck you alright! And leave me alone, ain't nobody stuntin your lil dirty ass.", she said with a roll of her eyes and neck.

"Dirty? Bitch…" Tiffany must have struck a nerve

because this nigga went straight to the extreme by grabbing her hair at the roots from behind then yanking her body to his chess. "You just don't know who the fuck I am.", her snarled in her ear.

She could smell the weed and alcohol on his breath and knew that this nigga was drunker than her. But it was all bad because when she turned her head to look him in the face, his eyes were wild and he had powder residue under his nose. This fool was geeked out of his mind.

"No the fuck you didn't! Let go of my fuckin hair you goofy ass nigga!", she snapped clawing at his wrist.

He yanked her head around a bit, causing her to lose her balance in those heels then smacked her viciously across the mouth. "Calm down bitch!"

Tiffany felt the blood in her mouth and lost her got dam mind....

TWWUH!!

She spat every drop of liquid from her mouth right into his face and gave him everything she had. Her parents ain't raise no bitch and she wasn't about to start nothing new. She punched, kicked, scratched, and bucked with the energy of a wild animal, but this nigga was not letting up. She might've been a feisty little firecracker but was no match for a horny drunk gone off that white. In the middle of her assaulting her assaulter, she felt a fist being driven into her belly with the force of a mule kick, then a punch to the bridge of her nose, breaking it on impact. Tiffany fell to her knees with all of the fight knocked out of her and felt herself being dragged into a dark alley. Scraping her knees on the pavement, she tried her best to regain her composure but the alcohol was helping the fight against her and she became helpless. The smell of garbage and piss filled her nostrils overwhelmingly and she knew what was to come next. "Please…. Please let me go!", she whined. "Don't! I'm only sixteen!"

Her attacker stood her up against the wall and drilled his fist into her face twice while holding her up by the throat.

"Shut up bitch! Ain't talking that slick shit now huh?" "Please! Back the fuck up off of me! You tripn hard as…"

BAM!!

Tiffany felt another blow to the head and blacked out. But only for a moment as she came to, feeling her dress being torn violently away from her body.

"Noooo…..", she begged barely above a whisper. "I'm sorry…. Please…."

Her words were cut short as she felt a 10 ½ thick ass dick ramming its way into her untouched vagina. The wind was knocked out of her with the first stroke and her eyes flew open. She held her attacker in a death grip as he drilled and pounded her pussy relentlessly with no remorse. She felt herself split from his thickness all the way to her asshole and she damn near fainted. Her attacker then gripped both of the back of her kneecaps and pushed her knees into her armpits, bracing all of his weight on the back of her thighs. Throwing all hips and stiff dick into her stomach, he fucked this little girl like a porn star and there was nothing that she could do about it. She felt his piece get harder and longer because of the pressure that her tight pussy applied around his shaft, and it seemed like he was touching her liver. Noticing his pace picking up speed and the pounds becoming harder, she prayed that this was a sign of it all being over but her hopes were short lived when she felt a strong hand wrap around her throat. The pressure from the choke hold forced her eyes to bulge and the look on this man's face read death. He was stroking with so much force that her backside bled from scraping across the cement bare, and her pussy was now numb from the overload of pain. But she couldn't breath. She tried to speak, to beg, to warn him that he would kill her. But she was powerless. The vessels in her rites began to burst, making them bloodshot red as black spots closed her vision. Her attacker wrapped his other hand around her throat and squeezed so tight that she thought that he would snap her neck. He then pushed every inch of him inside of her then came long and hard as death came to collect another soul....

"Ssss....oooohhhhh papi! Not so deep!", Keeyanda whined. "Who's ass is this?"

"Mmmm, you know it's yours papi. Buy that dick is thick as fuck daddy!"

Julio had Keeyanda on her side, throwing nine inches of rocks up morning dick in her ass as he laid behind her, one of her legs cocked up with a grip around her throat, sucking on her neck.

"You better tone that shit down before you wake the kids.", Julio hissed.

Keeyanda just laid her head back into his chest, tooted her plump ass up against his rock hard abs and allowed him to push that dick up her spine. That were married for sixteen years and every morning it never failed. They would suck and fuck each other straight out of sleep before starting their day.

"Ease up papi...I can't breath."

Julio knew that when his wife said that , she was ready for him to come. He then squeezed her throat tighter causing her to gasp, folded her legs up even more, and began to slow grind that dick just the way she liked it. Keeyanda knew what her man liked and allowed him to be aggressive and dominate her sexually on every way possible. Reaching behind her with one hand, she clutched one of his ass cheeks and pulled his stroke deep in her ass while slowly throwing out back on him.

"Cum for me papi... give me that fat dick and show me you love me daddy.", she wheezed, barely able to breath.

The way she moaned and purred drove Julio crazy every time and he bit down on her collar muscle then shot up in her club in the most savage way possible. Keeyanda just embraced the sweet pain as she felt the think warm fluid fill her ass up instantly. Julio felt his wife clawing at his fingers then released the sex grip from around her throat.

BAM! BAM! BAM! BAM! BAM!

"What the fuck?!", Julio snapped, jumping out of bed grabbing his pistol.

"I'm about to beat somebody's ass!", Keeyanda said running on Julio's heels.

These two were always ready to give up the business since day one. They did everything together so if one had a problem, they both had a problem.

BAM! BAM! BAM! BAM! BAM!

Julio cocked back his glock and peeped out of the living room window and his eyes grew wide. Keeyanda was about to swing the door open, 380. In hand when Julio snatched her up and whispered in her ear.

"That's the jakes outside baby."

"What? Why the hell would 12 be banging on my fucking door at five in the morning papi?ç

"I don't know but take this pistol, gather that work out of the room and sneak the kids out the back."

Keeyanda gave her man a quick kiss and ran off to do what she was told. That's what Julio loved about his wife. She knew how to keep her mouth shut and so what was asked of her without asking questions. She knew the drill. Once Keeyanda was out of sight, Julio swung the door open and was met by two cops. They both looked him over but the male quickly looked away while the female could not steer her vision away from all that glossed up dick that dangled between the legs of this sexy ass Puerto Rican nigga. Julio just grilled them both.

"Can you please put some clothes on sir.", the male officer asked with a slight attitude. "You never seen a dick before? The fuck you want?"

The female officer snickered and toll the lead. "Do you have a daughter by the name of Tiffany Rodriguez?"

"Keeyanda! Pantalones par par favor! "

Julio continued to grill the jakes as Keeyanda came to the door handing him a pair of sweats. She wore a short tight fitting silk robe that her huge breast were spilling out of, giving the male officer a hard time.

Literally!

"What's the problem papi? Why this stinking vato bang on me door huh?" "They asked about Tiffany."

"Tiffany!", Keeyanda snapped. Looking at the officer then rolling her eyes, Keeyanda turned inward to the house but never leaving the door. "Tiffany! Bring your ass to the door chica!"

"Ma'am, that won't be necessary.", the make officer advised. "Hey cabron!", Julio snapped. "You speak to me eh?"

"Your daughter is not home sir!", the female snapped back, now running short on patience for the testosterone show.

"What the fuck you mean, she's not home? She's in her room.", Julio said in confusion.

The female officer then held up a photo. "Is this your Tiffany?"

Keeyanda snatched the picture of her only daughter then looked back at the jakes. "What the fuck did she do?"

"She's in the hospital ma'am."

"Hospital? How? She's supposed to be sleeping in her room!"

"I can't answer that but she was raped and badly beaten almost to death."

Keeyanda bolted through the house towards Tiffany's room and found it empty. Her heart twisted at the sight of the empty bed and the butterflies began to go crazy in her belly. Rushing back down the stairs, Keeyanda collided with Julio and saw the look of desperation in his eyes.

"She's not the papi.", she said shoving him out of the way, headed back to the front door. "Take us to her."

The male officer grew a smug smile and spat, "That's not our fucking job." "You watch your mouth puto!", Julio said coming up behind his wife.

"Or what motherfucker?!"

"Everyone calm down ok!", the female officer pleaded. "Suck my dick aight!"

"Excuse me?"

"You heard him chica!", Keeyanda smacked. "Our little girl is in the hospital and we can't get a fucking ride? You brought this shit to my front door and won't help? Yea, suck his dick bitch!"

"Alright! That's it!", the male officer said pissed. "Hands behind your back lady!" "Fuck you!"

"Touch my wife and you'll need a ride to the hospital tough guy!" "Is that a threat sir?", lady cop asked.

"Take it how you wanna bitch!" Keeyanda spat.

The male officer got bold and grabbed Keeyanda's wrist and....

WHOPP!

Caught a nose breaking cross hook as Julio pulled his wife into the house. The female officer went for her taser as Keeyanda attempted to close the door but had it slam into her grill as the male officer kicked it in. The lady let Julio ride the lightning with one foot in the door and caught a lamp to the side of her head. Keeyanda was in savage mode and went for the male officers gun as Julio yanked the taser prongs from his neck. Seeing his wife wrestle the stronger man for the pistol, he joined her side and scooped the man up off of his feet from behind and dropped him on his neck.

BOW! BOW!

Julio fell into his wife's arms as two slugs blew out his throat and left cheek from behind. Falling with the weight of her dead lover, Keeyanda squeezed off five rounds hitting the female twice in the vest, and one to the elbow, causing her to drop her weapon. Laying under Julio's body, she aimed up at the male officer who was stuck in surrender.

"Don't do nothing stupid lady!", he tried to reason. "It's not murder yet. You leer is live, you'll see the streets again."

Keeyanda pulled herself from under the dead body and made distances between her and the jakes. "I need an ambulance!", the female officer pleaded. "I'm gonna bleed…." **BOW!**

Keeyand shot that bitch in the face! No way was she going to live after killing her other

half in front of her. Training the gun on the other officer, she could tell that he saw death in her eyes as she stood silently staring.

"Mommy…"

Keeyanda gasped as she turned to see her eleven year old son standing in the middle of the steps. That was all that the officer needed to make a move for his pistol. Keeyanda heard him before she could turn to see him and reflexively up the gun and fired. The slug slammed into his vest but he kept coming and was able to clutch the gun. Keeyanda had a death grip on that glock and he was catching hell trying to take it from her. She gave him a solid knee to this midsection, causing him to jerk the gun around violently and....

BOW!

The pistol went off blindly. Keeyanda twisted the gun out of his grip, stepped back and blew his chin off. The officers body spun as she popped him again before he could hit the ground. Turning around to grab her son, she panicked that he was gone.

"Neeko!", she hollered. "Neeko baby we gotta go!"

She ran up the stairs thinking that her son got scared after the gunshot. She came across the spot where Neeko previously stood and saw blood. She froze in shock seeing drops of blood leading down the steps.

Her head slowly turned as her vision followed the blood spots back down the steps headed to the kitchen. She quickly followed the trail to the kitchen and the tiny spots transformed into globs. Walking into the kitchen, Keeyanda found her son hiding in the pantry shaking holding his stomach.

"Neeko baby! Come! We have to go baby!"

"Mommy....", Neeko barely whispered. "My tummy hurts..."

Neeko crawled out of the pantry, removed his hand and blood poured from his belly as he began to sob uncontrollably, reaching up to hug his mommy. Keeyanda broke down in tears at the sight of her son.

"Shit Neeko! Come!"

She scooped her son up and searched the officers for their car keys.

"I love you papi….", she said to her dead husband. "Promise to see you soon my love." She did the dash to the hospital flying through the streets, hoping her son made it. Pulling up to the emergency entrance, she ran inside with a semiconscious Neeko.

"Help! I need some fucking help!"

Keeyanda rushed the nurses station and laid her son on the counter. An elderly nurse saw all that blood spill out of this pale faced child and clutched her heart.

"Oh my Lord!", the nurse said. "Nancy! Get the doctor! I'm gonna pray for this baby." Nurse Nancy punched in a few numbers in the phone, spoke a few words, then rushed to retrieve a gurney. "Father God, I call on you because one of your most precious creations is in need of your grace and mercy. I beg that you…"

Keeyanda lost all hearing blanking out as the nurse prayed for the survival of her son. Moments later, two more nurses and a doctor came rushing out of the back and placed a dying Neeko on the gurney and wheeled him away. An assistant tried to get some information from Keeyanda but she was out of her mind. She witnessed her husband get murdered in their own home, her baby boy shot damn near to death, and her only daughter raped and almost killed all in one night. She stood bare foot, half naked in a silk robe in the middle of the hospital intake area. A few police officers came on and approached some people that were waiting. A couple questions were asked and the individuals pointed to an oblivious Keeyanda. As the officers approached, Keeyanda heard the keys and snapped out of her daze. She felt a stranger's hand grip her shoulder….

"Ma'am…"

At the sound of the officer' voice, Keeyanda spun around and without second guessing, reached out and snatched the pistol off of the officer's hip.

"Holy shit! Calm the fuck down lady! Let's not get hasty."

Keeyanda just backed up slowly, pointing the gun back and forth at the two officers without saying a word. She peeped the female officer hand eased towards her second pistol and gave the 'bitch really' looked as she trained the pistol on her. Keeyanda backed up to the nurse's station and snapped her fingers at the older nurse.

"Come her chica!"

The nurse shuffled around the counter and stood a few feet away from Keeyanda. "Yes baby.", the nurse said lovingly.

"What's your name mami?" "Rosetta. But you can call me Rose."

"Ok Rose. My daughter came in here not too long ago. Tiffany Rodriguez. She was raped?"

"Oh my Lord...", Rose sympathized. She knew just who Tiffany was because Ross was the one who cleaned her when she was brought in. "Yes baby, I know about Tiffany."

"And you prayed over my son. Neeko.", Keeyanda said still looking at the officers. "Mmhm. God will see that child through too."

"I'm Keeyanda.", she lightly sobbed. Kee knew what was to come. "Ok Keeyanda. Let me pray for you baby."

Keeyanda snickered. "No thank you chica. I need a

bigger favor from you." "Anything baby. Tell momma Rose what you need."

Keeyanda let a lone tear fall down her face then turned to Rose. "Take care of my babies momma Rose."

POW!

Keeyanda shoved the gun in her mouth and blew her brains out. A few people ran out as the officers flinched in shock. Nurse Rose slowly bent down, grabbed the gun, and passed it to the officer. She then knelt over Keeyanda.

"I promise to take care of your babies..." She closed Keeyanda's opened eyes then took a deep breath.

"Father God, I call on you because one of your fallen angels is in need of your grace and mercy...."

Chapter Two

"Where the fuck is my phone?", she whispered looking around her room which was a mess. Clothes all over the floor and bed, trash over flowing the small garbage can in the corner of the room, hair and skin products scattered across the dresser and blunt guts littered the window sill.

"Uuuugghhh! I need my fucking phone!"

The room looked like a nuclear bomb had went off inside of it and no seventeen year old girl should be living like this. The only way that she was going to find that phone was if it rang.

"Momma Rose!", she opened her room door and screamed. "Momma call my phone!"

"Maybe if you'd clean that mess up, you'll be able to find it!", Momma Rose yelled upstairs from the kitchen table.

She was reading her bible and singing spiritual hymns, as she did everyday after work. Her grand kids were in constant need of the Lord's grace and mercy. They wouldn't even know how to pray for themselves, so she did it for them. Momma Rose

looked over at her cellphone and debated whether to give Tiffany's cell a call. Ever since Tiffany's father was killed by the police in his home and her mother Keeyanda killed herself in the same hospital Tiffany was taken to after being raped and nearly beaten to death, Rossetta Bess aka Momma Rose had raised Tiffany and her younger brother Neeko.

On the same night of her rape and death of her parents, the then 9 year old Neeko was shot in the abdomen when his mother Keeyanda was tussling with an officer over his service pistol. As if the trauma from the gunshot caused him to act like a hellcat, 12 year old Neeko was a bad little motherfucker. And that was putting it mildly. He was constantly fighting in school, skipping classes, smoking weed, stealing out of stores, stealing out of Momma Rose's purse, and the list goes on. A problem child at its finest.

Tiffany on the other hand was a whole different kind of trouble. She always stayed out late, coming in at 4a.m. on a school night high on weed and pills as well as drunk. Rose knew that Tiffany was fucking because empty condom boxes were always in her trash can as well as crusty panties filled the dirty clothes hamper. She stole all of her dress attire so they all were too revealing, showing ass, camel toe, cleavage, whatever. But Momma Rose never gave up on them babies. She had promised Keeyanda moments before she took her life that she would look after her children. And that's what she would do until her last breath. Neeko walked into the kitchen headed to the fridge and the smell of potent weed smoke assaulted Mine Roses nostrils…..

"Neeko…come to Momma for a second baby."

Little Neeko made his way to Momma with his head down texting on his phone…

WHACK!!

"Dam Momma!"

"Don't you", *WHACK!* "Dam Momma me boy! What I tell you about smoking that dope!" "Man, ain't no dope!", Neeko said picking himself up off of the kitchen floor. Momma might have been full of love, but she played no games with them kids and would reach out and bless their asses every chance she got.

"You on dope boy! Looka ya! You is high son!" "Maannnn…"

Momma swiftly raised her hand and Neeko dam near flinched his way into a seizure. "Don't man me boy. Now call your sister's phone."

"But she right upstairs. Why I gotta call get phone?"

"Because I fuckin!!. ", Momma took a deep breath. "Little boy, you're gonna make me lose my dam religion in this house. Now call that phone before I smack you in your shit!"

Neeko sucked his teeth as he began to text Tiffany's phone and ducked just in time to dodge Momma's Bible. She did not tolerate anyone sucking their teeth at her. Neeko grinned as he walked away calling his sister's phone.

A hip-hop tune could be faintly heard coming from behind Momma. Only thing back there was a refrigerator. Opening the fridge, Tiffany's phone was sitting next to a bottle of soda. Momma picked it up and went straight to the gallery to snoop at the pictures.

Tiffany had the most graphic videos and photos in her phone showing images that no seventeen year old should be caught taking. Momma placed the phone on the seat next to her, picked up her Bible and sat back down.

"Fanny!", Momma called Tiffany by her nickname. Fanny come get this phone!" Tiffany could be heard flying down the steps and skipping into the kitchen.

"Thank you Momma. Where was it?"

"Right there on the chair.", Mona nodded her heads nonchalantly. Tiffany twisted up her face in confusion and went to pick up the phone…

DOMP!

Momma Rose slammed the Bible across the back of Tiffany's head, causing her to fall forward.

"Momma! What the fuck?! Why would you…"

DOMP!

"You watch your dam mouth Fanny!" "But why would you hit me with a book?"

"You got them nasty pictures in ya phone gal, why? You too young and that's no way for a girl your age to be living."

Neeko walked into the kitchen snickering. Tiffany sucked her teeth as she was getting up and Momma swung the Bible, barely missing her mark.

"I'm out!", Tiffany mumbled as she stormed out of there kitchen.

"And you better have your tail in here at a decent time or ima bless your ass some more bitch!", Momma screamed at Tiffany's back. She then looked to Neeko. "And you can get the fuck out of my face!"

Tiffany slammed the apartment door behind her and was about to dial her best friend's number, but saw her sitting on the stoop in front of the building. Brionna Tsuni and Tiffany were like Thelma and Louise. Standing 5'3, 137lbs., mixed with black and Korean, Brionna aka Bri was a threat to any woman in her eye sight. At only sixteen, she was built like she ran her own household. Long bone straight jet black hair, honey wheat toned skin, thick pink lips and natural ash gray eyes gave her an appearance that looked like she paid for it. But don't let the pretty face fool you, Bri was all about action and a few hard headed bitches had to learn the hard way. Her Korean father made it his business to teach her kick boxing for self defense and she would dust a bird bitch off every chance she got. Tiffany was no slouch either. She kept a razor in her bra but her hands were a real problem. Growing up, she constantly had to fight them ugly hoes up off her until she earned her respect. When she first moved to Momma's neighborhood, the perverts wasted no time putting their bid in on the fresh meat. But her experience of being raped caused her to turn up really fast when someone pursued her aggressively.

Once, an old school pimp tried to shoot his shot and got cussed out something nasty.

One of the pimp's hoes thought it too be cool to try and check Tiffany for being out of pocket with her pimp. The moment her finger went in Tiffany's face, it was dam near chewed off, followed by a fist wrapping around her nappy ponytail with Tiffany's knuckles working overtime. Another hoe came to her fellow hoe's rescue and they began to give Tiffany the biz. Even though these were two grown women, Tiffany was not letting up. Going blow for now, stepping forward!

Suddenly, a loud deafening crack sounded off and a hoe rolled into the street, holding the side of her face. Tiffany saw the pimp move funny and another skull cracking noise sounded off, dropping the pimp.

Tiffany kept it hot on the hoe in front of her until a girl yanked the hoe by the side of her throat and smashed some brass knuckles across her nose. The hoe hollered, grabbing get face and took off! Tiffany spat out blood and twisted her hair on a messy bun.

Locking eyes with her savior, Tiffany just stared at the calm expressionless girl waiting for an explanation.

"Are you ok?", the savior asked.

"I'm good! I'm real good!", Tiffany said with a slight attitude. "I could've took them bitches to the grave on my worst day."

"Yea, whatever. Well, if you want…"

"Whatever my ass!", Tiffany snapped, cutting the savior off. "I didn't need your help alright. These bitches got a best chance and getting high than fucn with me!"

The savior burst out laughing, covering her mouth, waving Tiffany off. Tiffany grilled the girl for a few seconds then began cracking up herself.

"I'm sorry.", Tiffany apologized. "Girl thank you for helping me out back there." "It's cool. I owed the fat bitch an ass cutting for a while now."

"Oh yea? What's up with that?"

"Dumb shit! Everytime I come to the store and her trickin ass sees me, it's always 'Ming Lee this or Ming Lee that', or this lil Chinese bitch think she's cute. Bitch is just annoying as fuck yo, for real."

"Yea? Well I bet the bitch ain't on no Lee- Lee shit no more!", Tiffany capped. "I like you. I'm Brionna."

"Tiffany. But my peeps call me Fanny." "Call me Bri."

"A Chinese girl named Brionna?"

"I'm Korean and black. Last name Tsuni."

"Well, I'm no different. My peeps are Puerto Rican, Dominican and white. Rodriguez."

"Aight then Fanny. You got some hands girl! You were holding your own back there for real."

Yea, well I'm not with the bullshit. These hoes keep a problem so I'm solving em. It is what it is."

And that's how Tiffany and Bri clicked. Ever since then, the two were inseparable.

"Bitch I was just about to call you.", Tiffany sighed sitting on the stoop next to Bri. "You got some tree? I need to get fuckin high man."

"No but you know Lil Bird keep some gas. You want me to call him?"

Tiffany just rolled her eyes. Lil Bird was a young small time hustler who sold weed, and had a serious crush on Tiffany. At 15, Lil Bird was doing his thing with the little bit that he had and anybody could see that he had major potential to be big in the game. But with his mother on crack and his pops doing life in prison for killing a crack dealer he caught with his wife in an alley getting his dick choked on, he had no one to school or guide him so he was just living day to say, doing what he knew best.

"Like, girl?! Is he the only one you can call?"

"I mean, we could go to the projects but you know everybody gonna try to fuck, soooo….."

"This shit is for the birds man for real.", Tiffany sighed.

"Just give that lil nigga some pussy T, dam! We might can get some free weed from now on lol."

"Well why don't you fuck him?"

"Shit, I just might! So call him or naw?" "Just call him ok?"

Bri snickered while calling Lil Bird, placing the order. Neeko eagled out of the house and Tiffany saw the lust in her little brothers eyes. Neeko was all in over Bri and it showed real bad. He would stutter and fidget in her presence and she actually thought that it was cute.

"Guess she ran yo ass out the crib too huh?", Tiffany laughed.

"She want somebody to help her clean chitterlings. Ain't that a pig's asshole?"

Tiffany was cracking up. It was his innocence in always saying the most wild shit that drew everyone to young Neeko. Losing both their parents, Neeko shot and Tiffany raped, waking up in an orphanage together until Momma Rose could rescue them, nothing could become a threat to their bond and the love that they had for each other. Tiffany would do life with her hands up in a heart beat if you fucked with that one.

"He's on his way.", Bri said.

"Who on their way?", Neeko asked.

Tiffany rolled her eyes at Bri, then cut them towards Neeko. "Um…mind your fuckin business!"

"Whatever. You bitches are weird as fuck anyway.", he said walking pass them and up the street.

Bri's mouth fell open at the same time, Tiffany twisted her face up at her. "Bitch really?"

"Whatever. He's on the way. And a bitch need a drink. And a fat dick. Fat stiff one. So what you on?"

"Eww!", Tiffany laughed. "Not any of that shit! I like my pussy and the way she looks. Give me a 6-7 inches over a 9-11 any day!"

"Ha! Bitch you buggin. Friday having free ladies night arty the Rugh. If we get there before 10:30 you can get your 6-7 and I can get my 11."

"I said *NINE TO ELEVEN*!"

"Me wan-leven bish!", Bri said in her Korean accent.

Once again, Tiffany was cracking up. This bitch was always laughing. Caught up in the bullshit, they both let some random motherfucker sneak up on them.

"Say bitch! Run them pockets and them jewels before shit gets ugly."

Tiffany turned around to become face to face with a pistol gripped in a shaking hand.

Bri froze up, eyes wide.

"Yooo... you gotta chill...", Tiffany whispered staring down the barrel

"Aye ma nigga. It's broad day right now! Three o'clock! You really doing this shit!", Bri snapped.

He cocked the hammer back and upped his pistol.

"Girl please shut the fuck up and give him our shit.", Tiffany said taking off her jewelry. Bri just rolled her eyes and did the same. Tiffany reached out to give hers to and...

BLAOUW!

Brains went everywhere and Tiffany dam near passed out. "Hooo shot!", Bri screamed with blood splattered across her face..

Lil Bird had walked up a few ferry away and thought dude was just some random nigga trying to holla at the girls like usual, but when he saw that gun, he slid his glock 17 out of his pocket and sent ole boy to the dark side of the moon. Tiffany knew that the jakes would be pulling up any second because the whole hood was either in their window or coming outside and there was a dead body on the sidewalk with only them the standing over it. But Lil Bird had the gun in his hand.

"What the fuck Bird! You better get the hell from around here!", Bri said snapping out of it.

"Give me that dam gun! ", Tiffany said snatching the smoking pistol. "Here!", Bird said. "Take this too."

He passed them a big bag of weed and a roll of money then took off running up the block. Tiffany and Bri rushed into the crib and locked themselves in Tiffany's room.

Momma Rose was sleep so they were able to wash the blood off of them and change clothes unnoticed. But the nosey ass neighborhood watch bitch had been sitting in her window so when 12 pulled up, she told what happened like she did the shit herself! The jakes banged on Tiffany's door loud enough to wake up Momma Rose and they both panicked.

"Hide that fuckin gun!", Bri hissed.

Tiffany slid it under the mattress, thought about it, then dropped it in her panty drawer.

"What the fuck are you doing?"

"You said hide the shit right?", Tiffany snapped. "Ain't nobody coming in..."

"You about to send the both of our asses to jail. Bitch move!", Bri rushed pass cutting her off.

Grabbing the pistol, Bri went and lifted the top off of the back of the toilet bowl and dropped the dirty glock inside. By the time Bri returned, Momma Rose was walking in the room with two police officers. The lady cop walked in first with a male behind her and the weed could be smelled instantly. They were so nervous about the gun that they forgot about the smokes. The white man had his hand on his hip where his service weapon was, looking for the killer that he was told had came inside. The lady was more at ease.

"Where is he?", the cowboy asked accusingly.

"He who?!", Tiffany snapped. "And get the fuck outta my room while we don't have on any clothes!"

After showing, they both only slid on wife beaters that barely covered their vagina's. Young firm breast pushing against the thin material had him low key throwed off. But he had a dead body outside with a phony lead that the suspect was inside.

"He ran in here and..."

"And? What!? You got a fuckin warrant?", Tiffany spat cutting him off.

Momma Rose lost her mind... "Fuck a warrant. Bitch, get these people out of my house! You got somebody in here Fanny?"

"No Ms. Rose. You know we wouldn't…"

"Hush the fuck up little girl! Wasn't talking to you.", Momma Rose said citing Bri off. "if you got somebody in my house Fanny, you getting the fuck out too!"

"Nobody is in this room Momma."

"Can we search the room?", the cowboy asked Momma Rose.

She looked at Tiffany for a split second then moved to the side allowing 12 to come in. When the male officer walked further onto the room, the lady cop just grilled Tiffany. Bri noticed and elbowed her girl and nodded. When they locked eyes, Tiffany saw the lady cop broke her stare and eyeballed the bed. Sitting ruffled partially in the blanket was the nah of weed that Bird had passed. Bri caught on and without looking around, sat on the bed. Momma Rose was so into watching the man search, she seemed to not pay the lady cop no attention, let alone, catch onto Bri.

"I'm searching this bed area, get up!"

"You know dam well ain'tnobody in here!" Tiffany then turned to Momma Rose. "He looking for something or someone? Like where he at?"

"Get your ass off this bed!", Momma Rose grilled Bri and ignoring Tiffany. "Second time talking to your ass!"

When Bri got up, the jake shoke the covers and looked under the bed. Finding nothing, he was a bit pink in the face.

"You good? You find whatever the fuck you were looking for?", Tiffany sassed.

The jake rolled his eyes then looked to Momma

Rose.

"Well did ya?!", Momma Rose snapped. "Y'all get the hell out of my house and leave us the fuck alone!"

Pink fac took one last look around and stormed out. The lady cop gave a warning look at the girls and turned to leave. Her and Momma Rose suspiciously avoided eye contact as she left. Tiffany abs Bri were still too shook to be on point of something so inconspicuous.

"You better stay your ass in this house.", Momma Rose told Tiffany. Then looked to Bri. "And you can get the fuck out!"

Rosetta Bess slammed the door on her way out mumbling something about needing to pray.

"Yoooo...what the fuck just happened?", Tiffany whispered as she sat on the bed. "And you were trippin nut good thing I called Bird!"

"For real right?"

If Bri had never called Bird for the tree, who knows what would've happened. Bri pulled the bag off weed out of the crack of her ass and held it up to Tiffany's face.

"Get that shit....bitch stop playing!", Tiffany stiffened "So you ain't smoking lol?"

"And you rolling!"

They sat in the window with the door locked blowing smoke. "So you working your vibe or not?", Bri asked.

"You know I never got an I.D. since I lost Joy's.", Tiffany confessed.

"You know dam well Friday ain't gonna turn its

286

around. Plus then niggas only let you in because they wanna fuck, not because of that I.D."

"Well please tell me exactly what the fuck you trying to say?"

Bri twisted her neck at Tiffany's attitude and popped her shit still. "Because ya bloodline mixed up with all kinds of shit and Joy couldn't look close even with a $500 lace front abs a MAC kit!"

"Pppppp!", Tiffany laughed, choking and passing the blunt. "Girl you stupid! But I still don't have anything to wear."

"Like what we got on ever stopped is from shutting shit down when we walk in. Ass phat, pussy phat, belly tight, titties right, and my face *BEAT* with no makeup. Bitch so bad, I'll step in that muthafucka and tell these goofy ass niggas that I got a dick and they still gone fuck! "

COMING SOON!

She Ready Part I

She Ready Part II

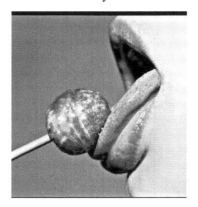

CREW III

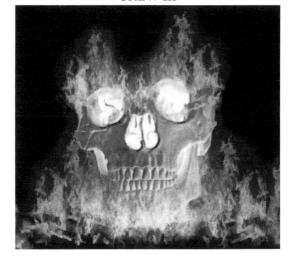

Made in the USA
Columbia, SC
10 October 2023

24220418R00161